Vienna

in

Violet

David W. Frank

Blank Slate Press | St. Louis, MO

Blank Slate Press is an imprint of Amphorae Publishing Group, LLC
For information, contact info@amphoraepublishing.com
Amphorae Publishing Group
4168 Hartford Street | Saint Louis, MO 63116

Publisher's Note: This book is a work of the imagination. Names, characters, places, organizations, and incidents either are products of the author's imagination or are used fictitiously. While some of the characters, organizations, and incidents portrayed here can be found in historical accounts, they have been altered and rearranged by the author to suit the strict purposes of storytelling. The book should be read solely as a work of fiction.

www.amphoraepublishing.com
www.blankslatepress.com

Cover Design by Kristina Blank Makansi
Interior Design by Elena Makansi
Set in Adobe Caslon Pro and Edwardian Script ITC
Manufactured in the United States of America

Library of Congress Control Number: 2015950847

ISBN: 9781943075102

Many people have promoted my musical life. I cherish particularly fond memories of Elliot Forbes, F. John Adams, Luise Vosgerchian and Robert Spillman. I also owe great debts to Spencer Huffman, who first introduced me to Schubert on the piano, and to Todd C. Gordon, who has worked valiantly over several years to help me in my attempts to sing Schubert's *Lieder*. But I dedicate this book to the person who had the most direct influence on my musicianship, with whom I played and sang the most Schubert, Frances Kleeman ("Auntie") (1918-2010) and to her sister, my mother Elizabeth Kleeman Frank, without whom none of what folows would have been possible.

Vienna

in

Violet

Introduzione

Maestoso cantabile

Franz Schubert (1797-1828) wrote more than six hundred songs. The pace at which he lived and wrote made it impossible for him to shepherd them all into public view. Many probably fell by the wayside, but, according to legend, there is one that Schubert hoped would never see the light of day.

Schubert usually promoted his works enthusiastically. Indeed, his livelihood depended on income from publication at least as much as from the performance of his works. Schubert also wrote with great facility and rarely looked back. Songs seemed to flow effortlessly from his pen, and he generally was more interested in producing the next one than in polishing its predecessor. Hence, Schubert's cryptic note to the publisher, Artaria, written a year before his death: "If the song of doom resurfaces, destroy it," has mystified scholars. (The phrase "song of doom" appears in a diary entry of Schubert's friend Johann Meyerhoffer in an entry dated April 19, 1822).

The recently discovered "Die Sonne und Das Veilchen" ("The Sun and the Violet") may be the song in question.

It was not published during Schubert's lifetime, nor afterwards when the great rush to get all of Schubert's work into print occurred. Although nothing in the song is blatantly sinister, an aura of unhappiness could be associated with it. There is, for example, the chance remark of Schubert's friend, the artist Moritz von Schwind (1804-1871), several years after Schubert's death about "the infusion of violet violence" tainting the memory of his otherwise tranquil "Biedermeier days." Another extant reference associates a Schubert "flower song" with several deaths that occurred in Vienna in 1822—a likely time for the song's composition.

The score of "Die Sonne und Das Veilchen" unquestionably displays Schubert's freehand penmanship. Though musically no masterpiece, the song is well-crafted in Schubert's style, without any extraordinary features in its piano or vocal parts. Schubert produced many works much better than this one, as well as a few not as good.

About the song's probable lyricist, one Eugénie von Nuelinger, almost nothing has come down to history. Indeed, her authorship of the poem is questioned. For one thing, she is not known to have written anything else. Her name does not appear in Schubert's score or anywhere in his other writings. Eugénie von Neulinger's contribution depends on a separate copy of the lyrics, discovered with the score. The handwriting of this text is clearly not Schubert's and appears to be feminine. The stationery bears a crest of a Von Neulinger family, but the poem is not signed. The name of Eugénie von Neulinger is inscribed in a different hand; some scholars believe it to be that of Michael Vogl, Schubert's long-time friend and collaborator.

Incidentally, it is only in the hand-written lyrics that the song's complete last line exists. Apparently a corrosive agent caused a small hole in Schubert's last page of, which Eugénie's manuscript conveniently fills.

The song evidently came before an audience at least once, sung by Vogl. In a letter to her daughter, Vogl's wife mentions hearing her husband sing it accompanied by Schubert himself. The duo frequently performed in Vienna and its environs throughout late 1821 and 1822.

In any event, for the sake of completeness—another drop in the ocean of appreciation which Franz Schubert never sufficiently enjoyed during his brief life—here is the first published appearance of "Die Sonne und Das Veilchen". Whatever the circumstances preventing its publication during the nineteenth entury, there is no reason to withhold it now.

–DWF

DIE SONNE UND DAS VEILCHEN
The Sun and the Violet

Words by "Eugénie von Neulinger"
Music by "Franz Schubert"

Summer mornings, a shaded, blushing violet
Would unfold to the rising sun:
"I must find a way
Your kindness to repay
For the golden thread you've spun,
For the golden thread you've spun,
For the golden thread you've spun."
Every evening, he'd shine upon his violet,
Who would thank him from the heart he'd won!

A season her message repeating,
To the sun by the violet was told;
But life, for a violet, is fleeting,
And, 'neath clouds of autumn bold,
The violet grew fragile and old,
'Til, at last, she succumbed to the cold.

Then, in the spring, when to call upon his violet
With delight came the evening sun,
Though he missed her face,
He found in her place
There were five* where there had been one!

Translation by David W. Frank

* The piano score has a hole in it at this spot, and the number is in dispute. A sole mark resembling a "t" remains in the score, leading some to suggest that the number is eight (acht), not five (fünf). The verbal manuscript is unambiguous.

Die Sonne und Das Veilchen

Words by "Eugenie von Neulinger"

"Franz Peter Schubert" (DWF)

Poco allegretto

sum mer morn ings, a shad ed, blush ing vio let would un

fold to the ris ing sun. I must find a way your___

thank him from the heart he'd won!

A sea son her mes sage re peat ing to the

sun by the vio let was told: But

life for a vio let is fleet ing, And 'neath clouds of au tumn

bold, the vio let grew fra gile and old, 'til at last she suc cumbed to the

cold Then in the spring, when to shine up on his

*Allegretto
scherzando*

Chapter One

Countess Eugénie von Neulinger thrived on audacity, but this time she may have gone too far. She was still in bed, amply protected by mounds of down and yards of linen, with a servant nestled discretely in the corner, professionally out of earshot, yet able to provide ocular proof that no impropriety transpired. Comfortable for her, the setting was calculated to cause her visitor maximum disquiet. Johann Michael Vogl, the current visitor, was keenly aware of the contrived awkwardness of his situation—invited to appear in the *boudoir* of a married woman at ten o'clock on a Tuesday morning. But Eugénie held her business meetings with whomever she liked in whatever locality suited her. Vogl, like most men who knew her, including her husband apparently, acceded to her wishes without resistance.

"Misha," the countess affected a carefully wrought expression of plaintive indomitability, "now that you've kindled my hopes, you must promise that the eunuch will accompany you."

"He's not a—"

"He might as well be. So unattractive." The countess permitted herself a tiny tremor of the shoulders.

Vogl smiled. "But the instant he sits down at a keyboard…"

"…he becomes an angel!"

"And now that he is in such demand in the salon…"

"I must have him!"

"I see no great difficulty, Eugénie," Vogl said with less confidence than he felt, "since I will be singing." He caught the hint of an exotic floral scent—roses? lavender?—as the countess lifted her bejeweled hand.

"He refused you last time. We settled on that Hauptnegler person. Let me speak with him personally."

"Emil Hauptnegler is a perfectly adequate musician, Eugénie. He'll perform impeccably for you. As for Franz…"

"Don't contradict me, Misha! Hauptnegler has no *feeling*. Even tin-eared Baron Lefkowitz says so. I must have that eunuch!"

"I'll ask *the man* for you."

"You'll tell him," said the countess. Then her tone softened. "The question is, tell him what?"

"If you offered him a florin or two…"

"I don't want to insult the eu—little man."

"Then a simple invitation to the *soirée* should serve. Franz will be honored to come as your guest."

"He has never accepted before," the countess said, pouting.

"He refused employment from you once, my dear, and then only because he was intimidated." Vogl coughed to mask this discoloration of the truth. "Eugénie, a small gesture of condescension on your part goes a long way. Such exalted rank, such grace…"

"Stop teasing me, Misha."

"He'll come as a guest readily enough. Once he's here, he'll make music. Why make such a fuss?"

"I can't send a man of no stature a formal invitation. Am I to become a laughingstock?" The countess's emerald eyes blazed. Noticing Vogl on the verge of acquiescence, she reduced their flame and said calmly, "I want him available to play on Thursday night. I'll pay him something, if I must."

"Eugénie. Is this some new intrigue?"

"Whatever can you mean, Misha?" The countess feigned shock.

"Forgive me for speaking plainly. This is not 1815. Vienna no longer belongs to adventurers and diplomats. On the street one sees only ordinary, blunt-thinking Austrians."

"I am Austrian."

"Eugénie, you are a cosmopolite." The countess, with a modest nod, apparently accepted this as a compliment. "I do not refer to your world-renowned beauty and wit," Vogl continued. "Vienna today belongs to people with a passion for order and respectability."

The countess stirred beneath her bed clothes. "Don't lecture me, Misha. I get quite enough of that from Georg."

"I merely remind you, my lady, that your husband is instrumental in maintaining the present order and promoting Viennese respectability."

"Pooh! Georg is not as straight-laced as you think. He manages his affairs freely and leaves me free to manage mine. Would you be permitted in here otherwise?"

"Whatever his other proclivities, Georg is ambitious, and now he answers directly to Baron Hager. When *tout le monde* ruled the city, power resided in the hands of those with access to the power mongers, I daresay to you, Eugénie. Now Metternich rules, and power belongs only to people who don't make visible waves."

"Misha, enough! I detest politics. The arts are my weakness. I simply desire Thursday's artistic gathering to be a success."

"But why Franz Schubert? The city overflows with starving musicians, any of whom would sacrifice a year's commissions simply for a taste of the pastries you serve. Though a few of Franz's songs are known…"

The countess's expression acknowledging defeat was most becoming, the precise raising of her right hand simultaneous with the lowering of her eyelids, "Ah, Misha, I can't get around you. There's one special requirement for Thursday."

Vogl expected no less. "What is it?"

"I understand that Herr Schubert writes quickly."

"When he is inspired to do so."

"How does one inspire Schubert to set a poem to music?"

"Why not ask him?"

"He'd accept?"

"That depends, Eugénie. Genius cannot be coerced. If Franz found the verse to his liking…"

"Ah, Misha, you've hit it. We must convince the … little man … that this verse is to his liking."

"This verse? What the devil are you talking about?"

"Imagine, Misha. On Thursday evening when he arrives, Franz Schubert receives a text, a little poem. Before my guests' amazed eyes…"

"Don't be a fool, Eugénie. Franz Schubert is no *improvisateur*, no performer of parlor tricks."

"Too bad," said the countess, sighing gently. "Then he needs the poem today, for you to sing it on Thursday."

"Eugénie!"

"I am rather behind in my household accounts, but if a few weh weh will kindle his artistic fires—" The countess chased the rest of her utterance into the ether with a vague wave of her hand, stirring up another hint of that exotic fragrance.

"He can use the money," Vogl said, once he understood the alarming dimensions of the countess's proposal, "but in matters of music, Franz cannot be bought. He follows his heart. He used to read poems voraciously and worked on ones that inspired him. At present he is not writing songs. He's obsessed with his opera."

"His opera?"

"Alfonso und Estrella. He and Schober talk about it constantly."

"Schober. That one." The countess lifted an interested eyebrow. "He's still in town?"

"Regrettably, he is. His influence over Schubert is not healthy."

"Certainly not if he keeps the little man from setting poems to music. We must redirect Herr Schubert's inspiration."

Vogl thought for a moment. "He may give special consideration to the work of a friend."

"Then tell him that the poem comes from you, or perhaps Herr Schober. Let me spend half an hour with Schober, and he'll oblige."

"I will not involve Franz Schober in any of my business, Eugénie. On that point I am firmly resolved."

"Very well. The mechanics of our enterprise are in your

hands. Present Franz Schubert with a poem. Have him set it to music. Perform the creation at Thursday's *soirée*. *Natürlich*! Everything's settled." The countess then dropped her imperiousness and instantly softened. "You will do this for me, won't you, Misha?"

"I'll do what I can," Vogl sighed, "but I won't involve Franz Schober. I don't approve of him."

The countess favored Vogl with a look of arch disappointment. "Misha, impending old age is turning you into a prude."

Vogl let the remark slide. "Where is this magnificent epic that Franz Schubert must immortalize?"

"Not written yet," the countess replied lightly. "Stop by this evening at six. He'll have a good twenty-four hours. Now, leave me. I really must dress. I expect several callers this afternoon."

Vogl bowed. "I'll stop by after this afternoon's rehearsal."

"At six!"

"All right, at six. Good day, *Contessa*."

The countess raised herself on her pillows. "You may kiss me once, for old times' sake."

"Ever the same Eugénie," sighed Vogl, leaning over to peck the proffered cheek.

Chapter Two

Descending the steps of the von Neulinger establishment, Johan Michael Vogl almost collided with a man going up. Both heads were tucked down in deference to windswept snow, the last gasp of a morning squall. No harm occurred, but Vogl obtained a glance at the youthful face of a man he didn't know. Through muttered apologies and awkward sidestepping on the stairs, Vogl concluded that the man was, like himself, Austrian, and, if his overcoat and scarf were any indication, wealthy. Undoubtedly this was the first of the countess's "afternoon callers." Vogl experienced a pang of something akin to jealousy.

What a fool he was. There were many perfectly innocent explanations for a well-dressed young man to call at the von Neulingers when the count was away. Vogl had received his summons by private messenger that morning. The young man probably received similar treatment. The city, indeed the entire world, teemed with young men who'd sacrifice greatly for a good word from the house of von Neulinger.

Angrily, Vogl cut this meditation short. The reason for the young man's visit did not concern him. If, God forbid, the man were a special friend of Eugénie, who was Vogl to begrudge the man an experience for which he would probably pay all the rest of his life?

Did one ever live down one's youthful indiscretions? Vogl mused as he directed his tread through the abating snow towards the Wipplingerstrasse. Would he ever free himself from thralldom to Eugénie von Neulinger? More than a decade had passed since that fateful, bewitching encounter with Eugénie Schutzmacher, his little Jennie, the last and undoubtedly the wildest of his adventures. He had been in his thirties, well past time to be sowing wild oats, and his mad infatuation had not fallen beneath the cloak of youthful indiscretion.

Vogl smiled at the memory. How they had met! A story suitable for treatment by Schiller or Kotzebue. The Tyrolean village and his stranded acting troupe, the cellar of her father's shop, the desperate need for refuge from impending French bombardment. She, a frightened seventeen year old, embraced the tall stranger out of sheer terror as the bombardment began.

The embraces soon became something else entirely. Vogl recoiled from the memory of his disappointment when the French withdrew. While the rest of the troupe talked of nothing except the return to Vienna, he begged the manager to remain in the village for an extra week, an extra hour.

Some years later, Vogl himself brought Eugénie to Vienna—having an opportunity to "make an actress of her," as he explained to the theater manager—at the precise moment history chose to crown his Jennie Destiny's Darling. Their longed-for reunion ran exactly two weeks. Her stage career ended at its debut, when an English Viscount, Lord Bellingham, one of the many involved in re-defining the world after Bonaparte, invited her to sup with him after the performance. She never trod the boards, nor shared Vogl's bed again, although she appeared in the boxes often enough, always with an entourage replete with uniformed men and women almost as dazzling as herself.

It was said that Princess Eugénie (as the world enviously rechristened her) knew more about what many kings and councilors thought regarding the future shape of Europe than they knew themselves. If they didn't understand the intricacies, she explained them. More than once, Eugénie came to him secretly backstage, not, alas, to rekindle their conflagration, but in hurried search of a costume piece or prop to embellish a masquerade, the details of which she never divulged. Rumors abounded about blood spilt on her behalf. Some gossipers of position high enough to speak with authority claimed that her smile could turn a duke into a pauper, or vice versa. Vogl ruefully witnessed his Little Jennie thriving everywhere in the dangerous carnival that was Vienna.

But she knew when to stop. Within a month after the Congress's last delegate returned to his fiefdom, she married Georg von Neulinger, a dashing widowed officer in the service of Chancellor Metternich. In the seven years following, as the lid of respectability clamped ever more firmly on the city, Eugénie von Neulinger transposed her public self into a sophisticated, charming hostess, famous for the *gemütlich* atmosphere of her salons, which attracted the finest minds of Europe. Access to the von Neulinger establishment was a prize esteemed almost as highly as admittance to the Sonnleithners'.

"No more," Vogl said aloud, again curtailing his musing. He never had an honest inkling of what went on in Jennie's heart. He felt relieved that he no longer cared—very much. "But here I am, once again, operating on her behalf, promising to push the most innocent of all men, Franz Schubert, into harm's way," he muttered. "*Schwammerl*, the little mushroom, does not understand the *beau monde*."

For proof of his friend's naiveté, he needed only to recall Schubert's previous summons to the von Neulingers' some months before. Franz refused. "I intend to spend that evening with some friends," he said.

"The same friends you see every day," Vogl replied with veiled exasperation. "Unlike the von Neulingers, they don't pay you. And you are passing up a chance to meet one of the world's most beautiful women."

Schubert was adamant. "I will not relent for love or money."

The glittering prospect of possible prestige meant nothing to him. That one simple sentiment virtually guaranteed another year, perhaps an entire lifetime, of impoverished obscurity for Franz. He lived for three things only: his pipe, his comrades, and his music. Alas, none of them did him much practical good. Every time Vogl saw him, Franz seemed a little paler, a little puffier. There was no man easier to persuade to accept another glass of wine, another helping of potatoes. True, Franz could rarely afford to buy these or most other viands himself. Vogl admitted that, in the matter of diet, he was one of Franz's nemeses.

As for other friends ... Well, there, perhaps Vogl was too harsh. Wasn't he now heading towards the home of young von Schwind, who graciously provided Franz a haven after the falling out with Mayrhofer? But von Schwind, like Vogl himself, could do so little, particularly in the face of that blackguard Schober, who actively subverted anything Franz's other friends attempted. It was Schober who turned Franz from the path of songwriting, just when it showed signs of becoming profitable, to work on an impossibly risky opera. He kept Schubert out all hours in all weathers, at great risk to the composer's constitution.

All the while, Schober touted his "prerogatives of genius," an obvious euphemism for indulgence and irresponsibility. Perhaps Schober had the temperament, strength, and charm to profit from such madness; Schubert would only come to grief by it. Yet little, loyal *Schwammerl* followed Schober everywhere, oblivious to the danger the man personified.

And then there was the music, the thread that bound Schubert to everyone's heart. Here was a true God-given gift. But a more sensible Almighty would have supplied some means for Schubert to gain material advantage from it. True, Franz wouldn't starve as long as he tapped that seemingly inexhaustible vein of song in his heart, but under the best of circumstances, Franz would never enjoy a substantial income. Now he was banking on an opera! Even if *Alfonso* were another *Figaro*, Franz could never navigate it to the stage through the maze of backbiting confusion comprising the life of the theater.

To be heard today, one had to write like an Italian and fight like a Prussian; tomorrow, it was likely to be the other way around. Rossini visits the city, and everybody is mad for *La Centerentola*. With Weber's new sensation, the complete version of *Der Freischütz* on the horizon, everyone parades their "common German heritage." Italians fear for their lives until the next earth shattering phenomenon comes along—a week later. One heard rumors that the French, out of fashion since the time of Mozart, were preparing a new invasion.

"What difference does it make?" Vogl grumbled loud enough to discourage a street vendor of chestnuts from offering his treasures. Vogl passed by unawares. Schubert heard no musical voice but his own, and Vogl feared that the swirling tides of Viennese popular opinion would drown him.

The snow stopped as Vogl reached his destination. After a moment of trepidation, he raised the brass knocker and let it fall heavily on von Schwind's door.

"I believe Herr Schubert is upstairs," the parlor maid informed him, "but I'll look in the study."

"That won't be necessary, Fraülein. I have only a few minutes, and I know how Franz hates having his work interrupted."

That was a lie. Vogl himself hated to interrupt his friend's work, Franz's only economic supply line. Even more than its prospect of financial independence, composing kept him, however temporarily, from the clutches of that despicable Schober.

"Ah, *meine süsse* Vogelein," Schubert exclaimed, hurrying down the stairs toward Vogl. "Aren't you rehearsing this afternoon?"

"I am. I have an invitation for you."

"Tell me about it as we go to the coffee house. It's more or less on your way. I'm ravenous."

"Have you had a productive morning, Franz?"

"Good heavens, I've forgotten my pipe! Wait here while I fetch it, won't you, dear fellow?"

Waiting, Vogl observed that the air was clearing, becoming colder. Instinctively he adjusted the lapels of his overcoat.

"Here we are. Now tell me of this invitation."

"The day after tomorrow, *chez* von Neulinger."

Schubert blanched. "Impossible!"

Vogl expected this. "I know of some who will be most disappointed," he said with a sad smile.

"Your old friend, the countess?"

"I refer to myself…."

"You don't need me. Try Hauptnegel, or Schimmel. He's always in search of patronage."

"And some Fröhlich sisters."

Schubert stopped in his tracks. "Anna?"

"Josephine," said Vogl, quickening his gait.

"Wait a moment, my dear fellow."

With amusement Vogl slowed down. Schubert needed five full strides to catch up with the much taller man. He seemed slightly short of breath. Vogl continued, "Josie and I hope to perform a duet…"

"That magnificent voice!"

And with that, Vogl knew he had prevailed. "She will be less enthusiastic when she learns that it's impossible for you to attend."

"I'm meeting Schober. You know that Weber is bringing *Der Freischütz* back here?"

Of course Vogl knew. Everyone knew. In every salon, rathskeller, and coffee house in the city, battle lines formed, critical weapons were honed. Rumors circulated behind closed doors from the grandest palaces to the humblest hovels. An educated listener could deduce the sentiments of an apartment's occupants simply by noting the musical phrases that wafted down from their parlor pianos. Amateurs plunking out hoary airs by Paisiello were declaring war on those insisting on broadcasting the works of Beethoven.

Austrians heard their precious German language sung but only as comedy, in music halls of the second tier. No one equated these frivolous musical plays with dignified Italian opera. Weber's greatest coup was securing the city's Central opera house for the performance. His brilliantly disingenuous disclaimer, "Had I known Viennese customs better, I would have sought out a more modest venue more suitable for this venture," apparently lulled the Italians into a false sense of security. They allowed him access to their most powerful citadel.

In fact, the previous October, a miniaturized performance of *Der Freischütz* received a smattering of positive attention. However, no Germanophilic ideologue, nor any of the city's really important critics, thought the performance worthy of notice. Weber, in another political master stroke, did not conduct the performance himself. How important could this new work be?

It was only after news of *Der Freischütz's* performance in Berlin, the full four-hour spectacle, with its innovations "starting with the overture," its "majestic effect" and its "powerful influence over all truly German souls" filtered into Vienna did the Italians realize they'd been duped. The Viennese public, asserting itself as Europe's elite cultural arbiter, demanded the right to assess the groundbreaking opera, in all its glory, themselves. Opera fanatics from all walks of life, "from clerk to king, from peasant to princess," virtually forced the Italian establishment to bring *Der Freischütz* back.

Weber heeded the call and was *en route*, with his piece refurbished, a company of hand-picked singers, and a promise to supervise every aspect of the production—including wielding the conductor's baton—himself. Neither Weber nor *Der Freishütz* suffered from obscurity this time. Large wagers, arguments, and reputations hung in the balance. All this in advance of the first rehearsal. Vogl's only surprise was that Schubert knew of the brouhaha.

"What of it?" he asked.

"We're going to show von Weber the score of *Alfonso*."

"A week before his arrival?"

"Don't poke fun, you ninny. Schober and I are considering how to approach him. What, if anything, in the score needs changing, that sort of thing. We're meeting on Thursday."

"And for that, a meeting with someone you see every day, you pass up a chance to perform with Josephine Fröhlich?"

"That does seem silly, doesn't it?" Schubert admitted.

Vogl nodded his head solemnly. How typical of Schubert to forget any business consideration in view of a moment of musical gratification. "I'll tell you what. If you attend the countess's *soirée*, I will approach von Weber myself on your behalf."

Schubert smiled with delight. "Done, my good man!"

"But there's one other thing," said Vogl. "A wager."

"Well, don't look at me to supply collateral," Schubert said with a laugh. Schubert's continual brushes with destitution were the long-standing matter of jest between them.

"In a manner of speaking, I've done just that," said Vogl.

"What? My eyeglasses? A lock of my hair?" Schubert laughed more, adding, "I won't sacrifice my pipe. You know I have nothing else."

"You have talent, facility, and invention."

"And look what they've done for me. A garret room in a draughty house—"

"Melodrama doesn't suit you." Vogl cut his friend off sternly. "You're not starving. I've told a certain skeptic of my acquaintance that you can set a poem of twenty lines to music in less than twenty-four hours."

"Can't everyone?"

"The song must have a complete piano accompaniment."

"Nothing simpler." Schubert paused for a moment. "I presume the poem is in German?"

"I assume so."

"You haven't seen it?"

"No one has seen it."

"I sense a trap, Michael. What if the poem is in Hotentot, or worse, Hungarian?"

"I doubt my skeptic is as devious as that." Actually, Eugénie was capable of any deception, but Vogl did not expect her to exercise her wiles on a practical joke. "I'm to pick up the manuscript this evening and perform it at the von Neulinger *soirée*, with you providing the accompaniment, at nine o'clock Thursday night."

"Very sporting of you. Well, 'I shall win for you at the odds, if I can'."

"'For this relief, much thanks'," Vogl said in perfect, precise

English. He then finished in German. "I leave you now for the theater."

"Bring the blasted thing here," Schubert said, "to the coffee house. I won't budge, I promise you."

Chapter Three

Vogl quickened his pace against the cold, which ironically intensified in brightening the afternoon sun. He arrived at the Hofoper a few minutes after the start of rehearsal.

"Ah, Herr Vogl, how kind of you to join us," Assistant Manager Schmidt barked at him. Schmidt's obligatory sarcasm lacked conviction and, after dispensing with that formality, Vogl was ignored. His part in the piece, Bildman's *The Empress of the Common*, was small, and he had played it before.

Sensibly, Schmidt was working on the scene that needed the most attention, the festive celebration of village maidens led by the bewitching "Katarina" that preceded Vogl's own appearance as the merchant who joyfully announces the impending arrival of his student/soldier son Hernando. Vogl tried to convince himself to review his twelve measure *duettino* with Katarina. She was, after all, the underlying cause of the

Hernando's unbearable heartache in the third act. More to the point, the Katarina *du jour*, Frau Anna-Marie Donmeyer, was a perfectionist who did not take kindly to unprepared co-workers. Vogl witnessed several of "La Donmeyer's" impromptu scenes during the course of his career, though he had never triggered one. Today was not the day to tempt fate. Desultorily, he roused himself from a seat at the back of the house to search out a score.

Something on the stage arrested him; not something, someone. Fresh faces were part of the landscape at the Hofoper. Its frantic production schedule consumed quantities of choristers. Yet this girl stood out. Why? Her attire, Vogl decided disingenuously; to be precise, her shoes.

Among the maidens, she alone wore slippers without heels. The other maidens, who would be slipper-shod when performing before the public three weeks hence, by consensus, remained true to the low-heeled fashion of the street, oblivious to the demands of theatrical verisimilitude. Seasoned maidens knew managers' preferences. Vogl continued to study the newcomer and noticed further variation from standard rehearsal dress: a certain opulence in the fabric of her pale blue frock, the ivory ornament adorning the velvet band around her neck. And again there was that fresh, young face.

Vogl turned to his colleague, tenor Peter Thym, a man his age cast as his stage son Hernando. Peter awaited the still distant moment when Hernando appeared on the scene and became instantly infatuated with the fetching Katarina.

"Who's the new one?" Vogl whispered.

Thym whispered back, "You missed Schmidt's introduction. She's Kunegunde Rosa."

"Kunegunde?"

"Some bureaucrat's daughter. Frankly, I doubt she'll remain long in the profession."

"Perhaps not," Vogl muttered.

Indeed, some on-stage confusion proved that Fraülein Rosa lacked her co-revelers' experience with maypoles and the intricate contortions of limbs and torsos their appearance on stage invariably inspired. That Schmidt was hiding his exasperation suggested that the new girl enjoyed some sort of protection. Someone at the Hofoper owed someone else a favor.

What drew so many pretty girls to the stage? Moreover, why did so many men support their aspirations? If the lady failed, she lowered herself in her sponsor's affections. If she succeeded, the sponsor might never see her in private again. Vogl winced in memory of his own sponsorship of his darling Jennie.

Still, this Kunegunde Rosa was no Eugénie Schutzmacher. Fraülein Rosa appeared completely earnest in response to Schmidt's corrections, truly contrite over every misstep. However ineptly, she took her responsibilities seriously. Jennie, in her first and only stage production, by sheer force of personality, had made sure from the first that everything on stage revolved around her. She hurtled through the Hofoper like a comet, leaving chaos in her wake.

Vogl, inured to uncalled-for interruptions of his thoughts by his memories of Eugénie, shook them off. What interested him about Fraülein Kunegunde Rosa? Her name—that must be it. Blame her father. Imagine, an Austrian bureaucrat who appreciated Voltaire. But Kunegunde had more than a name. Vogl glanced again at her shoes and decided to learn more about her.

"We resume in ten minutes," Schmidt proclaimed, "at which time, *mein Herren*, we will be ready for you."

Vogl and Thym nodded in response and headed towards the wings. Although his entrance came from stage left, Vogl headed upstage right.

While the other ladies of the chorus dispersed, chattering and readjusting their garlands, Fraülein Rosa remained on stage during the break, reviewing her dance steps. Smiling, Vogl waved greetings at some of his cast mates until, with impeccable, professional timing, he stopped. Kunegunde's outwardly sweeping arm slapped his lapel. Only then did she notice him.

"Oh! Forgive me, *mein* Herr," she stammered, blushing, "I was so intent … I did not see you there."

"Think nothing of it, Fraülein." Pretty enough, Vogl thought.

An earnest gleam animated her pale blue eyes, and her auburn hair emitted sufficient luster; but Vogl saw nothing extraordinary. Her age—only a year or two past adolescence—surprised him. Most protégées were either a little younger, hence utterly irresistible to a certain kind of man, or a little older, more experienced. Most of her ilk observed other girls' procedures before attempting the game themselves. Perhaps Kunegunde found a different path to the stage. At any rate, she was almost certainly the youngest maiden in this particular lot. Vogl knew the histories of several of the others, in some cases quite extensive histories, featuring lovers, husbands, and occasionally, children.

But he was wasting time. This girl no longer interested him. His devastating experience with Eugénie Schutzmacher cured Vogl's weakness for mad infatuation, or should have. He immediately thought of half a dozen women whose charms he found more inspiring. He began an apology for interrupting her, but she interrupted him.

"Forgive me. Are you not Michael Vogl?"

"A piece of him."

"You were Pizarro."

"Fraülein, I assure you, I have always been Vogl."

"No, no! In honor of my thirteenth birthday, my parents took me to see *Fidelio*. You were Pizarro."

How flattering to be remembered. "I was."

"What a magnificent performance!"

"Thank you," Vogl said, as Kunegunde continued.

"When Leonora held a pistol to your forehead, I was awestruck. I never envied anyone so much as I envied her at that moment."

Vogl could not reply.

"Oh!" Kunegunde stopped with a blush. "Have I said something I shouldn't?"

"Not at all, Fraülein, not at all. Herr van Beethoven was truly inspired when he created that moment. Too bad today's piece is a comedy. Otherwise, I'd find you a pistol to point at my head yourself."

"Oh, but I don't want to … I mean, I didn't mean …"

The conversation ended as other ladies returned to the stage, among them Anna-Marie Donmeyer, who said with a trace of iron in her voice, "Michael, that is my spot."

"And mine is off left," Vogl responded suavely. "I shall return shortly."

"In character," warned La Donmeyer.

"Delighted to be working with you again, my dear."

"If your *tête-à-têtes* are finished for the day, Herr Vogl," Schmidt chimed in, "we will commence where we left off. Ladies, please start with the sweep to the left. Music!"

Two or three fell swoops later, Vogl entered as the merchant with his glorious news. Schmidt's and Donmeyer's demands occupied him for the rest of the afternoon and permitted no further interaction with Fraülein Rosa.

Chapter Four

S tars were visible when Vogl mounted the steps of the von Neulinger establishment for the second time that day, precisely three minutes before six.

"Punctuality is the actor's chief virtue," he muttered sanctimoniously. No one heard him. Indeed, he dared not risk the wrath of Eugénie, whose high jinks often demanded intricate timing. He was immediately admitted into the foyer, where he took a moment to catch his breath. Almost at once the front door opened, but Vogl did not encounter Eugénie. Instead, he saw the strange young man of the morning, now dressed in evening attire. Politely Vogl drew himself to his full height and uttered a polite, "*Guten abend.*"

The youth dashed past him and out the door without so much as a nod.

This breach of etiquette startled Vogl. He asked Diederich, the servant manning the door, "Is that young fellow late for the theater?"

"I wouldn't know, *mein* Herr."

"He certainly seemed in a hurry."

"The master's son rarely stays in one place very long," Diederich replied, before he bowed and withdrew.

Vogl knew of Heinrich, Georg's son from his previous marriage, but until that morning, Vogl had never seen him. Eugénie had mentioned Heinrich from time to time but always seemed slightly embarrassed when his name came up. What woman needs reminding that her husband had a life before she appeared in it? How odd that in the span of ten hours Vogl and Heinrich's paths crossed twice.

Vogl recalled that Heinrich studied in Heidelberg. Why Georg thought fit to send his son there was unknown. The venerable German university boasted an excellent reputation to be sure, and more than a few fathers sent wayward sons there to keep them out of mischief. Whether Eugénie's reticence regarding her stepson derived from any dust in the young man's attic, or from Eugénie's own private demons, Vogl had never learned.

Vogl considered the man's attire interesting. One expected an officer's son to become an officer, especially if that son attended university at Heidelberg, but Heinrich wore no uniform. "Youthful rebellion," Vogl mused, "the Teutonic male's one inalienable right." From the look of him, Heinrich had reached the age to confront his father. If Vogl's experience with his own father was any guide, Heinrich wanted to outrage the old man as much as possible—for a year or so—before accepting, in one way or another, his progenitor's authority. That was the Austrian way.

Perhaps the young man needed Eugénie's help. Heinrich

might well desire step-motherly intercession on his behalf, perhaps advice regarding an affair of the heart. Such diplomacy was Eugénie's *forte* in pre-Metternich days.

Of course in those days, any man entering Eugénie's sphere, young, old, military, civilian, married or single, became her slave. Vogl still wondered whether he was fortunate or not to remain beneath Eugénie's notice most of that time. Life at her beck and call, though not dull, was uncomfortable. But that was all so long ago. Contemporary legend claimed that Eugénie no longer prowled the slave market. As Vogl's brain foundered in these unhelpful waters, the parlor door opened again. Diederich announced that the count awaited him.

The antechamber Vogl entered artfully impressed the visitor with its opulent austerity. Tasteful expenditure radiated from its parquet floor through its mahogany furnishings, right up to the ceiling, still showing vague ghosts of ghastly baroque decoration under a thin coat of pale blue paint. Along opposite walls stood two sideboards. On top of the left one, a silver ornamental coffee service glistened; on the other reposed a set of crystal decanters glistening with their amber contents. Brass sconces lined the wall, and between them hung various paintings—largish still-lifes of comestibles over each sideboard, flanked by small portraits, one supposed of previous von Neulingers. Single chairs, upholstered in red and silver, flanked the sideboards, but the place was hardly a sitting room. It felt like an overdressed interrogation chamber.

Eugénie sat in a chair by the sideboard with the decanters. Her husband stood by her side, with one hand on the back of her chair. Vogl appreciated this composition of impeccable decorum. The von Neulingers always paid exact attention to detail.

Adopting his best formal manner he said, "I bid you good evening, Herr Count. Good evening, Countess."

Von Neulinger acknowledged Vogl's words with a small bow. Vogl, as always, was impressed with the man, who radiated both confidence and self-discipline. He wore his full regalia—a uniform the color of caramel crème, with epaulettes and medals, golden frogs on the jacket, and a crimson sash. On another man such trappings might appear foolish, but the count's face forestalled any sense of frivolity. His gray eyes revealed nothing but steely confidence. Although close to Vogl's age, as streaks of gray in his reddish-brown hair attested, the count maintained every inch of his well-mastered military posture, refined by frequent visits to Vienna's stables and dueling clubs. He looked considerably stronger than Vogl, himself no weakling. Eugénie's consort was certainly no milksop.

As for Eugénie, she displayed a dazzling array of jewels on a gown of dark blue velvet, trimmed with silver. It played nicely with the fabric upon which she perched. One glance confirmed that the von Neulingers operated among Vienna's most important couples.

"We are about to attend an emperor's reception for the ambassador from Tuscany," von Neulinger said quietly.

His voice had a surprisingly high timbre. Vogl always felt surprise that the count was a tenor. On the stage, such a man would be played by a baritone. Regardless of tone, the count's remark was an implied order to make his business snappy.

"We could perhaps offer Herr Vogl a glass of wine." Mischief was in Eugénie's voice.

Choosing tact, Vogl said, "If such an offer were made, I'm afraid I must decline. I'm expected at the theater."

"What do you perform tonight?" asked the count, his politeness metallic.

To cover for his little lie, Vogl began a response to the effect that his evening duties required him only to watch the performance, when Eugénie saved the situation.

"Tonight, Herr Vogl plays the role of the messenger," she said, "for me. Here is your missive."

From the sideboard Eugénie extended a sealed lavender tinted envelope. Vogl read the inscription, written in Eugénie's elegant script with careful underlining: "To Fraülein Schikaneder - By hand."

A faint smile at Eugénie's duplicity crossed his lips. She took such pleasure in artifice. Her path to the title of countess rarely displayed examples of undue circumspection or discretion. Her primary weapons were magnetic beauty and the constantly disquieting impression that she was one—only one—step ahead. The legion of men still under her command proved the strength of her stratagems.

Vogl fell in step like the rest. "The lady will receive her invitation forthwith," he said with his own slight bow. "And now, I must go."

"We will see you at Thursday's *soirée*, will we not?" asked the count.

"I would not miss it for anything."

"Michael is providing the evening's entertainment," said Eugénie. "I'm sure he'll divert us better than this gathering at the Hofburg tonight. How I deplore these formal occasions. I much prefer quiet, intimate evenings at home."

A quiet evening with seventy guests, thought Vogl, but he said only, "Until Thursday, then."

"Come, Herr Vogl," said the count, "we'll walk out with you. Eugénie?"

He offered his arm. Eugénie dutifully rose and took it. Her gesture ushered Vogl into the hallway two steps ahead of them.

Vogl felt some misgivings at this unexpected act of condescension. Von Neulinger was not stupid. Did Eugénie believe he had no suspicions? Perhaps he simply had no illusions. Eugénie employed intrigue as naturally as Signor Rossini employed *crescendi*, whether or not such effects were strictly necessary.

Vogl felt the count's eye upon him, but fought down the impulse to dart out the door when the von Neulingers donned their outer wraps. He waited patiently. Perhaps the count wanted to show off the fur trim of his cloak. It came from an exotic mammal Vogl didn't recognize, perhaps North American. Vogl's fears dissipated when the von Neulingers' mounted their coach and dashed off towards the Hofburg without offering to deliver him to the Hofoper. Now he was free to march to Café Lindenbaum, his actual destination. Schubert awaited him there.

Chapter Five

Alone on the street, Vogl looked unhappily at Eugénie's envelope. The choice of addressee, "Fraulein Schikaneder," a mere afterthought on Eugénie's part, caused him some worry and no little pain. To her, Schikaneder was just a name, but Vogl remembered a man—a man dying destitute in a madhouse in 1812. He often spoke of the aging rascal in the time when Jennie was his.

Vogl watched Emanuel Schikaneder create the role of Papageno in 1791. Three years later, Vogl, under Impresario Schikaneder's watchful eye, created the role of Publius in a never-to-be-forgotten experience, introducing Mozart's last opera, *La Clemenza di Tito*, to the public. Schikaneder launched Vogl towards his present fame at the very moment his own star waned. Those magnificent days were long gone. Mozart passed into legend, and Schikaneder was virtually forgotten. How sad that, to Vogl, these men remained quite real, human, alive. Vogl saw himself, like them, on the verge of oblivion.

He shook off his melancholy aloud. "I shall not end up like Schikaneder, or Mozart either." He, like them, served the gods of Art faithfully, but the gods did not consume him. He maintained perfect physical and mental health, and he employed a resource that neither of these great masters possessed—a sense of proper proportion. He foresaw the twilight of his stage career and saved for it accordingly, not merely financially. Not trusting popular opinion—that most fickle of friends—to sustain him, he chose better allies than either Mozart or Schikaneder ever had, a lifetime of trusted friends from the theater and elsewhere, not to mention his library.

"*Gott im Himmel!*" Vogl shook himself again. "This isn't the time to contemplate retirement," he said loud enough to startle a passerby.

The man's reaction reassured Vogl. He still served his gods with great energy. Now they commanded him to fulfill a sacred duty: preserve the young genius Franz Schubert from forces of darkness such as consumed Mozart and Schikaneder. He quickened his step.

At the Café Lindenbaum, Vogl encountered the situation he expected and feared. Schubert, camped at a table at the back, was so engaged in animated conversation that he didn't notice Vogl's arrival. Schubert's companion showed only his back, but Vogl recognized from the dark, undisciplined locks just touching the dyed velvet collar of his maroon coat Schubert's librettist, Franz Schober. Schober: third-rate poet, second-rate actor, , first-class libertine.

Vogl considered Schober another of his great indiscretions, although not of the romantic kind. Six years before, Vogl, always one to promote youthful talent, consented to perform the role of the count in *Cosi fan Tutte* for a young upstart company of which Schober was a member. Schober's role as a servant didn't disguise his aristocratic breeding and bearing, his dashing good looks, his superbly graceful manners. Schober's earnest enthusiasm when speaking of the great dramatic heights he hoped to achieve appealed to Vogl—then. In the first bloom of their association, which lasted several weeks, Vogl took a personal hand in the fiery, young performer's career. Six years later Vogl regretted his good intentions.

Vogl soon learned where Schober's greatest talents and interests lay—the fields of self-indulgence and seduction. His off-stage antics suggested that he took the cynical themes of da Ponte's satirical opera for his personal creed. Vogl was no saint, but he fully understood the difference between youthful exuberance and unmitigated predatory behavior.

Vogl saw Schober use their association as a conduit into Vogl's set of acquaintances among Vienna's social elite, usually not for artistic support but rather for personal, often unsavory, gratification. At that point Vogl took decisive steps to distance himself from Schober's machinations. The sequel justified Vogl's decision. Schober's artistic career advanced little, but scandals featuring his name grew by volumes.

The one redeeming grace was that Schober introduced Vogl to Schubert. Five winters before, Schober dragged the reluctant, resentful Vogl home with him to introduce yet another new "genius." Schubert, the genius in question, was hopelessly incapacitated at the meeting, barely able to stammer out how honored he was to make Vogl's acquaintance. He was utterly unable to perform any music.

Fortunately, Schubert's music spoke for itself. Within weeks Vogl began to include the little man's compositions in his own vocal recitals; within months Vogl and Schubert were performing together. For Vogl the collaboration was a joy. Schubert was everything Schober wasn't—a genuine talent driven by immortal forces with only incidental attachment to the physical world.

Vogl stood within earshot of the conversation for several moments, waiting for someone to notice him. From what Vogl could gather, *die zwei* Franze debated about how much of their opera to present to Carl Maria von Weber when he arrived in Vienna. Schober expressed his views *forte*, bordering on *fortissimo*.

"If the third act is too long, the master will tell us."

"But why show him material of which we are unsure? Act two ..." Schubert's voice was no match for his friend's in volume, but it resonated with sincerity.

"Weber won't touch a fragment. Give him the complete score."

"But the third act remains incomplete ... in its soul."

"Schwammerl, operas have no souls, any more than women do."

Vogl chose that moment to intervene. He stepped forward. "*Grüs Gott*, Franz. *Guten abend*, Herr Schober." He wanted to leave no doubt regarding which man he considered his friend.

Both men answered at once, Schober with a cool nod, Schubert with unabated animation. "Misha, help me convince this donkey that two perfect acts are better than three imperfect ones."

Schober became all obsequiousness. "We value your opinion, Michael."

"Since I haven't studied this masterpiece and I, like you, have never met von Weber, I doubt my opinion is worth very much. I'm actually here on another matter." Vogl brandished Eugénie's envelope.

"My commission!"

Schober seized the opportunity to joke. "Schwammerl in the military? Little Franz, one doesn't need to don a uniform to attract the fair. Please reconsider."

The remark produced the desired effect on Schubert. He smiled as Schober hummed the first two bars of "*Non piu andrai*" from *Figaro*.

"Herr Schober, please leave us for a while," Vogl went on steadily. "This matter is urgent for both of us."

"Yes," said Schubert. "I am Misha's second in an affair of honor. We are to prove that the pen is not mightier than the chord."

"Very well," said Schober. "I have other engagements this evening. I was hoping you'd join me, Franz. There is a certain young lady …"

Vogl said nothing. He merely dangled the envelope before the composer who sighed. "I must decline. The muses beckon, and they demand more than corporeal mistresses."

"So they do," said Schober with apparent good humor, "and that is why it is important to snub them every now and then, to keep them in their place. I can't persuade you, Little Franz?"

"I have promised Herr Vogl my services for the next twenty-four hours."

"Then farewell. *Guten Abend*, Herr Vogl."

"Schober," Vogl acknowledged with relief, but Schubert continued.

"Franz, wait. You must witness the battle. We take the field Thursday at the von Neulingers. You shall be my guest."

Schober paused. An entrée into a von Neulinger event was not to be sneezed at. "Can you grant me an invitation?"

Of course Schubert couldn't. Even he recognized that fact, but conventional etiquette did not supply the last word on the matter. "No. You can't come as my guest," said Schubert. "You must be part of my entourage; my page ... turner." He laughed. "Misha and I insist upon it, don't we?"

Vogl, wanting nothing of the sort, held his tongue.

"Let's decide the issue Thursday," said Schober. He left the coffee house without another word.

Vogl watched the departure. "I don't approve of that man."

"Oh, Schober's decent enough, once you get to know him."

"I've known him a long time. Decent sorts pay their tavern bills, and they stay off the Annagasse."

Schubert peered over the tops of his spectacles. "Oh? Have you been following us?"

"Of course not! But I have it on reliable authority ..."

"Misha, what reliable authority?" Schubert said with feigned scorn. "You, who follow the most profligate of professions—the theater. If some actress sullies Franz Schober's good name ..." Schubert, shaking his fist in the air, broke off with a laugh. "Or do you refer to your beloved Aurelius? Now there's reliability for you, but how a long-deceased Roman emperor comes to learn of the deeds of Franz Schober, I cannot imagine."

"Very well. My warnings fall on deaf ears."

Schubert blanched. "Never mention deafness in the presence of a musician. They say that van Beethoven is afflicted with it."

"Don't change the subject, Franz. I say once more that Schober is a bad influence on you."

"Misha, I can take care of myself."

Falser words were never spoken, thought Vogl, though he let the matter drop.

"But, come to think of it," Schubert continued, "I may have leapt from the gate too soon regarding this Thursday. Who knows if we'll have any pages for him to turn? Tell me about this little *billet doux*."

"At the moment, I know no more than you, Franz."

"Then, for God's sake sit down, and let's see what our adversary has in store for us." Schubert took the lavender envelope from Vogl's hand. "The color seems promising," he said. Then he passed the envelope under his nose. "Hmm. Unscented. I take as a bad sign." Schubert opened the envelope and extracted its contents. "Here we are. '*Die Sonne und das Veilchen*,' submitted anonymously but transcribed in a very feminine hand. Do you suppose we have some sort of philosophical debate? Give me a moment."

Vogl took the seat vacated by Schober and watched his friend adjust his spectacles to read. Shifting attention to the detritus on the table, Vogl reflected on the degree of disorder in Schubert's simple life. Mixed in with pages of three different newspapers were more than a dozen pages of manuscript, some with words, some with musical notations on them, many crumpled. An inkwell, two pens, and a sharpening knife sat near Schubert's right hand, although the dried ink on one nib and the cleanliness of the other, suggested that little writing had occurred for at least the past hour. Partially buried under a broadsheet was a plate with what looked like breadcrumbs on it. Nestled behind the plate, Vogl perceived the caramel-colored bowl of Schubert's partially filled pipe. By the composer's left hand rested a small crystal glass with a *soupçon* of wine in it. It dawned on Vogl that one roll and one paltry glass of wine were all Schubert had consumed that day.

"I'm going to have something, Franz. Would you like some more wine?"

"Dear fellow, I thought you'd never ask," said Schubert quickly tossing down the few drops remaining in his glass. "And could we get some bread with it?"

Vogl summoned the waiter who no doubt had tactfully avoided Schubert's little nest for a long time. With a few brisk instructions supported by a few gulden, the waiter replaced the newspapers with wine, bread, and some sausages.

Dining slowed the tempo of their immediate project. Schubert's appetite for Wienerwurst outpaced his appetite for literary disquisition. He ate rapidly, silently, barely able to maintain proper decorum with knife and fork. The young artist's tragedy, thought Vogl. On the days when one could afford to eat, because one's art was in demand, one forgot to eat, because one was overwhelmed with the art. At least that was Schubert's predicament. Left to himself, Schubert would starve. Vogl considered himself a general in the army of the composer's supporters who refused to let the calamity come to pass. Tonight, Vogl won another skirmish in the active campaign to keep Schubert's body and soul together.

Vogl sipped his wine, shuddering at the thought of how

Schubert's evening might have gone. True, Schober would willingly pay the bills, or rather absorb Schubert's debt into his own, but he'd supply no food. Only wine and, almost certainly, women. Not even song. When Vogl last called upon Schubert the morning after an evening in Schober's clutches, Schubert was incapacitated to the extent that they canceled their afternoon rehearsal and scratched out a wretched performance in the evening. A similar fiasco at the von Neulingers could destroy them both.

At last Schubert finished the last morsel of bread and returned to work by lowering his spectacles and reaching for his pipe. "I'm now ready again to confront 'The Violet'. Misha, do you have a match?"

The reason Franz's postprandial pipe still contained tobacco was that Franz habitually forgot to take any matches with him when he left home. He was too shy to ask a stranger for a light.

During his second reading of the poem, Schubert started nodding. Then came a moment of humming. Theatrically, Schubert folded up the paper and, with a knowing wink, returned it to its envelope. Vogl asked impatiently. "What do you make of it?"

"E-flat major," said Schubert, smiling. "I hope you don't find the key disagreeable?"

"Franz stop talking nonsense. Will you set the poem to music?"

"The problem seems quite straightforward. The meaning of the poem remains somewhat obscure ..."

"Then let me see it!"

"But its central sentiments are clear enough," Schubert

said, depositing the envelope in a pocket behind his lapel. "Our impetuous bard includes a hazard or two in this somewhat confused allegorical narrative," said Schubert patting his coat pocket, "but nothing insurmountable. Yes, E-flat should serve."

"Choose any key you like, Franz, but, if you encounter difficulties I can assist—"

Schubert lifted his surprisingly sturdy hand from his breast. "Let's not alter our usual arrangements. Stop by von Schwind's tomorrow evening."

"I'm performing tomorrow."

"Well, Thursday afternoon then, and we'll use the piano there to rehearse for the evening. I promise not to write anything you can't sing."

Vogl was accustomed to accommodating artistic temperament, but he couldn't resist saying, "I have no doubt of that, Franz, but I must know the poem's contents."

"Tut tut, Misha. This is no longer a mere poem. It is my song. Until I hear from my muses, I won't discuss it further."

"Just don't write anything you can't play, little wanderer," said Vogl with poor grace.

"Now Misha, don't be upset. A little suspense will do you good. Let's talk of something else. What have you heard of *Der Freischütz?*"

"Not a word."

"But you will introduce me to von Weber."

"If I can. But Franz, you must realize that he's preoccupied. The production of an opera is, at best, an arduous undertaking. Since Weber is doing everything, both preparing the singers and conducting the orchestra, not to mention staging the piece, he won't receive many social calls from strangers while he's here."

"Schober thought of that. We'll delay our approach until after the performance."

An ugly thought passed through Vogl's mind. "Franz, does Weber expect you to approach him?"

"Well, no, but …"

"Does he even know of your existence?"

"Not exactly, but …"

Vogl noisily planted the palm of his right hand on the table. "Do you expect to meet with a personage who will be more in demand than the pope while he is here, without so much as a preliminary introduction?"

"It's not as bad as all that…"

"You must be mad!"

"Misha, hear me out. We haven't made contact with Weber directly, but we have great hopes…"

"I have great hopes of becoming Persia's next potentate!"

Schubert remained unperturbed. "We needn't meet in person. Weber only needs to see our manuscript. Salieri promised to broach the subject."

"I suppose that's something," Vogl muttered. Antonio Salieri, long retired from his place as Vienna's preeminent opera composer, had been Schubert's teacher. Weber was probably shrewd enough to pay his respects to the grand old man of Viennese musical life, if only to appease the Italianophilic faction of the city's opera fanatics.

"We have additional strategies. Schober has written a poem to honor von Weber. We will find out where he's staying. If all else fails, we'll wait outside until he appears.

And if you help us—"

"I thought you only wanted me to facilitate the social amenities at a pre-arranged meeting."

"That too. But aren't you always welcome at the Theater an der Wien? Can't you approach the maestro during a free moment of rehearsal?"

"I can, and dash all your hopes at once. Franz, you know better than to interfere with an artist in the throes of creation."

"Well, afterwards."

"I'll do what I can," said Vogl shaking his head. Schubert's cavalier attitude didn't shock him, familiar as he was with his friend's impracticality. Franz did not know how the world worked. He earnestly expected a letter from an old teacher, a flattering poem, and his acquaintance with Vogl to deliver *Alfonso und Estrella* into Weber's hands. If by some miracle Weber received the opera, the odds against the piece ever reaching the stage remained astronomical. Vogl expected the next few days to provide Schubert a sobering lesson. Perhaps Weber's inevitable snub would induce Franz to produce works that brought in some money. Vogl saw his role in the upcoming drama clearly: soften the inevitable blows.

"Franz, what do you say to some Linzer torte?"

"Misha, I'm honored to accept."

Shortly thereafter the men cordially parted. Schubert walked back to his room at von Schwind's; Vogl found a horse-drawn cabriolet to take him back to his lodgings off the Ringstrasse. Schubert presumably sang himself to sleep with visions of sun-drenched violets; Vogl contented himself by reading a few pages of Epictetus before succumbing to dreamless slumber.

Chapter Six

I t is not true that no work gets done in Vienna before noon, at least not in so well-managed an enterprise as the Hofoper. To prepare for the evening's *singspiel* (one of Hiller's tested war-horses that Vogl had ridden to general acclaim several times before), Vogl appeared at the unlikely hour of 10:00 a.m., to participate in a three-and-a-half hour brush-up rehearsal. Assistant manager Schmidt dismissed Vogl at noon with obligatory sarcasm, ordering him (unnecessarily) to return at 6:00 for the evening performance.

Vogl didn't leave. Schmidt planned to work on Act III of *The Empress of the Common* during the afternoon. Vogl didn't appear in the act but he decided to wait for the start of that rehearsal in response to a thought that disrupted the tranquility of his breakfast: Who would portray Fraülein Schikaneder?

Eugénie von Neulinger's mysterious poem came to Vogl under the cloak of an invitation to this fictitious person. Only someone with the social naiveté of Franz Schubert refused invitations to the prominent von Neulingers. Moreover, the count was shrewd. He'd seen the invitation; he expected a response. Someone—someone not known to the count— ought to answer the call. Not without qualms, Vogl prepared to approach Kunegunde Rosa.

The village maidens were to assemble at two, to provide appropriate choral response to Katarina's complaints about Hernando's effect on her turbulent heart. As Vogl hoped, Fraülein Rosa appeared well in advance of the hour. As a tyro, she wished to vocalize in advance, even for a staging rehearsal. Vogl knew he had plenty of time for his mission. The other more jaded maidens arrived at rehearsals at the last minute, and settled into the rehearsal process as situations demanded. Of course, one expected La Donmeyer to flutter in a few minutes late, to remind everyone of her importance.

Vogl positioned himself strategically at the *repetiteur's* piano and happened to be running through the final measures of "*Ganymed*" when *Fraulein* Rosa approached. Vogl finished the phrase and rose from the bench. "*Guten Tag*, Fraülein."

"*Guten Tag*, Herr Vogl. That's a lovely piece. I'm not familiar with it."

"It's a song by my friend, Franz Schubert."

"Schubert? The one who set "*Erlkönig*" to music?"

"The same."

"Why, I love that piece! Do you know it?"

With a trace of surprise Vogl said, "I perform it all the time. I had the honor of introducing it to the public."

Kunegunde's jaw dropped. "How wonderful for you! Such exciting music! One can almost see the lightning flash and the torrents of driving rain. You say you know the composer? You are very lucky."

This girl certainly knew how to prick his vanity. Vogl and Schubert performed together all over Austria. Vogl always did his utmost to promote Schubert's talent and "*Der Erlkönig*" in particular, but he naturally assumed that audiences came to hear *him*, no matter what he chose to perform. On the bright side, the girl's lack of knowledge about his professional life boded well for his present purpose. He interrupted the flow of her words.

"Fraülein, I can introduce you to Herr Schubert."

Kunegunde gasped. "Impossible! What would I say to such a powerful personality?"

The idea of Schubert as a powerful personality caused Vogl to smile. "Have no fear on that account, Fraülein."

"Well, perhaps, if someday…"

"Fraülein, Schubert and I are performing tomorrow night. Will you join us?"

"After the performance, you mean?"

"It's an informal occasion. A gathering at the von Neulingers." The von Neulinger name apparently made no impression on Kunegunde, so Vogl continued, "Please come as my guest."

"I doubt my father will approve."

"Fraülein, I'm not suggesting anything improper. I insist on meeting with your parents before we venture anywhere."

"I'll ask for permission this evening. Father seemed impressed yesterday when I told him I met you."

"He, too, remembered my Pizzaro?"

"Oh. He's seen you several times. He didn't mention any

particular role. He usually sleeps through operas, or so Mother says."

Vogl sighed. Getting a compliment out of Kunegunde Rosa was as difficult as getting a bass note from a piccolo. He returned to the business at hand. "If you do attend the von Neulinger soirée with me, I have an additional request."

A tremor of fright passed over Kunegunde's face, followed by an expression of determination. "I won't sing with you."

"Nothing quite so taxing. I merely want to introduce you under an assumed name."

Fraülein Rosa almost giggled at the thought. "Me? Intrigue? How exciting! Do I wear a mask?"

"Hardly, Fraülein. Just assume a different surname for the evening."

"What's wrong with my own surname?"

"Nothing. Indeed, if your surname is Schikaneder, you won't have to change it."

"It's Rosa. Kunegunde Rosa," she added with an absurd curtsey.

"I'm honored, Fraülein Rosa, but tomorrow I need a Fraülein Schikaneder."

"I'll do it—gladly—if my father permits."

"Then let's leave it at this: I'll escort you home after your rehearsal. Will your father be available then?"

"Oh, yes. He stays at the gallery only half a day on Wednesdays."

"Then it's settled. One thing, Fraülein. Let's not mention our charade to your father."

Kunegunde favored him with a mischievous smile, the

first sign that the girl was capable of flirtation. "Herr Vogl, I no longer feel compelled to tell my parents everything."

Noticing others arriving for the start of rehearsal, Vogl quietly withdrew. Throughout the afternoon and his dinner hour, Vogl experienced unanticipated bouts of self-doubt. He preferred life to be simple and straightforward. While he exercised a certain degree of diplomacy to advance his career, he scrupulously avoided the sort of duplicity in which he now found himself a participant—except when compelled by Eugénie.

Vogl maintained an iron self-discipline that over time had tempered itself into steel. In the theatrical world he enjoyed a reputation for complete reliability. Though not strictly pure (in worldly terms) in his service to the muses, he never allowed sensual, financial, or romantic temptations to distract him. He saw too many who succumbed—to bottles, to cards, to lovers—and refused to let any such catastrophe befall him.

He understood the dangers so well that his responses were a series of maxims. "Applause is the only stake worth playing for," he warned gamblers. "Save your histrionics for the stage," had long been his attitude toward the throes of romance.

He had rules for stage performance, too. "Beer before Singspiel, wine before opera; and just one glass!" He usually found this libation a reliable method of focusing his artistic powers.

However, this evening's glass of beer was not producing the desired effect. "Women!" he heard himself mutter, meaning Jennie. Like a fool, he was embroiling himself and others in a situation of unknown complexity, for Jennie's sake. Almost a decade after their brief, tempestuous affair, he remained under her spell. What business had he recruiting innocent youth to facilitate traffic in cryptic communications through mysterious music? Why was he protecting the secrets of a woman who quite possibly was using her wiles to draw another lover into her web? Perhaps it was because Jennie chose courses exactly opposite to those Vogl chose for himself.

Where he resisted temptation, Jennie plunged in with both feet. While he scrupulously avoided all distractions from his career (once Jennie abandoned him), Jennie jumped ship at the first opportunity. Until her marriage, Jennie's perfidy in matters of personal politics was almost as well established as Vogl's reputation for loyalty.

"This current enterprise takes on the character of a philosophical debate," Vogl told himself.

Essentially, Vogl was happy with his life choices, and Jennie seemed happy with hers. His self-denying pursuit of Truth through Art gave him satisfaction of a kind that Jennie pursued through personal gratification and the manipulation of emotion and temporal power. Which course was right? Which course—his or Jennie's—produced greater happiness? Viewed in this light, the upcoming soirée assumed the contours of a desperate battle.

Vogl paused. Philosophy was all well and good, but the sophisticated world of Eugénie von Neulinger was no abstraction. Real people, unequipped to adjust to the whirlings of that world, faced having their lives redirected, damaged, or destroyed.

Consider her influence on him. When they met in her father's cellar, Vogl was pursuing an honorable courtship of a diplomat's daughter. After his tumultuous time with Jennie, Vogl wrestled his conscience into submission and was ready to try again for marriage. But by then the diplomat's daughter was happily married to a silk merchant and pregnant with the first of her six children. Vogl was still a bachelor.

Now Vogl felt responsible for bringing two potential victims into Jennie's world: the as-yet-untested Kunegunde Rosa and the hopelessly over-matched Franz Schubert. Vogl vowed that any associations formed between these young artists and Eugénie would remain temporary and tangential. He valued his clear conscience as much as Jennie valued her ability to emerge ahead of the rest.

He fretted more about Fraülein Rosa than Herr Schubert. Franz at least had his talent to shield him. A scoundrel like Schober might waylay him for an evening or two, but in the end, some wisp of song dragged Schubert back from whatever abyss threatened. Once the muse captured him, Franz heard no other voice.

But what of Kunegunde? She was appealing enough to attract all sorts of interest (cynics always placed the highest value on fresh blood), and Vogl had no idea where the girl's head or heart lay. He regretted the impulse to provide a Fraülein Schikaneder for the evening, even as he reminded himself that the risks of serious trouble resulting were slight. He was on the verge of abandoning the enterprise when he returned to the theater precisely at five to escort the young lady home, according to his promise.

Vogl waited discretely in the theatre lobby and ignored Thym's knowing leer when Kunegunde rushed to join him. A carriage awaited, but Kunegunde lived not far away, and she preferred to walk in the gathering dusk. Vogl dismissed the carriage and offered his arm. She took it.

Vogl had not escorted a young woman home in such a manner for quite a while, and the first few paces of their journey down the street felt rather awkward. Vogl, at six-feet tall, covered nearly twice as much ground per step as the girl, who did not release his arm. Muttering an apology, he adjusted his stride. With a good *andante* gait established, Kunegunde looked up at him.

"Herr Vogl, may I ask you something?"

"One may always ask. One may also choose not to answer."

"Is Frau Donmeyer happy?" They walked on for several steps. "Oh, I see. You choose not to answer," she said with a blush.

"Not precisely, Fraülein. I just don't know what to say. Why do you ask?"

"Frau Donmeyer walked off the stage when Herr Thym missed an entrance. They say it is nothing unusual."

"I see," Vogl said with amusement. "How long did Frau Donmeyer stay off stage?"

"A full five minutes!"

"No more?"

"No."

"Then rest assured, Fraulein. Frau Donmeyer was not unhappy. She is an accomplished, dedicated *artiste* who does not like to waste time. I assume Herr Thym apologized?"

"He did, but she said nothing. And then they sang a duet."

"How did it go?"

"Oh," Kunegunde said, blushing, "it was beautiful, really exquisite."

"Then everything is all right. With an incompetent singer, her fits of pique continue for hours."

"Good. Then I didn't do any lasting harm."

"You?"

"Herr Thym missed his entrance because he was talking to me."

"Don't blame yourself for that, Fraülein. Herr Thym knows what he's doing."

"He was showing me a more graceful way to manage Cherubino …"

"Cherubino. The schnauzer? Oh you poor child!" A loathsome moment in *The Empress of the Common* required that Katarina, on the brink of leaving the village forever, bequeath her incongruous lap dog to another maiden. Naturally, as the newest recruit to maidenhood, Fraülein Rosa was put in charge of the little beast.

"Cherubino's real name is Rolf. In the opera they call him…"

"Schmutz. I know, Fraülein. Rolf and I are old acquaintances. The last time we met, his nickname was Pierrot, because French opera was in vogue. Rolf, like La Donmeyer, is not particularly fond of the French. He nips."

"That's what Herr Thym said. While showing me a sure-fire way to control Rolf, he missed his entrance."

"Ah. Now I can answer your original question. Anne-Marie Donmeyer is quite happy, as long as the fauna remain in the forest and don't upstage her. In return, Fraülein, may I ask you a question?"

"One may always ask," Kunegunde said with a smile—a truly lovely smile.

"What draws you to the stage?"

"Why, nothing."

"I don't understand."

"This opera was my father's idea. He disapproved of my hanging around the gallery all day."

"The gallery?"

"My father manages the Oberes Belvedere Gallery. Do you know it?"

The artlessness of the question all but flabbergasted Vogl, who immediately resolved to abandon his project of letting this girl accompany his descent into espionage. The Belvedere Gallery, pride of the Habsburgs, was the envy of all Europe. Its manager was a person of consequence. Masking his disappointment, Vogl rose to the immediate occasion.

"My dear, I performed there. Afterwards the Crown Prince toured me through the collection personally." This was not a happy memory for Vogl. His tour occurred in late 1815. He was Jennie's invited escort, until Jennie sent him off into the sunset alone while she remained with the Crown Prince. During the ensuing seven years, Vogl avoided the Oberes Belvedere Gallery, despite the magnificence of the artwork inside.

"That was before my time," Kunegunde said matter-of-factly. How far before caused Vogl some consternation. "Anyway, Father's the first manager they've ever had, and he started his tenure only last month. We really haven't settled in yet."

Perhaps Vogl's masquerade was salvageable after all.

Kunegunde continued, "Father says that the gallery is dangerous for me. He thinks I'll meet the wrong kind of people."

"I see," said Vogl, not seeing at all. What sort of parent

considers painters and their aristocratic patrons the "wrong kind of people", yet thrusts his daughter into the opera world as an improvement? Obviously someone with enough egalitarian sentiment to name his child Kunegunde.

"But I think," said Kunegunde, "Father just wants me out of the way. One of his friends from home …"

"Home?"

"Salzburg. But we were living in Prague. As I was saying, when Father learned that one of his old flames worked at the Hofoper, he asked her to find a place for me. Thus I am now Rolf's keeper."

"Fascinating," said Vogl sincerely. Herr Rosa promised to be an interesting acquaintance.

"We turn here," Kunegunde said. "Our house is at the end of the street."

Vogl easily convinced Kunegunde's parents to allow him to escort her on the following evening. His name and more to the point, the von Neulinger name, carried the day. The only difficulty lay in persuading the old man not to join the party, but eventually Rosa saw the advantages of waiting until he was fully ensconced as manager of the Belvedere Gallery and in a position to return their hospitality.

So satisfied was Vogl with his afternoon's success that he gave a sterling performance of Herr Heller's Singspiel that evening, untainted by any other concerns. After the performance he went home, took a celebratory glass of wine and headed straight to bed feeling at ease with the world.

𝄢

The sound of a marching band stirred him. It sounded like *La Marseillaise*, but in A-flat minor! Vogl, shivering at an open window, witnessed an odd procession. In a cart, bound together and headed for apparent execution, were Franz Schubert and Kunegunde Rosa—Schubert smiling and singing; Kunegunde weeping. Behind the cart, came Franz Schober, who pelted the two with rose petals. Schubert looked up, and catching Vogl's eye, demanded quite distinctly, "Misha, grab my spectacles. You'll find them in my pipe."

On that absurd note, Vogl awoke, surrounded by silent darkness. Dawn remained hours away, but Vogl recognized the depths of his dread of the byzantine world of Eugénie von Neulinger. He slept no more.

Chapter Seven

"That's a D flat, Misha."

"Yes, of course. Nice touch."

"Kind of you to say so. Shall we take that phrase again?"

"All right, perhaps with a slightly grander *rallentando* at the finish."

Rehearsal progressed smoothly. True to his word, Schubert had not written anything that challenged Vogl's voice, or from what Vogl gleaned from the sketchy scrawl on the piano's music rack, anything beyond Schubert's imperfectly polished pianistic ability. Musically, they would satisfy Eugénie von Neulinger's demands. Additionally, Vogl found *"Die Sonne und das Veilchen"* quite to his taste.

Of course he did not share his opinion with Schubert. The composer never sought other musicians' appraisals. When criticized, he became morose; when complimented, flustered. In either of these conditions, Schubert's hands became hammers, imperiling his piano accompaniments. Vogl always let Schubert's music speak for itself. His highest compliment was merely to sing the golden lines again. Schubert sought no greater reward.

"No, that's too much," said Schubert sharply. "Too slow."

"But it's the culmination of the song," Vogl protested. "A little *tenuto* at the apex ..."

"We are singing of violets, dear fellow, not oxen. That was too slow!" Schubert confidently asserted himself about music, at least with Vogl. Vogl generally let the little maestro have his way—in rehearsal. "Take it again, and be careful with my D flat!"

Forty minutes later, the duo deemed *"Die Sonne und das Veilchen"* ready for its impending public debut. Schubert and Vogl then discussed the other pieces on the program and the order of their performance. They agreed to invite Josephine Fröhlich to sing *"Gretchen am Spinnrade"* as a solo encore after she and Vogl performed Mozart's *"La ci Darem La Mano"* duet. Throughout these mundane preparations, Vogl felt his anxieties of the night before return. When Schubert went upstairs to retrieve some additional music, Vogl revisited their source.

Paradoxically, the main problem was that nothing was amiss. Vogl saw no sinister significance in Eugénie's new song. Innovation added zest to an evening's entertainment, but why this particular poem? As Schubert noted, it told a simple story, rather like a folk tale, but Vogl saw no compelling moral sentiments amongst its innocuous words. Vogl tried to dismiss the issue. Schubert's setting made the song likely to please, and that was Vogl's only relevant concern.

But his worries persisted. Vogl's best theory—that Eugénie, determined to present these words in the best possible light, recruited the best parlor musician in Vienna to bolster them—was unsatisfactory. Eugénie never doubted her powers. Her minions were mere adjuncts to her brilliance. She paid them little attention. Furthermore, Schubert was not Vienna's most highly regarded composer, even excluding Beethoven, whose ungovernability and contempt for aristocratic patronage kept him totally out of Eugénie's reach.

Vienna teemed with songsmiths; Eugénie knew, or knew of, dozens of them.

Maybe Jennie wanted Schubert precisely because she did *not* know him. What a terrifying thought. Schubert's transparent innocence and unfamiliarity with aristocratic circles implied that ulterior motives loomed behind the song. Vogl hoped fervently that the only obligation for him and his small entourage was to perform the song and be done with it.

Schubert's light tenor voice interrupted Vogl's meditation. "Sorry for the delay, old man. I'd misplaced my pipe." The composer's blue-grey eyes were barely visible above a bunch of large black portfolios with paper peeking out precariously from every side. "Has Schober arrived?"

"Not yet."

"He's due at five," said Schubert dropping the folders on the top of the fortepiano. "I thought to arrange this stuff as we ride over," he explained, "but since Schober isn't here, I'll start now."

At precisely that moment, Schober appeared at the door. "Disruptive as ever," Vogl muttered. Schubert gathered up his bundle and hurried from the room.

"Franz, one moment. Will you need these?" Vogl indicated the pages of music still on the piano's music rack, the sketches for the accompaniment of *"Die Sonne und das Veilchen"*.

Schubert stopped in his tracks. "*Mein Gott*, yes!"

"Don't worry, I have them."

Vogl gathered the pages and headed after his friend, retrieving en route several pages fallen from Schubert's bundle.

"Almost a disaster," Schubert laughed, as Vogl exchanged curt nods with Schober.

Vogl hired a coach for the evening, and the three men rode in reasonably comfortable silence—the stillness of a temporary cease-fire. Vogl sat next to Schober facing Schubert, who occupied himself by arranging his papers. Occasionally a page escaped Schubert's grasp, and Vogl or Schober, whoever was nearest, retrieved it. When the coach stopped, Schubert jumped up.

Vogl was amused. "We are not there yet, Franz, but now that you're up, will you change places with me?"

"Why?"

"You'll see in a moment," said Vogl, reaching across Schober for the door of the coach. They were at a rear door of the Schloss Belvedere. Vogl dismounted to escort Kunegunde Rosa.

She stood in the doorway, ready to go. Vogl cleared the first hurdle without difficulty. After exchanging the requisite pleasantries with her father, Vogl, his misgivings multiplying by the second, ushered her to the waiting coach.

"Herr Schubert, Herr Schober, permit me to present Fraülein Schikaneder, who will be joining us this evening."

Schober lit up instantly. "*Enchanté, Mademoiselle*" he said, smiling as he offered his hand to help Kunegunde into the coach.

Schubert lit up in a different way. His face turned red as a sugar beet as he muttered, "*Guten Abend*," and buried his face in his folders.

Kunegunde's "I'm delighted to meet you, *mein Herren*," was perfectly polished.

Vogl found the ensuing ten minute journey entertaining. He sat across from Schober. Kunegunde sat on his right side, back to the coachman directly across from Schubert, who continued to bury himself in his music. Kunegunde exercised all her wiles to engage Schubert in conversation while Schober fought to get the girl's attention.

"Is that the music for this evening's entertainment, Herr Schubert?" Kunegunde chirped. She received a grunt in return.

"Will you show it to me?" she continued.

"Don't worry, Fraülein," said Schober. "Once Franz finds himself a keyboard, you'll hear it all." Schubert looked up with a tentative smile.

"I hope you play "*Erlkönig*", Kunegunde went on undaunted. "I've attempted it myself at home, but it's quite difficult."

"No Schubertiad would be complete without "*Erlkönig*", said Schober. "When Herr Vogl is not there to give it the magnificent treatment it deserves, someone always sings it."

"Do you ever get tired playing all those octaves, Herr Schubert? " In response, Schubert looked quizzically at his right wrist. Schober tried a different tack.

"Forgive me, Fraülein, but may one be permitted to know your first name?"

"Why, it's…."

Vogl was himself curious to hear her response. She assumed the surname of Schikaneder for the evening, but whether she planned to assume a complete alter ego remained to be seen. Vogl's curiosity remained unsatisfied as Schober continued, "It's not Franz, by any chance is it—or Frances?"

"Why no!"

"You see, aside from Herr Vogl, our host here, all our surnames begin with the same sound: Schubert, Schober, Schikaneder. Herr Schubert and I are both named Franz, and so I wondered if…"

Schober was finally rewarded with a blushing smile from Kunegunde. "You may call me Juliet."

"Charming!" said Schober. "Franz, we could write a little canon,

Fortune called, so they obeyed her:
Schober, Schubert, Schikaneder!
Not a one of them stayed sober,
Schubert, Schikaneder, Schober!

"The devil! Franz, how dare you have a surname I can't rhyme?"

Vogl completed the cycle:

"Everyone within the Stüb' hurt:
Schikaneder, Schober, Schubert!"

Schober laughed, and Kunegunde turned her smile on Vogl. "Really, Herr Vogl, I'm surprised at you."

"You can't have all the fun, Herr Schober."

Schubert remained immersed in his portfolios.

"You see, Fraülein, I'm Franz's wordsmith. We have an opera in the works."

"Franz," Schubert said at last, "I can't discuss the opera now."

"An opera, Herr Schubert," said Kunegunde. "What is it about? Will we hear any of it tonight?"

Kunegunde at last got what she played for, a verbal response from Schubert, an embarrassed "No, Fraülein, not tonight."

Schober began to regale the company with a synopsis of the turgid plot of *Alfonso und Estrella*, but their arrival at the von Neulingers forestalled the recitation.

There followed some debate about approaching the house. As invited guests, Vogl and Kunegunde should go up the steps to the front door. As a hireling, Schubert belonged at the servants' entrance. Schober, as a hireling's hireling, belonged with Schubert. Yet Vogl habitually demanded that when he and Schubert performed together they were treated as equals to each other and to the invited company, as guests. In fairness to his hosts, in those cases Vogl arrived with the guests, not in advance of them. If Vogl mounted the steps with his entire party this evening, Schober became an equal, a relationship Vogl preferred to disavow.

The final complicating factor was that Schubert, of course, had not eaten. He'd be offered to share in the meal given to the servants before the guests appeared, but time was running short. More important to the adventure was that Schubert familiarize himself with von Neulinger's piano before playing it in front of others. Too many well-to-do patrons of the arts viewed musical instruments as sculpture, often with insufficient regard to the sounds they emitted. Both Vogl and Schubert had struggled heroically with badly-tuned instruments. If heroic measures were required to make the evening successful,

Vogl wanted to be forewarned.

At last Vogl decided to drop off Schubert and Schober at the servants' entrance, then return to the coach and take a short drive with Kunegunde in order to arrive with the earliest guests. At the last minute, Schober chose to remain in the coach with Kunegunde, promising to go straight to the servants' hall upon his return.

"But Franz then, you'll miss supper," Schubert pointed out.

"Never fear," Schober replied, "I always travel prepared with sustenance." With a flourish, he produced a flat bottle from his coat. "Will anyone share in my repast?"

Vogl and Kunegunde both declined with good humor—in Vogl's case, feigned—but Schubert took a swig, "To fortify myself for the coming ordeal."

Vogl formed a new plan: escort Schubert to the front door as a guest, but dispatch him directly to the kitchen, then return to Schober and Kunegunde, take a short coach ride and come back with two additional guests.

Diederich, von Neulinger's steward, foiled it. Standing in the open doorway, he ushered the two musicians inside and told Vogl that the countess wanted to see them. Only Vogl's hand on Schubert's arm prevented him from taking flight.

"How delightful," Vogl said suavely, tightening his grip. "I'll inform the other members of our party." Vogl was loath to leave Fraülein Rosa alone with Schober, even for a minute. "Franz, please tell the countess that I'll be along forthwith."

"Michael," Schubert stammered, but Vogl was gone.

"This way, Herr Schubert," said Diederich.

𝄢

Franz Schubert had been in aristocratic establishments before, so he was not overawed by the opulence surrounding him as he passed through the dining room into the von Neulingers' grand salon. Only after they started up the stairs did Schubert's knees begin to quiver. When they reached an antechamber and the servant announced his name, Schubert needed all of his will to enter.

A glittering vision confronted him. The countess, in not-quite-full regalia, sat on a horsehair divan and extended her bejeweled hand towards him. All was assembled carefully, from the delicately crossed ankles above white satin slippers up to the ever-so-slightly raised eyebrows and the slight opening of the lips. The velvety "Herr Schubert, *enchantée*," coming from her throat, with imperceptible movement of her rouged lips, was equally polished.

Schubert almost fainted. His eyes focused on the outstretched hand with rings on all but the index finger and thumb. Should he take it—kiss it? What if he made the wrong decision? At the last moment he thrust his own arms behind his back and managed an awkward, silent bow.

The countess merely broadened her smile. "And where is our friend Michael?"

"Misha … Michael is telling the other members of our party where we are. He'll be here directly."

"Good. I so want to thank you for your extraordinary efforts. Please sit down, Herr Schubert." The countess indicated a straight-backed chair to her left.

Schubert did not want to sit. He wanted to vanish. How could he sit? He was still wearing his overcoat, which hung down to his knees. Undressing in the countess's presence, even if only to the extent of removing his overcoat, was unthinkable. He began, "Pardon me, your highness …"

The countess interrupted with a tinkling laugh. "Don't tease, Herr Schubert. I am no princess, merely a countess."

Schubert blushed, "Oh! I beg your pardon, your majesty."

The countess favored him with an admonitory lifting of an eyebrow. Then she laughed again. But she didn't renew her offer of a seat. "I hope my request was not too burdensome, *mein Herr*."

"Not at all," said Schubert when he realized that he was supposed to speak.

"Thank you for obliging me on such short notice. But the task is completed?"

"Yes … in effect."

"In effect? What do you mean?"

"You see, your … frau—countess, there's the piano part not fully copied. I can finish it before the guests arrive," Schubert added, hoping to be dismissed.

"Can you not play it from memory? You've just written it, after all."

"I can, but with people around, I prefer to have music in front of me."

"Most interesting, Herr Schubert. I'm fascinated by the workings of the musical temperament. But the text is fully transcribed? Misha has his part?"

"Oh yes. I finished that yesterday."

"Where is Misha?" asked the countess, voicing the question pounding in Schubert's own head, "It is not like him to keep his old friend waiting."

9:

In fact, Vogl was searching for the countess at that very moment. He lost several minutes persuading Kunegunde and Schober to enter the house. Schober wanted to take a ride around the ring with Fraülein Schikaneder who, to Vogl's dismay, did not object. Indeed, had Schober not made the mistake of partaking once too often of his flask, Vogl might not have prevailed. There was further delay at the front door, depositing the two in a sitting room and assuring that servants kept an eye on them. In an ill-considered maneuver to prolong chaperonage, Vogl reminded Diederich that he knew his way around the house and did not need an escort. Before mounting the stairs, Vogl saw with relief Kunegunde sitting at the von Neulinger's piano. Schober retreated to his bottle, lacking the decency to ask for a glass.

Vogl went to Eugénie's dressing room but found the door locked. Now having the choice of finding Eugénie somewhere to his left or somewhere to his right, Vogl chose incorrectly. At last he heard Eugénie's velvet voice uttering petulant tones. "I will not have my evening ruined!"

Vogl swept into the room in his best leading man manner: "I am here at your service, *Contessa*! I beg a thousand pardons if I have caused any distress." Schubert smiled at the gesture. Eugénie didn't.

"Good evening, Michael," she said coolly. "Are you in good voice this evening?"

"Anything less would be unpardonable, my lady."

Eugénie softened. "So our little artistic venture has come to fruition," she said, favoring Schubert with a smile calculated to charm, but which caused the little man to look at the floor. "The question now is, when to introduce it?"

"I'll sing it for you now, if you wish."

Eugénie smiled at Vogl. "That won't be necessary. I'll wait with the rest of my guests. However, I want the song to create an indelible impression. Should we start with it?"

"It is unwise to begin with something climactic."

"Then how will I know which song it is? I'm afraid, Herr Schubert, that I know very few of your compositions."

Schubert said nothing, so Vogl said, "I'll introduce the song before I sing it. Permit me to decide on a suitable moment …"

"Misha, I want to know in advance. I may need to postpone the maiden voyage."

"Then signal us."

"That I would prefer not to do. I have it. We will have dancing. Herr Schubert, do you play dance music?"

"With pleasure, my lady. Are waltzes permitted?"

The countess let out a genuine laugh. "*Natürlich*! And Mazurkas too, if you have them. We are quite daring here. Michael, after you've sung a while, take a rest. Sing the new song fourth after the dancing."

"A brilliant solution, Eugénie."

"Now go back downstairs. I expect my husband at any moment."

"Of course, *Contessa*." Vogl gallantly took Eugénie's hand and brought it to his lips. When the same hand was extended towards Schubert, he again bowed with his hands behind his back, spun on his heel, and left the room leaving Vogl behind.

Vogl caught up with his friend at the top of the stairs. "The countess Eugénie is impressive, is she not?"

"Oh, she seems very nice," Schubert said earnestly. "Does she know how to dance the mazurka?"

"It's best to assume that the countess knows everything."

Chapter Eight

T he flurry of activities at the von Neulingers did not prevent a normal evening from passing in the rest of Vienna. By six-thirty that evening, three new corpses had attracted official attention, one in the canal, one in an alley, and one on the edge of the Glacis military drilling ground on the city's western side. Already one plausible perpetrator was in custody as officials scrambled to preserve the veneer of security essential to the city's reputation as well as the morale of its more respectable citizens. Given such efficiency, most residents of the city found ways to contain their savagery, preferring to mask most lethal intentions beneath civilized words.

Indeed, a stone's throw away from the von Neulingers, another gathering was taking place. In his own townhouse, Count Moritz von Merlinbeck hosted an improbable quartet: himself, his Countess Zdenka, and two Germans, Instruktor Jurgen Himmelfarb and Professor Johannes Barenberg. They spoke in anticipation of the impending musical soirée, to which they had all been invited.

"We are preparing for war!" Instruktor Himmelfarb asserted, "and we must keep our minds on it."

"Surely you exaggerate," von Merlinbeck said meekly. "After the devastation caused by the Corsican bandit, no one has much taste for such conflict."

"Unless they are assured of instantaneous and total victory," Himmelfarb responded.

"Impossible," said the count.

"Not if the reports from the Urals are true. Decisive action now will alter the face of Europe forever."

Despite being the youngest member of the group, Zdenka took charge. She spoke with authority. "Meine Herren, haste will destroy us. Tonight we go only for good company and light entertainment. Don't expect anything of a serious nature."

"Our time is short, and our resources are limited," grumbled Himmelfarb.

Jurgen's patience was the most limited resource, thought his taciturn colleague, Barenberg.

Himmelfarb was a man of action who consorted with scholars like Barenberg and other elements of civilized society, not by choice but by accident. Four years earlier, a beam fell from an entryway to a silver mine and broke his arm. The next day Himmelfarb prevailed in a debate with the person he deemed responsible for the loose beam "with his left hand," as it were, choking the truth out of the engineer with the arm unencumbered by a sling. Himmelfarb then took over from the engineer as a supervisor, expecting to return to his regular duties when his arm recovered.

Then came Barenberg, a professor from Munich, who understood everything that connected the mathematics of mining to European politics, but nothing about practical methods of extracting metals from the earth. Certain representatives of the Prussian government sent Barenberg on exploratory missions. Barenberg, in due course, found Himmelfarb.

The association wasn't always easy, but it functioned. Himmelfarb, fortunately and atypically, was literate and displayed rudimentary awareness of civil behavior. Barenberg, who reserved his snobbery for those who pretended to understand Leibnitz as well as he did, tolerated his associate's not infrequent solecisms. Barenberg eventually prevailed upon his superiors at the university to employ Himmelfarb, purely in an advisory capacity.

The notion of Himmelfarb ever talking to an actual student amused some and alarmed others. Barenberg made sure that such a travesty never occurred. Himmelfarb's title, "Instruktor," was honorary and ironic.

The two academics' presence in Vienna was the upshot of a sort of mining accident. While deciding how best to cross an alluvial plain on their way to a coal seam, miners in the Ural Mountains stumbled upon a vein holding vast quantities of platinum. Until that moment, scarcity of the element rendered it of interest to only a few. However, platinum *cognoscienti* fully appreciated its value if it ever appeared in bulk. A British scientist, Lord Wollaston, had discovered ways to make the metal malleable.

The Russians knew what they had in terms of raw material. The English knew how to transform the material into invincible weapons. Germans like Himmelfarb knew where and how the Russians were digging. Germans like Berenberg knew what the English were capable of. Hence, the race was on to scoop up the platinum first.

Rumblings from the Urals inspired the Prussian government to send Himmelfarb and Berenberg to Vienna, where an English force seemed to be gathering. The bearing and polished behavior of the Austrian aristocrats appealed to Barenberg, at least in a theoretical way, but they bothered Himmelfarb. He resolved problems by clawing through mud and dust with physical force, not by indulging in endless chatter in immaculate rooms. Barenberg's problem-solving methods involved secluding himself for hours at a time so that numbers formed patterns in his mind. His students and colleagues were largely irrelevant distractions to him.

Although he was Himmelfarb's superior, not only in rank but, he believed, in every other way too, Barenberg encouraged his colleague to talk for them. Himmelfarb didn't mind; his very contempt for the power and importance of words released him from inhibitions that governed more polished negotiators. Himmelfarb said what he wanted when he wanted.

"Tonight I shall confront the British …"

"Please, Instruktor." The Countess Zdenka stopped Himmelfarb with the shocking maneuver of placing her hand on his knee. Indomitable among workingmen, Himmelfarb lost much of his effectiveness in the company of women, especially women as attractive as the countess. He generally ignored women he couldn't avoid, but Zdenka compelled his attention. Her light touch stopped his tongue more effectively than a beam falling on his head in a mineshaft.

"In Vienna one must arrange all the cards before playing the hand," the countess explained. "Tonight, we'll learn about the other players. Armed with that information, I shall guide you properly."

Himmelfarb remained unsatisfied. "I don't like palavering. We are prepared to make a simple offer once we get a straight answer to a simple question. Why not do it all tonight?" Encountering only silence, Himmelfarb continued, "What do you say, Johannes?"

"Would anyone else like another brandy?" the count interrupted.

Receiving muttered refusals from the others, Merlinbeck rang for a servant, who appeared, bottle already in hand.

"I trust the countess," Barenberg said gravely, as the servant withdrew. "We're in a foreign world here, Jurgen. The Merlinbecks are natives. Our instructions are to put ourselves in their hands. We will undoubtedly thrive under the Merlinbecks' care." It was a long speech for him, but the high stakes of their enterprise justified the effort.

"Herr Professor," said the countess, turning to Barenberg, "Allow me to correct some misconceptions." Zdenka's means of controlling Barenberg differed from those she employed on Himmelfarb, but they were equally effective. She appealed to the man's sense of reason, couching everything she said in terms of impeccable logic. Barenberg invariably succumbed.

"While my husband is dyed-in-the-wool Viennese, I come from Óbuda, a little city in Hungary." The countess's precision regarding detail was one of the reasons Barenberg trusted her. "Secondly, I am far from infallible. I only promise you my best efforts on your behalf. I can't guarantee success."

The countess's frankness increased Barenberg's trust. "Finally," she added with a steady gaze from her doe-like eyes, "I prefer being addressed by name, not by title. Please call me Zdenka." As of that moment, Barenberg's trust in the countess crystallized.

"Another?" the count half offered, half ordered.

This time Himmelfarb accepted a second brandy to match the count's fourth. Zdenka and Barenberg still nursed the remains of their first drink. "What shall we drink to?"

Appropriate toasts crossed every mind: "To control of the continent," thought Himmelfarb.

"To expanding horizons," thought Barenberg.

"To Eugénie's damnation!" thought Zdenka.

But the honor went to the count, who said cheerfully, "To platinum."

♪

The word "platinum" also echoed in the residence of the British ambassador.

"This rare metal," the ambassador explained to his retinue before embarking on the evening's excursion to the von Neulingers, "may become vital in the defense of The Empire. Lord Wollaston of the Royal Society informs me that platinum, in sufficient quantities, will alter the military situation on the continent permanently and incalculably. Should one control it, one becomes invincible on the battlefield. It is one of the hardest substances on earth. Until recently, it was thought that there were insufficient quantities to make it useful for the manufacture of military ordnance. The Russians' discovery in the Urals has changed all that. Thus, the safety of the Crown depends on our activities tonight. Do not let Tagili slip from our control. We must corner the market before anyone else understands the value of the material.

"We will turn a lot of heads when we arrive with Tagili in tow, so exercise extreme caution. I need hardly remind you he is not in our pocket. He may be operating outside the scope of the Tsarists. He wants a quick profit and will sell to the highest bidder. He has our offer, but he intends to entertain others. Tonight's situation is fraught with danger. Isn't that so, Sir Thomas?"

The question bore the barb of rebuke, but Sir Thomas showed no sign of discomfort, except for raising and steadying his nodding head. Truth to tell, he saw little change in the international landscape since the Congress of Vienna. Any political turmoil Britain suffered because of his lack of vigilance, he considered a paltry expense compared to the wealth of pleasure diplomatic jaunts provided. In his opinion his country's political machinations, win, lose, or draw, if one could tell the difference, changed nothing.

Sir Thomas joined this Austrian expedition not to serve the King, but for the spring shooting and fishing in the Hartz Mountains. When told that his route ran through Vienna, he accepted with alacrity, anticipating sport of a different kind. "Quite so, Your Excellency," he replied to the ambassador's dig.

"Pay particular attention to our hostess," the ambassador continued. "If there's any jiggery-pokery in the wind tonight, she'll be at the heart of it."

Again, the ambassador's stern gaze and unspoken

condemnation rested on Sir Thomas. Unfairly perhaps, the ambassador considered the lord's behavior, specifically when confronting a certain kind of woman, a principal reason that the Crown had no foothold in some important German seaports.

Perhaps Sir Thomas had let the ball drop ocassionally, but he maintained his desire to participate in the game. The evening before him held out the prospect of a tantalizing reunion. Young Jennie! Curiosity about her development during the seven years since their last encounter consumed Sir Thomas Bellingham. He took one last drink and wondered vaguely if Vogl would be there.

$$\mathbf{9^{:}}$$

"*Vot Ya*," Pyotr Dmitrivitch Tagili sighed and adjusted his green sash studded with medals he had manufactured himself—a costume piece, to be sure. He needed it to provide sufficient *cachet* to his imposture. He felt it was sufficient. Not bad for an itinerant clerk who, until a few weeks prior, had been staring at his last kopek.

Tagili, the son of a serf, was an opportunist. At the age of five he taught himself to cipher by studying papers left on a writing table by the land-owner's son and parlayed this ability into ways to spare himself from field work.

From his perch behind desks, Tagili developed a shrewd understanding of others' careless ignorance and relied on it to make his way in the world. For forty-two years he bluffed his way around the Tsar's dominion and beyond, serving various landowners and their offspring in various capacities, always willing to change his allegiance to whoever offered him the most reward. This policy enabled Tagili to see large swaths of society but had also brought him his share of vicissitudes. He knew destitution as well as times of relative comfort.

This time he hoped to arrive in the realm of the well-to-do with the wherewithal to remain there permanently. He had no master to assuage, no associate to circumvent. He stood alone in his assumed stature of exclusive representative of vast mineral rights.

Five weeks earlier, he had been transcribing accounts in a dingy office in Cherdyn. Among the papers that passed through his hands was a geological report mentioning the discovery of vast deposits of a mineral thought "very rare." Tagili pocketed the report (along with a tidy portion of the payroll funds he was asked to register) and, as far as his mining company was concerned, disappeared.

He didn't fully understand the value of his holdings, but he knew where to take them—Vienna. He had observed first hand just how much one could accomplish there.

As soon as he arrived in the city, Tagili sought out old associates. He stopped searching the minute he found out that Princess Eugénie was still active. He went straight to her new address, and, though he left no card, had no formal means of introduction, he was given instructions regarding when and how he would be admitted. Eugénie remembered him.

He marveled at how well the "princess" (now Countess) had fared since the mad days of the Congress of Vienna. Tagili then had been a virtually anonymous attaché with a large military delegation from his homeland hoping to recover something after the downfall of the hated Bonaparte.

Because of his access to certain strategic calculations, the princess approached him, and the two soon discovered a sort of spiritual kinship as they casually outmaneuvered aristocrats who had power to wield, but lacked the brains to wield it.

In her he found an ally both powerful and cunning. They were never personally close—their business relationship depended on keeping their association secret. Further intimacy had been hindered by a language barrier, among other things—but from the princess, Tagili learned a smattering of German and witnessed first hand the difference between someone like him, who schemed merely to remain alive, and someone who schemed her way into the highest ranks.

Thus it was straight to Eugénie that Tagili came with his stolen maps and unsigned contracts featuring the word "platinum." It was she who directed him to the British—the people least likely to question his authority as a Russian negotiator. All Tagili had to do was keep to himself and hide behind his limited knowledge of English. The plan was working perfectly.

If all went well at the gathering, Countess Eugénie would snare a buyer for his papers, and arrange for him to receive the first installment of the proceeds. He would then be a wealthy man. By the time his fraud was discovered, Tagili, a talented escape artist in his way, would be long gone.

He had no illusions. However much he benefited from the evening's machinations, Eugénie stood to gain exponentially more. Perhaps before he left Vienna, he could persuade her to grant him a larger percentage of the proceeds. Time would tell. Now he needed to join his British host-captors and travel to the *soirée*. Making sure that the latch of his third-storey window had not been repaired since he dismantled it that morning, Tagili left his room, accepted the two elegant military attachés waiting to escort him, and descended the stairs.

𝄢

Eugenie von Nuelinger stood at the top of the main staircase surveying the field of the evening's upcoming battles. The wheels had been set in motion. *All is ready*, she assured herself. The tasteful mansion is immaculate, inside and out. The rooms to be employed are properly decorated; the right food and wines are plentifully supplied. Everyone important would soon be there. She had prepared an appropriately elegant *soirée*. It was time for it to provide her with her next victory.

𝄢

The reflection in the mirror nodded approval. All was prepared for either a delightful evening of conviviality and music or potentially, the hostess's final tribunal.

The fall of Eugénie von Neulinger would cause pain no doubt. Arguably, her friends would bear the loss better than her enemies. Love her or hate her, Eugénie excited the passions, provoking people to act. Her past provocations led people to folly or worse, humiliation. Friends, such as Vogl, had kept their sanity by keeping their distance. More vital passions such as the desire for revenge kept her enemies alive.

But there must be a limit to her influence. The shameful acts currently in motion might have strayed beyond all bounds. If so, they must be stopped. Yet, such a venture is risky and the night is young. All might yet be well.

All props are in place: the furniture, the food, the drink, the metaphorical Sword of Damocles. Eugénie might recognize it, might ignore it, might avoid it, or might bring its wrath down upon her.

A gloved hand at the door, A deep breath. An acknowledgement that the countess's *fate rests in her own hands. Let the festivities commence!*

Chapter Nine

With understated pageantry the *soirée* began. How different from 1815. During the Congress of Vienna, ostentation bespoke power. The new decade's game was to show just enough—a bracelet, a necklace, a jewel on a watch-fob—to prove one understood aristocracy. No longer was it appropriate to outdo the hosts in dress or bearing. In the uncertain times of 1815, today's prince became tomorrow's outcast. One made one's way by capturing the attention of others. By 1822, order prevailed and demanded respect. The art of social survival was to come close to one's hosts without threatening the existing social hierarchy.

In this regard at least, the von Neulingers put their guests at ease. Georg in uniform looked as dashing as anyone in the room, and Eugénie, a great natural beauty still, even without excessive adornment, dazzled. Their son Heinrich, although too young to boast many badges of success, stood tall with his father and step-mother. The pearl stick-pin in his cravat provided a perfect touch of superiority over other men of his generation.

Vogl's early arrival caused little concern. By rights he should have arrived after the insignificant guests, the clerks and similar petty bourgeois and their wives, upon whose happiness the harmonious functioning of the government depended. Vogl ranked among the city's most celebrated artists. He belonged in the next wave, with merchants and ministers, before the full-blooded aristocrats. These arrived whenever they chose and often timed their arrivals to be as disruptive as possible.

This evening, however, not even a prince of the blood dared arrive more than forty-five minutes after his invited time, not because of the count's name or rank, or because the line of his ancestors was venerably long, but because Georg von Neulinger served Baron Hager. Hager guaranteed the maintenance of public order. He performed with such skillful and dedicated ruthlessness that he was the most feared man in Vienna. His network of spies, real and rumored, was so powerful that people avoided Hager's attention at all costs. The merest breath of disloyalty to his wishes entailed grave consequences. Hager liked all things to run on time. Though Hager himself had no plans to attend, his minions were everywhere.

In any event, Eugénie covered Vogl's potential affront to etiquette by introducing him as "a dear family friend." Such a sop-to-the-gossips made little difference. The place of artists was the one article in the prevailing social code that was not completely ossified. Unestablished performers like Schubert were treated like servants, but established personages like Vogl were in great demand. They were entitled to large audiences pre-gathered anywhere they were invited.

Foregoing his right to an audience, Vogl stood next to Heinrich von Neulinger, exchanging unheard pleasantries with a procession of the city's most prominent denizens, and a handful of foreign guests. Vogl accepted this fatiguing chore happily, welcoming the opportunity to learn who was ascending and who was plummeting through Viennese society.

Most of the guests knew Vogl, at least by sight. Some even numbered among his friends. Almost all members of the minor orders visited the theater occasionally, and Vogl had maintained a virtually constant presence on the boards for more than a decade. Ministers and aristocrats, to the chagrin of some of them, knew Vogl because of their acquaintance with the countess. Indeed, Vogl was surprised that some of the guests ventured to appear at all. Straight-faced, Vogl received at least three of Eugénie's reputed former lovers, accompanied by their apparently unsuspecting, or perhaps merely complaisant, wives. Eugénie's value as a social ally remained inestimable.

Some of the guests were true enemies. Countess Zdenka Merlinbeck for one. Her ascendance to social prominence followed a trajectory similar to Eugénie's, albeit usually in her shadow. Merlinbeck once wielded significant power in the Austrian foreign office, power that reached its zenith when Eugénie befriended him. He married Zdenka only after Eugénie cast him off, just before Georg von Neulinger wrested the job with Baron Hager from Merlinbeck's grasp. Now Merlinbeck, well out of the limelight, showed his demotion in his bearing. Von Neulinger maintained his military posture; Merlinbeck looked jowly. Georg spoke with increased authority; Merlinbeck became an inconsequential mumbler.

Merlinbeck's wife Zdenka, however, had lost none of her fire; she sizzled with thwarted ambition. This evening, audaciously she came, escorted by two men in addition to her husband. Vogl admired her shrewdness. A single foreign escort might be dismissed as a lover, but the second German made this thought untenable. In any event, these two, with their unkempt beards and clothes so nondescript they bordered on the shabby, were unlikely candidates for romantic entanglement with the exotic, intoxicating Zdenka.

Zdenka introduced her Germans as Herr Instructor Himmelfarb and Herr Professor Barenberg, and offered no further explanation. Vogl watched Zdenka hold her host's hand for an unexpectedly long time before turning to the countess, and saying a little too loudly, "My dear Eugénie, ravaging as ever! Forgive me … ravishing!"

"Good evening, Frau Merlinbeck," Eugénie responded coolly. The ladies rested their fingertips on each other's shoulders and kissed the air a small but noticeable distance from each other's cheeks, parodying the manner of old friends.

Vogl next overheard Zdenka comment to her husband, "Of course I didn't insult her, Carl. It was an old joke we shared from our time backstage."

"Zdenka reached the peak of her powers as a chorus girl," said Eugénie, somewhat less volubly to her husband. "She was well known to the men of Vienna."

Though smiles punctuated this exchange, neither woman put forth significant effort to disguise their mutual enmity.

During the pre-concert reception Vogl experienced precisely three awkward moments. The first came when Diederich announced the entrance of Fraülein Schikaneder escorted by Herr Schober. To circumvent potential scandal mongers, Vogl wanted to treat Kunegunde as a total stranger, but she, all enthusiasm, said, "Herr Vogl, you told me this would be a grand occasion, but I never imagined how grand. The countess is even more beautiful than your description. How can I thank you enough?"

Fortunately, she and Schober were among the first guests to enter, so few people saw this exchange. Watching her stand by Schober for the next half-hour was unpleasant, but Vogl was powerless to intercede.

The next awkward moment made Vogl angry with himself. The arrival of Thomas, Lord Bellingham induced spasms of jealousy. Bellingham! The very man who escorted Eugénie from the theater and out of Vogl's sphere that horrible night in September 1815. As in the past, Bellingham came with the entourage of the English ambassador. He looked older and stouter but no less resplendent in his evening clothes. Bellingham's time with Eugénie in the old days was short. He soon surfaced among the multitude cast aside in favor of more promising prospects, but he had been first after Vogl. Irrationally, Vogl still blamed him for the destruction of his doomed relationship. How dare he return to Vienna? Did he hope to re-establish his ties to Eugénie? Unthinkable.

Vogl received no enlightenment from the correct, formal way Lord Bellingham and the countess exchanged greetings, or from the bow Bellingham gave him. Internally, he foundered between his memory and his imagination. Nonetheless, Vogl stammered in decent English and without noticeable anguish, "I am honored to see you again, Viscount."

Another member of the British ambassador's retinue captured Vogl's attention because he was not British. Indeed, he wore an odd suit in the pale blue color and cut of a military uniform, which it wasn't. An outrageous green sash displayed odd metallic studs that lacked the ribbons and insignia commonly found on medals. A complete absence of any facial hair, except for whiskers cut back so that they ended, absurdly, at the base of the man's ears, made him seem uncivilized. In 1815, such people were ubiquitous; this man clearly came from that dying breed. He seemed unembarrassed and unimpressed, standing out among the more proper guests. He was announced as Peter Tagly, but when he introduced himself to Vogl directly, with a bow too deep for the occasion and an inappropriate clicking of the heels, he identified himself loudly as Pyotr Dmitrovitch Tagili. A Russian. That explained a great deal about the person, but not about his presence.

The final awkwardness came with the appearance of Captain August Millstein and his buxom wife Annie. They arrived late, although they were not highly ranked among aristocrats. They weren't aristocrats at all. Annie was often called "the farmwife" behind her back. Millstein, however, was almost always seen standing on Baron Hager's right side on public occasions. It was said that Millstein's proximity to power proved that he almost instinctively understood all of his master's wishes, particularly the unsavory, deadly ones.

Yet Vogl felt more than the instinctive chill produced in the room by the presence of a man who might possibly hold all the revelers' lives in his hands. It was the realization that many of Hager's associates could be spotted. The footman in the English ambassador's retinue looked familiar. Vogl remembered seeing him, or someone uncannily like him, frequenting a bookshop outside of which "a terrible, fatal accident" once befell an outspoken opponent of Metternich. Several of the guests were introduced as clerks; yet these minor clerks did not carry themselves like clerks. Were they officers incognito? Even some of the women, presented as clerks' wives, took on sinister aspects. Vogl, with a shudder, recalled a metal glint coming from beneath the shoulder straps of one of the gowns. How many clerks' wives chose to carry concealed daggers?

"Herr Vogl, I have longed to tell you how much the Captain and I enjoyed you in *Figaro* last season."

Vogl emerged from his fog long enough to say, "You are too kind, Madame Millstein." Then, with great relief, Vogl detached himself from the line of hosts to locate Schubert. He fervently hoped that the night held only musical adventures in store.

Vogl knew where to find Schubert—in an underpopulated corner of the room far removed from the social center. At first he saw the back of Schober's head. Working his way across the room, he next saw the lustrous red hair framing the flushed, animated face of Fraülein Rosa, who faced the room with unmasked awe. His search ended when he heard the composer say, "No more for me, Franz, I have to play."

Vogl approached the group with a hearty, "There you are, Franz. Shall we begin?"

Kunegunde spoke then. "Thank you, Herr Vogl, for introducing me to such celebrated company. I've been in the city less than two months, yet I've heard of almost everyone. Herr Schober has been pointing the luminaries out to me. But we have a question. Is that woman over there Count Waldstein's wife or his mistress?" She indicated a woman with two strings of pearls woven artfully into her raven-colored hair.

"I know enough not to involve myself in wicked speculation, Fraülein, but I will tell you this much. That woman is the count's sister. Her greatest achievement, as far as I know, is to be the dedicatee of one of van Beethoven's piano pieces."

"I knew it was something like that," said Schober.

"Has Josie arrived?" Schubert asked suddenly.

"All three of the Fröhlich sisters are here with their parents," said Vogl. "Josephine will join us at the piano just before our first break."

"I have "*Gretchen*" with me," Schubert said with a sly smile.

"All right, Franz, I'll ask her," said Vogl with a smile in return. "*Gretchen am Spinnrade*" was one of Schubert's best songs, but being the desperate lament of a lovelorn lady, it rarely appeared in Vogl's personal repertoire. Josephine Fröhlich was one of the few amateurs in Vogl's acquaintance who did the song justice.

"And so I am resolved," said Schubert, theatrically draining his punch and thrusting the glass towards Schober, "Lead on, Misha."

During this conversation, servants arranged chairs in several rows before the piano, which was placed near the center of the floor. Enough von Neulinger guests were seated that a smattering of impromptu applause broke out as Vogl led Schubert to the piano. For once he was glad of Schober's presence behind Schubert. Schober prevented the little man from taking flight.

The world changed the second Schubert settled behind the piano. Without preamble and, as always, forgetting to see if Vogl was ready, he started the rapid burst of G octaves that launched "*Der Erlkönig*". By the time Vogl completed the song's first vocal phrase, all traces of Schubert's shyness were gone. It was easy for him to forget that there was any physical presence in the room. Together, Schubert and Vogl took their listeners through the terrible battle for a young child's life during a violent thunderstorm in a dark, haunted wood. At the final cadence, the audience, completely enchanted, responded with delighted applause.

For the next hour, the gods of music reigned. Vogl was in good voice. Ably abetted by Schubert, he assumed various identities—tortured father, moon-struck philosopher, cunning fisherman, even still-voiced Death itself—transporting his listeners over thrilling landscapes and startling vistas. Gone from the salon was the tension and suspense upon which Eugénie thrived. Private thoughts of romance, political or social advancement, even simple biological needs, receded. The inclusion of Josephine Fröhlich and a visit to Mozart's immortal *Don Giovonni*, provided a lovely pinch of variety. When she went on to sing "*Gretchen am Spinnrade*", several members of the audience, including Vogl himself, were moved to tears. Semi-consciously Vogl registered that first hour of singing at the von Neulingers' as among the happiest of his entire salon-singing experience.

The time for a break approached. Before Vogl began "Heidenröslein", the song chosen to end the set, he submitted to audience demands and elicited a promise from Fraülein Fröhlich to sing again later in the evening. The change in fortune may have come at that moment. The benign spirit that seemed to follow Schubert whenever he performed lost its predominance.

Between rounds of singing, as Eugénie promised, there was dancing. Schubert drifted upstairs to a second parlor and discovered another piano. Most of the younger guests followed, including Kunegunde and Schober. Vogl remained below. As efficiently as he could, Vogl pushed through the sea of compliments and commonplaces in hopes of finding more interesting conversation. In this, he was partially successful.

"Michael, give us your opinion on this," said Georg von Neulinger, who stood with Josephine's father. "Does *Der Freischütz* stand a chance? Herr Fröhlich maintains that German is a language fit only for the salon, that only Italian belongs on the stage."

Vogl again was dragooned into the debate dominating the city's cultural world. At least this time the conflict was civilized. In other corners of the city, and probably the room, the German-Italian controversy simmered close to full-scale war.

"That's not what I said, at least not what I meant," said Fröhlich. "When I say that Italians flourish in our opera houses, I mean that they control what gets produced there. They won't let an upstart like Weber challenge their authority."

"He has gotten this far. His opera will be performed next month."

"My point exactly. Someone in power here must have heard it in Berlin last summer and believes that it will fail. Otherwise …"

"My dear Fröhlich, you have a devious mind. Vogl, do you know anything of *Der Freischütz*?"

"Not really. But Weber is a dedicated artist with vast knowledge of the stage and of music."

"Without knowledge of Vienna, he will fail," insisted Fröhlich.

"He has a month," von Neulinger said blandly.

"A month to master Vienna? He needs a lifetime."

"Are we Viennese really that complex?" von Neulinger asked as Vogl drifted off in search of a glass of wine.

He next encountered the brilliant, pale-emerald eyes of Eugénie. "Misha, magnificent singing. You deserve a reward," she exclaimed, placing a gloved hand on his shoulder and levering herself up to kiss his cheek. "Don't forget, your fourth song," she whispered before letting him go.

"I shall endeavor to please in every particular," Vogl said, and Eugénie smiled at him.

"Herr Vogl, may I talk with you in confidence sometime?" It was Heinrich von Neulinger speaking, giving Vogl his first real chance to assess the young man. Beneath the veneer of respectability, Vogl sensed a grimness suggesting that, in the general scheme of things, Heinrich took himself too seriously. Heinrich's earnest gaze suggested only one thing.

He said, "I am hoping to establish myself as a playwright;. Can you advise me?" Vogl's suspicions were confirmed. He returned the response that served him for so many others. "Anytime."

Heinrich responded with a tight bow. "Not tonight, of course." His eyes darted around the room. Vogl suspected he sought out one or both of his parents and was prepared to bolt if they saw him.

"Of course. When you're ready, show me what you have and we'll discuss getting it to the stage."

Vogl's kind-sounding invitation often proved the best way to rid himself of pests seeking his intercession. Over the years, dozens of self-styled playwrights had thrust their works and themselves upon him. Most of them envied their perception of the playwright's life, but not the actual work. They usually came with a scene or speech in their pocket, but few had any inkling of what went into a full production. If the worst proved true and Heinrich offered a full script, Vogl would read it and offer suggestions for making it stage worthy. No one, not even Franz Schober, returned after learning their manuscripts' deficiencies. Sometimes Vogl felt that guiding the talentless away from certain public embarrassment, while sparing society untold quantities of worthless poetastery, was his greatest contribution to the world.

"I believe we have met before, Mister Vogl." This came from Lord Bellingham.

"Then I am delighted to make your acquaintance a second time," Vogl responded in his labored, albeit well-pronounced English.

"I haunted the theater, absolutely haunted it, when I was a delegate at the Congress of Vienna," Bellingham continued. "We met after a performance of some Shakespeare nonsense, the one with the fairies in it."

"*A Midsummer Night's Dream.* I played Oberon." The night he lost his Jennie.

"Quite a spectacle, as I recall. Done in German, of course, so I didn't understand a word of it. But I find the English version incomprehensible as well," said Bellingham with an abrasive laugh. "I enjoyed the dancy bits though."

"The dancers in that production were most charming," Vogl said, masking a trace of bitterness.

"Yes, those were heady days ... heady days."

"They say the world was remade in a matter of months."

"So they say, but the world is still with us. We still have a lot on our plates, I can tell you. I, for one, am glad. I never expected to see Vienna again, but after this dust-up in the Balkans ..."

"I'm afraid I am unfamiliar with the meaning of 'dust-up'."

"Well, never mind, old boy. I'm sure the whole thing's no more than a tempest in a teapot. Tell me about Vienna these days. All I hear about is this Weber chap."

"Von Weber?" Vogl took care to correct Bellingham's pronunciation and smiled. "*Der Freischütz* does seem to occupy everyone's attention at the moment, but if you are here two weeks from now, you might enjoy *The Empress of the Common*. It's a new work—a singspiel.

"German!" said Lord Bellingham.

"But with wonderful dances," said Vogl. "And the celebrated Anna-Marie Donmeyer plays the empress. You may remember her from your last visit."

"Donmeyer? Afraid not. I pay more attention to dancers than to singers."

Vogl knew that at least to be true. "Well, if you wish to see *The Empress of the Common*, leave word at the Hofoper. You can come as my guest."

"Thanks awfully, but I'd better steer clear of the whole business. Between us, old man, I don't fancy these Germans hanging about everywhere." Bellingham nodded towards Herr Himmelfarb, passing by with wine in his hand.

"Perhaps they intend to prepare us for von Weber," said Vogl, "though they don't look as though they're connected to the theater."

"Those two?" said Bellingham, again nodding at Himmelfarb, now standing with professor Barenberg next to Zdenka Merlinbeck. "I happen to know about them. They're sniffing about for Wollaston's plat'num. Please excuse me."

Lord Bellingham strode purposefully towards Herr Tagili, the incongruous Russian. For a moment disengaged from conversation, Vogl wished he were more proficient in English. What did Bellingham mean by fancy, clear steers and dirty plates? And what on earth was "Wollaston's plat'num" aside from being odorific and unpronounceable? But more than anything, he smarted from being called an old man. True he was fifty-four years old, but he considered himself a youthful fifty-four.

A few minutes later, the guests regathered for the second half of the concert. Things did not go well. Except to change pianos, Schubert had not stopped playing during the break, and his fingers were tired. He slipped over some of the thirds in the *vivace* section of "*Der Wanderer*," a recently published song, chosen to open the second set. Schober's buffoonery didn't help. He spent the break reveling, dancing, and drinking with a little too much of the latter. He ripped the final page of "*Der Wanderer*" as he flipped it and started to laugh. Vogl saw Kunegunde snicker also.

Hoping to suppress the brewing hysteria, Vogl decided to change the second song of the set, announcing the more somber

"*Lob der Tränen*" in place of the planned "*Frühlingsglaube*", forgetting how much more taxing on the pianist the "Praise of Tears" was.

Schober rendered the entire stratagem moot by dropping all the music on the floor. Eventually the song was performed to respectful applause. Vogl, still hoping to salvage something, remembered his promise to Josephine Fröhlich and invited her back to the piano.

New problems developed. Schubert only had "*Gretchen am Spinnrade*" and "*La ci Darem La Mano*" for Josephine to sing. Josephine was unfamiliar with most of the other songs Schubert had with him. Eventually, they selected "*Geheimes*", a recently written song that Schubert thought he could play from memory. How the gods must have laughed at that moment in the song's final verse:

"She casts her eye around the assembly;
But she only seeks to apprise
'Him' of the next sweet tryst."

Although the rendition was far from perfect—Schubert's memory was not quite flawless, nor was Josephine's, for that matter—it was received with delight, particularly by the hostess, if the increased sparkle in her eyes and the appreciative nod she turned in Vogl's direction were any indication. Before Vogl could return to the fore, Lord Bellingham, who apparently was not as indifferent to female singers as he claimed, made his own contribution to chaos, a cry of "zncore!" This was taken up by Tagili, his Russian companion, then by some other guests.

There was nothing for it but to ask Josephine to sing something else. In a flurried conference with Schubert, they settled on—again with unconscious irony—"*Der Tod und Das*

Mädchen". Vogl had sung the song solo in the first part of the program, but as it was a dialogue, he agreed to do it again with Josephine singing the part of the dying girl and Vogl singing the inexorable monotone of death.

The fading D major chords at the end of the song signaled the end of Josephine Fröhlich's contribution to the tragic fiasco that followed. She bowed gracefully to her well-deserved applause and withdrew.

Vogl, remembering the plan he made with Eugénie, faced a dilemma. He promised to sing Schubert's newly commissioned song as the fourth song of the set. "*Death and the Maiden*" pre-empted the spot. The song's appearance in the first half suggested that no one would take its reappearance as a special signal. However, Eugénie's exact terms were "your fourth song." Josephine had sung the third one.

Thus Vogl did something he later regretted.

After smiling Josephine back to her seat, he said, "My friends, Herr Schubert and I have the pleasure to announce a special treat for you. We now perform a song prepared exclusively for this glorious occasion. With all humility, we wish to dedicate this piece to our gracious hosts, the Count and Countess von Neulinger." Vogl paused artfully and then joined in the applause that followed. "We give you the premier public performance of "*Die Sonne und Das Veilchen*".

Schubert's simple E-flat introduction transfixed the audience. Not that the song was one of Schubert's best, but mingled amongst the listeners were a few who understood Schubert's remarkable talent. More than a few shared Vogl's conviction that the plump little man was a genius. They hung on every note. Unfortunately for the composer, except for Vogl, few of these kenners cared about the business of music. They took Schubert's ability for granted, the right of all Viennese, citizen or transient, to have continual access to the greatest sonorities in Europe.

As the song took its dramatic shift to C minor, Vogl found himself wondering who Eugénie's secret recipient was. He couldn't tell by looking. Every once in a while an audible sigh escaped a listener's lips, or a head flew back as if propelled by inexorable force, common responses among Viennese audiences. It was important to be seen as having a special affinity for music, whether one did or not. Still, certain people behaved uncharacteristically. Georg von Neulinger, for example, took only casual notice of music and usually spent his time surveying the rooms in which it was made. But tonight he was as involved as anyone in the violet's inevitable fate. Similarly, Vogl noticed Lord Bellingham's rapt interest. Was his foppishness a façade? Captain Millstein's head bounced as if the song were a march, and he became momentarily disoriented when the song's tempo shifted. Vogl knew several military men who experienced music only in terms of the parade ground. Not all of them were fools. Some actually understood what they heard better than they chose to reveal.

On the other extreme, Heinrich von Neulinger and Kunegunde Rosa treated the gently lyrical song as a dance. Vogl knew nothing of Heinrich as an auditor, but his behavior during this song was uncharacteristic from the habitually stiff young man. Berenberg, the German and Tagili, the Russian, provided a hint of comic relief. They remained stoically immobile, both physically and emotionally throughout the performance. Perhaps Tagili's knowledge of German was insufficient to understand the song's simple, yet cryptic story of a violet passing beneath the sun's benign gaze. Try as he might, Vogl deduced nothing.

The song reached its close. Vogl approached Schubert's pet D-flat with a *ritardando* a little grander than good taste indicated, and for greater effect closed his eyes and all but whispered the final phrase, "there were eight where there had been one."

Schubert finished the song's tiny coda, and there followed a moment of complete silence. Then, gratifyingly, the audience burst into spontaneous applause. Bowing in acknowledgment, Vogl noticed many heads turning to the back of the room where the von Neulingers sat. Several rose from their chairs.

Eugénie had fainted.

Professionally, Vogl completed his bow and extended his right arm towards Schubert, who rose to accept his share of the glory. Until that moment, Schubert was hidden behind the music and had no idea what was going on. When he saw the commotion and deduced its cause he muttered to Vogl, *sotto voce*, "The countess is pleased!"

Chapter Ten

The rest of the *soirée* passed in a blur. Vogl later remembered few details. Fainting in rapture was a common phenomenon in those days when great artists were considered superior beings. The procedures for assisting those who succumbed—smelling salts, warmed moistened handkerchiefs—were equally familiar. Eugénie soon recovered enough to exit the salon on her own feet. Her husband remained, firmly insisting that the performers continue. Three songs later, just before Schubert and Vogl reached "*Ganymed*", their customary finale, Eugénie returned, presumably fortified by some wine, looking none the worse for wear. The concert ended, and the pre-arranged "simple supper" commenced.

Post-concert time was usually onerous for Vogl. The aftermath of the von Neulinger *soirée* was particularly so. The guests moved towards various tables of food. Schubert quietly withdrew upstairs to accommodate those who wanted more dancing. This was not a formal duty, but among such a fine array of society, Schubert found safety only behind piano keys. Vogl realized that unless he took a plate of food upstairs, Schubert would go hungry.

Before gathering provisions for his accompanist, or himself for that matter, Vogl fended off several guests voicing their opinions of the evening's entertainment. He took the fawning praise of his voice and the gentle barbs about false notes and the like with good grace. Whenever anyone praised one of Schubert's songs, Vogl mentioned the publisher. With this ploy he hoped to help Schubert. The more people who approached Diabelli or Artaria mentioning Schubert, the more likely these men would accept Schubert's future submissions.

To the several people who praised *"Die Sonne und das Veilchen"*, Vogl took a different approach. The song was unpublished; Vogl thus suggested that interested parties talk to Schubert directly. He hinted that they could commission their own songs from the little master. No one would, of course; nor would Franz necessarily oblige them if they did.

Vogl recognized the futility of his efforts. The audience came from Vienna's civil service, not its musical promoters. Members and minions of the State security apparatus showed little concern for musical novelties. Even if someone took Vogl's advice, Schubert would gain little. Profits from a single sale were negligible. Besides, Franz lacked the diplomatic skill to take advantage of patronage. Nonetheless Vogl adhered to his policy of trying any path to support his friend.

Vogl's greatest discomfort came from the performance itself. He was urbane enough to hide his dissatisfaction, but he worried. Neither the count nor his son said a word about the music, and Eugénie's dramatic reaction flummoxed him. She never lost her composure in such a way. The role of helpless female was not part of her repertoire. Of course, Eugénie's tactics included unpredictability. Perhaps Eugénie feigned her response to signal someone. Still, Vogl was uneasy.

Supper was ending by the time Vogl assembled a plate of cheese, pastry and bits of sausage to carry up the stairs, following his ears to the room whence the ländler emanated. Before he reached his destination, Diederich tapped his shoulder. "Please follow me, *mein Herr*. The countess wishes a word with you."

Plate in hand, Vogl followed Diederich to Eugénie's dressing room. The countess sat alone and, ever conscious of her reputation, ordered Diederich to wait outside the door. Then her eyes flashed. She hissed angrily, "Misha, you've ruined everything!" Vogl thought he caught an uncharacteristic note of panic in her voice.

Supposing she referred to his little speech of dedication, Vogl replied, "I attempted to carry out my commission to the best of my ability."

"Did you? Was it then the eunuch …"

"Leave Schubert out of this! I assume full responsibility for everything."

"You don't know what you are saying!"

"You gave me a poem. Franz set it to music. I sang it."

"Yes, you sang it. I was a fool to trust you."

"If I have failed to satisfy, I beg your pardon."

Eugénie did not waste time with recriminations. "I don't want your apology. Nor did I call you here to chastise you. What's done is done. You now must make what amends you can."

"If it is in my power …"

"It's probably *not* in your power," Eugénie sneered, "but you can do this. Leave this"—out of nowhere an envelope appeared in Eugénie's hand—"on the hall table as you depart. Leave the plate."

Feeling more than a little foolish, Vogl placed Schubert's food on the dressing table and took the envelope from the countess. On it was written merely "*Die Sonne und Das Veilchen.*"

"Put it in your pocket." Vogl did so. "Stop by tomorrow morning. You have not heard the last of my displeasure for your ineptitude."

"I have rehearsal," said Vogl.

"Stop by before. Now we shall go downstairs to speed the parting guests." Eugénie stood up and clamped herself onto Vogl's right arm. She propelled him out of the dressing room like his jailer, not his hostess. She then produced a radiant smile, presumably for Diederich's benefit, marched to the top of the stairs and proclaimed, "*Messieursdames*, I give you our titan once again."

Vogl bowed at the ensuing wave of applause, at which point Eugénie released him and floated down the stairs to her husband. The guests understood their cue and began to gather their wraps—all wonderfully correct. Vogl waved them a final farewell and went to fetch Schubert.

Eight people still danced in the upstairs room, Heinrich von Neulinger, paired with Kunegunde, two clerks and their wives, and one clerk's wife's sister in the clutches of Schober. Vogl tried to stop Schubert's playing by placing a hand on his shoulder. Unperturbed, Schubert muscled his way to a full cadence.

"We must go," said Vogl.

"Surely we have time for one more Ländler," Schober said, laughing.

His partner supported him, but Vogl responded, "The other guests have gone."

The clerks hurriedly ushered their wives from the room. For government employees, even those attached to Hager's ministry, no personal gratification was worth breaching etiquette.

"I must join my parents," said Heinrich. "Thanks to you, I've enjoyed this evening, Herr Schubert and Fraülein Schikaneder." Then, with a small bow, he left.

"Now I may dance with you at last, *shoene* Juliet," said Schober smiling at Kunegunde. "Franz, play something really good."

"No more dancing for me," said Kunegunde.

Vogl was not unhappy to see her disengage herself from Schober.

"Then Franz, play something else. Perhaps one of Mr. Field's nocturnes?" Schober said, rescuing a glass of wine left unfinished on a windowsill.

"Oh, play something of your own," said Kunegunde, seating herself on the piano bench. Schubert stiffened.

"Only one movement, Franz," Vogl warned, "then come downstairs."

"Only one, Misha?"

"It's late, and we must get Fraülein Schikaneder home."

"Thy will be done," said Schubert.

After a moment's thought, he launched into the *allegretto* movement of his sixth piano sonata. To these charming strains,

Vogl watched the last von Neulinger guests vanish into the night. His upstairs entourage provided him the perfect excuse to leave last. The calming strains of the *allegretto* provided him reasonable assurance that Schober would not again inflict himself upon Kunegunde. When he returned to the upstairs room, he saw Kunegunde's head resting languidly against Schubert's shoulder. She did not prevent him from playing.

The von Neulingers retired to their rooms before the movement ended, leaving Diederich to let Vogl's party out into lightly falling snow. As per instructions, Vogl unobserved, left Eugénie's letter on the table by the door. On his way out, Vogl received a parting shock—from Diederich. "Shall we see you tomorrow morning, Herr Vogl?"

The remark had its probably calculated effect. Vogl was shaken. The innocuous sounding question confirmed Vogl's fear that, while waiting outside the Countess's door, Diederich heard every word of what passed between him and Eugénie. Whose desire was that? Potentially crushing wheels were clearly in motion, all too probably with Vogl directly in their path.

Chapter Eleven

Though midnight approached, the day was not finished for everyone. Vogl shepherded his little band to their lodgings without incident. As he escorted Kunegunde to her door and saw her safely inside, Schober left the group on the same street and vanished into the night. Schubert, exhausted from his hours at the keyboard, dozed all the way to his lodgings at von Schwind's, where he was hustled inside and presumably up to bed. Vogl arrived at his own home twenty minutes later and read himself to sleep with a few lines of Epictetus.

At Count von Merlinbeck's home, life was as quiet, though not as contented. On his arrival, the count ordered himself a nightcap delivered directly to his room. In the *boudoir* adjacent, the countess paced restlessly, reviewing her fortunes. She suffered, although not from her husband's diminishing interest in her. That was almost a relief. She had not expected marriage to close all doors to romance, and it had not. Count Merlinbeck gave her prestige, and in the past her marriage offered her access to power, but after the birth and early death of their first child, Merlinbeck lost interest, first in the outside world, then in his family. Zdenka seethed in frustration.

Tonight her gall boiled because of Eugénie von Neulinger, who lived the life Zdenka desired. As far as Zdenka was concerned, Eugénie stole it from her. Eugénie's tentacles reached everywhere. Her favor remained in constant demand. Recollection of how Eugénie outpaced her still inspired Zdenka to fury. What a dolt she'd been to believe that she had stolen *shoene* Moritz from the green-eyed guttersnipe. Eugénie planned it all along. She exploited the man's interior weakness at the same time she polished him up as one of the city's elite leaders. Zdenka's greatest coup, persuading an aristocrat to abandon his mistress in order to marry a "little gypsy girl with no family," thus became her greatest disaster. Sooner or later Eugénie would pay.

The *soirée* fueled her bitterness. The two Germans on their tiresome diplomatic mission and their military concerns dealt Zdenka a fresh hand, albeit a weak one. Who cared about the rights to mine platinum, whatever that was? Still Zdenka resolved to stay in the game as long as it lasted. If Eugénie's husband were somehow involved in these arcane negotiations, a nice, direct avenue for revenge might emerge. If not …

Zdenka continued her pacing.

𝄢

At the English ambassador's residence, the entourage retired quietly to separate rooms. The ambassador detained Thomas Bellingham, inducing him to stay with a welcome snifter of brandy. The ambassador's informal briefing on the state of political affairs was decidedly less welcome. "Why can I not impress upon you, Thomas, the seriousness of our mission? We cannot let access to such quantities of platinum escape our control."

"Surely there must be other sources of the mineral," Bellingham muttered in feeble defiance.

"No doubt, but they haven't been discovered. Control of platinum in abundance might undo the current world order in a matter of months. If Bonaparte had such an abundance before Waterloo, we'd be singing *La Marseillaise* now."

Bellingham shuddered, possibly at the thought of mastering so much French.

"I'm glad you now appreciate what's at stake. I expect you, therefore, to review your slipshod behavior this evening as part of your report on what you gleaned—or failed to glean from this evening's proceedings. Your long-standing acquaintance with some of our major adversaries could be of inestimable value to His Majesty's government, but you must maintain proper vigilance. I shall expect your full report by eleven tomorrow morning. Good night, Thomas."

Bellingham shuddered again. He was useless before noon, so he saw a long night before him. Pleasant dreams would have to be postponed.

Similarly, two floors above him Pyotr Dmitrovitch Tagili, wasted no time in dreams. "*K'chortu*," he swore under his breath in Russian, the only language he clearly understood. Something had gone wrong. Tagili lacked the communication skills to figure out what. All he knew was that his British hosts had whisked him away as soon as conveniently possible, and the countess had not given the agreed-upon code word when she bade him her formal farewell.

He reviewed his options. He could try to leave Vienna immediately, but even if his escape went as planned, he'd be a pauper. How long dared he stay before word came out of the Urals that he had no authority? Tagili knew and loathed the life of poverty, but a life in Siberia or in an Austrian prison would be far worse.

He had to communicate with Eugénie one more time. Only she could tell him if any chance for profit remained. But with the English growing ever more vigilant, the Germans growing more restless, and the French more interested in the situation, arranging a meeting was, to say the least, challenging. Nervously, Tagili stared out the window with its defective latch. He noticed a few falling snowflakes. His gaze continued in their direction for quite a long time. He saw a tremendous storm taking shape.

𝄢

Not everyone went straight home. At least three of Eugénie's guests ended up at an unregistered *weinstube*. Actually it was the cellar of a building occupied by a clothing merchant during the day. The authorities allowed establishments like these to operate after eleven. Occasionally, they helped the government unearth or observe potential trouble makers, or when it served the ruling powers' interest, to prepare trouble of their own. Many regulars came, most of them subsidized in one manner or another by Baron Hager.

This particular hornets nest, in order to function as a

spider's web, maintained a veneer of *gemütlichkeit*, complete with the all the trimmings: a large array of bottles, a larder stocked with cheese and pastries, and, of course musicians, a violinist and a pianist. The place was presentable enough to entice unwary souls such as now entered, men who felt that sneaking an illicit drink or two under the authorities' noses made them heroes.

Count von Neulinger's son Heinrich, first of Eugénie's guests to arrive at the rathskeller that night, was not a regular, but was known on these premises, the nightspot nearest his home. Anticipating the need to release tensions after "playing his father's game" at the *soirée*, he had asked a couple of friends to wait for him there. Heinrich drained his first brandy in one theatrical gulp, for his friends' benefit. His second drink arrived simultaneously with the two Germans, Himmelfarb and Barenberg.

The Germans presented studies of mixed emotions, observed carefully by the suddenly alerted regulars. They shared the satisfaction of finding the place without involving the von Merlinbecks. Barenberg had discovered it during one of his many nocturnal head-clearing rambles, rambles made necessary by the difficulties of his mission, not the least of which was keeping his more volatile colleague in line. After the *soirée*, Barenberg bluntly declined the Merlinbecks' offer of a ride back to the inn where they resided. It was out of the Merlinbecks' way, and Zdenka's husband obviously was eager to get home.

The men sought somewhere to confer privately. The *soirée* delivered "the simple answer" to Himmelfarb's simple question, and Himmelfarb had a simple response: "Too much!" Barenberg agreed with his colleague, but the two men differed on how to respond.

"Back to Bavaria," was Himmelfarb's choice, but Barenberg favored explaining the situation to Countess Zdenka and receiving her advice.

"Women are no good in matters of this kind," Himmelfarb insisted loudly as they entered the *weinstube*.

"Perhaps you are right in the main," professor Barenberg said, "but the countess is an exceptional woman." He wanted to quiet Himmelfarb so that they could begin more disciplined consideration of their options.

"On that we agree," said Himmelfarb, still volubly. "To the countesses of Vienna!" he continued, assuring the covert attention of every spy in the cellar.

The exact moment when matters spun out of control may have come as early as the moment Himmelfarb summoned the waiter. "Beer," he demanded, "Bavarian beer, if you have it, for me and my companion. We need something to purify the air around here."

The remark echoed throughout the cellar. One of Heinrich's friends picked it up and quipped, "Imagine, Bavarian beer in a Viennese *weinstube*!" Himmelfarb didn't hear this retort, but he noticed three young dandies snickering. He scowled.

"Forget them, Jurgen," Barenberg said. "We have more important matters to consider."

Himmelfarb acquiesced and muttered, "They don't understand us here." But it was too late.

"I recognize them," Heinrich von Neulinger told his friends. He went over to further the acquaintance effected by the formal introductions at his stepmother's *soirée*. His intentions were friendly; he did not want these two barbarians believing that Vienna lived solely on rigid social conventions.

With wine-muddled heartiness, he approached the Germans.

"*Grüss Gott, Meine* Herren, or perhaps I should say, in deference to the hour, *Guten Morgen*." Heinrich prided himself on his ready wit.

In reply, he received only a puzzled stare from Barenberg, who faced him, and a grunt from Himmelfarb, behind whom he stood. The Germans didn't remember him.

Heinrich persisted, "Were you not at my parents' house earlier this evening?"

The question was purely for politeness' sake. The Germans stood out like sore thumbs.

"Last night, Passarello," one of Heinrich's friends corrected jovially, hoping to establish his own reputation for wit.

How Heinrich received the name of an obscure character from an obscure English play as a nickname need not concern us, but the name had its role in what followed.

Himmelfarb grunted again. Barenberg, recognizing the young man at last, said, "Oh, yes," and rose as Heinrich offered his hand.

The gesture was unfortunate. In extending his hand to meet Barenberg's, Heinrich brushed the top of Himmelfarb's head. The German rose and spun around with unexpected agility. He was several inches taller and quite a bit broader than Heinrich. "That was your mother's house, eh?'

"Stepmother's," Heinrich explained, still pleasantly.

"Tell her something for me."

The remark took Heinrich aback, but he did not abandon his mission of good will. "Anything."

At that moment the waiter returned with two mugs of beer, and all the negative forces in the cellar fell into alignment.

"Tell her, 'Too much'," Himmelfarb bellowed. "Now leave us—puppy."

Himmelfarb's last word might not have been meant for Heinrich's benefit, but Himmelfarb was no master of the stage-whisper.

"Do you insult my family, sir?" Heinrich asked, more disoriented than angry.

"Passarello, step away from this," a friend counseled.

The tinder was set. Of all people, the waiter ignited it. He was the brother of the violinist—an Italian. Working after hours in Vienna taught them the value of discretion with rowdy customers, also the power of music to sooth savage breasts. But in Vienna music itself was sometimes combustible. The wrong hymn outside the wrong church or a German march played too close to a Frenchman's residence occasionally created significant disturbance. Naturally the waiter, his brother, and the pianist knew the dangers. When things became exceptionally tense, they turned to a piece certain not to offend anyone, a set of variations by the German Ludwig van Beethoven, composed in Vienna derived from the aria *Nel cor piú non mi sento* by the comfortably dead but still highly regarded Italian, Giovonni…

"Paisiello!" the alarmed waiter shouted to his brother.

The person who shouted, "Keep the damned Italians out of this!" is unknown, as is exactly who performed which deeds in the ensuing melee, but before the regulars in the cellar tossed all the brawlers out into the street, Heinrich's hat was crushed, Doktor Barenberg took a face-full of beer, and considerable amounts of furniture suffered abuse as some glassware suffered fatal injury.

As Barenberg helped him stagger back to the inn, Jurgen Himmelfarb found himself picking splinters out of his bleeding skull—splinters of a *verdammte* Italian's shattered violin.

The whirlwind in the *weinstube* was the most visible of the disruptions that blemished a typically quiet night in Hager's Vienna. Four arrests resulted from the regrettable confusion described above. These four were soon released without serious inconvenience. Elsewhere, a proper ratio was maintained—six corpses and thirty-five arrests. Did anyone require further evidence that the forces of order remained in the ascendant?

𝄢

Guilty! All suspicions confirmed! No doubt remained. The only recourse was retribution—final and immediate. Well, not quite immediate: One must allow time for the witch to fall asleep naturally in her bed before sending her off to a more permanent resting place. Satisfaction may wait that long—just a few minutes more. All that's required now is a little patience.

Everything is still. Falling snow outside dampens everything on the street. What is the line from Shakespeare? "That this blow might be the be-all and end-all." So be it. The end of doubt. The end of shame. The end of wickedness. It is now time. All will be well. Exit Eugénie.

Agitato e mysterioso

Chapter Twelve

At 6:30 on the morning of Friday, February 15, 1822, Franz Schubert awoke highly agitated after less than four hours of sleep. Upon arriving home the previous night he discovered that five pages of *Alfonso und Estrella* were missing—the crucial five pages where the unscrupulous Adolfo announces his repentance, the very pages Schubert intended to review with Franz Schober later that day. With von Weber expected in the city at any moment, the situation was critical.

Schubert tried to concentrate. At once his mind flew back to the previous evening, to the home of the aristocrat Georg von Neulinger, and his and Vogl's soul-stirring performance. Even in retrospect, Schubert savored the presence of so many eminent people under one roof—so many beautiful women— all there listening to his music. With a sigh, he recalled the countess, a legendary beauty reputed to have been Vogl's lover at one time. He smiled at the memory of the ever charming

Frölich sisters—if only Josi had Kathi's looks, or Kathi had Josi's voice. Then he remembered the fascinating stranger Vogl had brought along, the red-haired Fraülein Schikaneder. Schubert shook his head rapidly to dispel these visions. He threw off his blanket and rolled out of bed.

Immediately he faced the grim aftermath of his night of enchantment. His stiff back and dizzy head offered a mere prelude. How foolish he was to accept any invitation with von Weber's arrival so near. He had to channel all his energies in von Weber's direction. Schubert groped for his spectacles and found them on his nightstand. Perhaps the intoxication of the previous evening caused him to miscount. Alas, a hurried shuffling of the papers on the small table that served as his desk confirmed his earlier fear—five essential pages of *Alfonso und Estrella* were gone. Schubert forced himself to stay calm.

The solution to the mystery—not an altogether pleasant one—appeared once Schubert realized that other music was missing as well, including the folder holding the music Schubert took with him for the *soirée*, his rapidly composed song, *"Die Sonne und das Veilchen"*. There was nothing to do but to walk over to the von Neulingers' and retrieve the music. If he didn't dawdle, the round trip would take less than an hour. He'd start right after breakfast.

"You are up early this morning, Herr Schubert," said Frau Stieglitz, von Schwind's nominal housekeeper and, effectively, Schubert's landlady, "and you returned so late. Young Moritz was home before you last night."

"Good morning, Frau Stieglitz," Schubert grumbled. Accustomed to the landlady's garrulous tendencies, he paid little heed.

Frau Stieglitz continued, "Coffee is prepared. Rolls and butter are on the sideboard."

Schubert helped himself to three.

"So many? If this keeps up, we shall raise your rent," said Frau Stieglitz, half in jest.

"I had no supper last night," Schubert recalled somewhat sheepishly.

"And out so late. You artists! Moritz is the same. You with your music paper, him with his sketchbook, always scribbling."

"There will come a time, Frau Stieglitz, when an original sketch by Moritz von Schwind will be worth more than this entire establishment. Mark my words."

"Well, until that time arrives, give me two ducats a week. If you insist on stuffing yourself, I'll have to charge more. Here." In contradiction to her words, Frau Stieglitz placed another roll before him. "I'll run to the baker for more before Moritz wakes up. I have the time."

"I'm going out on an errand now, Frau Stieglitz. Would you like me to stop at the baker's on my way back?"

"Certainly I'd like it, Herr Schubert, but you won't remember. I'll go myself, *Danke Shoen.*"

Her reply caused the composer a spasm of regret. Schubert loved the patisserie a mere three streets away. True, he rarely entered it, for he rarely had the wherewithal to purchase its wares, but he associated the exotic scents of vanilla, nutmeg, and similar delicacies emanating from the place with home in rather complex ways—his city, his rarely seen father and siblings, and times of earlier comfort when his mother still lived. Indeed on more than one occasion the aromas from that bakery were all that sustained him between the modest breakfasts and suppers Frau Stieglitz provided. The moment passed. The composer had other things on his mind.

"Very well. If Herr Schober shows up, tell him to wait."

Frau Stieglitz looked at Schubert quizzically. "I've never seen that fellow before noon, but I'll tell Hilda."

"Thank you, Frau Stieglitz," said Schubert, rising from the table and heading for the door.

"Forgive me, Herr Schubert, but are you going out in this weather without a hat?"

A hand to his head confirmed his landlady's observation. "Good heavens, no! I'll be right down."

Twelve minutes later, after locating his hat and correcting some missing note stems on a manuscript, removing his coat, washing his hands, returning hatless halfway down the stairs, then, after securing his hat, retrieving his coat, stopping at the bottom of the staircase to deliberate whether to take his pipe (and deciding against it), Schubert again arrived at the front door. When he opened it, Frau Stieglitz was returning from the bakery.

"Still here, Herr Schubert?" she chirped. "Will you be dining here this evening?"

But Schubert hurried down the front steps without giving an answer.

Finding von Neulinger's house took longer than expected. The street was just off the Heldenplatz, but in the grayish light of the morning, Schubert didn't locate it at once. He passed the place twice before recognizing it. He was confused because two burly men stood at the door. One held a club.

Marshalling all his courage, Schubert approached. "Good morning, *mein Herren*. Is this the home of Count von Neulinger?"

"What of it?" snarled the unarmed guard.

"I have business here."

"What sort of business?"

"You see, last night I left some papers inside …"

"Then, *mein schatz*, you are out of luck. We have strict orders not to admit anyone."

"But I'll be only a moment. I know just where I left them …"

"And they'll stay there. Is there anything else?"

"Please. The papers are of no importance to anyone but myself, but I need them desperately. Could one of you gentlemen retrieve them for me?"

"Our orders are to keep pests off the premises," the unarmed guard said. His remark caused his armed companion to snort, perhaps in amusement. Like an accidental blow on a kettledrum, it was not a reassuring effect.

"Then can you at least send for someone? You see, I performed here last night. I'm sure Herr von Neulinger, or better yet, the countess…"

"The countess? You won't be seeing her this morning. Between us, *mein schatz*, you don't want to disturb the count today. Now be off."

The armed guard stirred slightly.

Schubert backed away in confusion. Wondering what to do next, he saw a familiar shape at the head of the street. With a look back at the guards, he trotted forward to intercept a welcome friend, Michael Vogl. "Misha! Thank God you're here!"

Vogl looked surprised. "Good morning, Franz. They summoned you too?"

"Summoned? No, no. You see, I left some pages of my opera here, and those two men..." Schubert indicated the guards, whom Vogl noticed for the first time, "won't let anyone in."

"We'll see about that," said Vogl. He approached the guards. "Your master awaits us."

"We are to admit no one," the unarmed guard responded.

Unflustered, Vogl continued, "Your orders are out of date. I rode here with Herr Diederich. He's tending to the carriage. I am to wait in the vestibule for him."

The guards traded looks. They seemed uncertain but disinclined to move. The armed one said, "Anyone could learn Diederich's name ..." but before he could say any more the door opened behind him. Diederich himself appeared.

"Herr Vogl, enter please." Diederich retreated inside.

Schubert, who stood gaping throughout this exchange, felt a tug on his sleeve. Quickly and quietly he slid in behind Vogl and tried to move as confidently as his friend past the suddenly deferential guards.

"But what about this other ..." were the last words he heard as the heavy wooden door shut resolutely behind him.

Once inside Schubert withered under Diederich's startled gaze. The steward paused for a moment, then accepted the *fait accompli*. "You will wait here, *bitte*," he said before progressing upstairs.

"Thank you, Misha," Schubert said with relief. "I'll just pick up my scores from the music room." Vogl grabbed his arm. "Misha, what is it?"

"Franz, something terrible has happened."

"What do you mean?"

"I don't know, but when I am waylaid on the way to rehearsal on orders from the count himself, it is not a social matter."

"Well, it's no concern of mine. I'll just get my music. Why is this door locked?"

Vogl said nothing. An uncomfortable silence settled upon them. It was not merely the cheerless anteroom. The whole house was unnaturally quiet. A half-filled glass remained on the marble-topped sideboard, a remnant of the night before. No one bustled about preparing for normal daily business. Not only that, the house was cold. No one tended the fires that provided the first line of defense against February's onslaughts. No servant other than Diederich and the guards outside was in evidence anywhere.

Vogl stood with his eyes glued on the staircase. Eventually Diederich came down. "Follow me, please. Both of you."

At the top of the stairs Diederich stopped. "The master is in the third room on the left."

"Eugénie's boudoir," Vogl half-whispered. Diederich stayed where he was. He did not again make the mistake of letting Vogl out of his sight. He observed Schubert also.

What greeted Schubert was perhaps the most appalling sight of his life—not the count looking disheveled and out of uniform or the two rather better-dressed officers standing on either side of him—it was the blood.

Spattered blood stained the count's shirt and the leggings of all three men. Blood defaced the wall behind them. A gathering pool of blood congealed on the floor beneath Eugénie von Neulinger's lifeless body. The countess lay sideways. Her partially severed head dangled over the side of her bed.

Schubert gasped, then gagged.

"Good morning, Herr Vogl." Officer that he was, von Neulinger remembered his manners. "You see why I sent for you."

Vogl mustered only a nod in reply.

Schubert fell under von Neulinger's gaze. It was even more chilling than Diederich's. "I did not send for that one." While Schubert struggled to formulate some response, the count continued. "No matter. He left with you last night. He might as well stay here now. These are two of my associates, Captain Millstein and Herr Doktor Nordwalder. They are commencing an official investigation."

More nods were exchanged. Schubert shrank back from this trio. The others, Vogl included, maintained their poise. Apparently, the count relied on disciplined formality to carry him through this ordeal. Only the rigidity with which he held his body suggested his discomfort. Millstein and Nordwalder were professionals, certainly representatives of law enforcement, the servants of the ruthless Baron von Hager. Schubert remembered them as guests at the *soirée*. Then, he noticed and appreciated the glitter of their medals. Now their icy formality frightened him.

Vogl avoided looking at Captain Millstein but paid close attention to Nordwalder. Sensible Viennese like Vogl treated Hager's minions with great care when they couldn't avoid them altogether. Though less aware of the power they wielded, Schubert experienced an animal sensation of fear. Instinctively he stepped behind his friend.

"Can you, either of you, shed light on this matter?" the count asked.

"Count von Neulinger, I am devastated … "

"I don't want your sympathy, Herr Vogl. I demand your assistance!"

"Of course … anything."

"When did you last speak with my wife?"

Vogl spoke slowly. "Perhaps a quarter hour before I left," he said. "The countess …"

"Her name was Eugénie, as you well know," von Neulinger said, displaying a trace of emotion.

"Yes, Eugénie. She wanted to speak with me about Herr Schubert's new song."

"What about it?"

"You see, she promised to provide an honorarium for the composer."

"So, you initiated the conversation?"

"Why, no. But I assumed that was the reason Eugénie wished to see me."

"And did she give you money?"

"No, she didn't. Eugénie merely expressed her opinion of the song."

"That was when she gave you this?" The envelope with "*Die Sonne und das Veilchen*" written on it appeared as if by magic. The seal on the envelope was broken.

Vogl showed no surprise. "Yes, that's right. She asked me to leave it on the sideboard."

"You know nothing of the letter's contents?"

"The envelope was sealed."

"*Natürlich.*" The Count spat it out as though it were profanity.

Schubert recalled hearing the word, in the countess's

effervescent voice only hours before.

A spasm of pain crossed the Count's face. "Is there more you can tell us?"

"About the letter? I'm afraid not" said Vogl.

"That's all," said the count.

"One moment, please." Doctor Nordwalder spoke for the first time. Schubert noted the man's bass voice, fitting for his somber demeanor. A singer with his attributes would make an excellent Adolfo, perfect for his opera. "Herr Vogl, the members of your profession are trained in manipulating weaponry are they not?"

"The works of Shakespeare and others require a certain knowledge of swordsmanship."

"Swords of all types?"

"For Shakespeare, the rapier, or rapier and dagger provide the greatest verisimilitude, as well as the most excitement for the audience."

"But you can wield other weapons. The broadsword? The saber?"

"I have impersonated many military officers. I've frequently worn a saber. I have no experience with the broadsword."

"Thank you, Herr Vogl. Forgive my intrusion, Georg."

The count nodded in Nordwalder's direction then turned again to Vogl. "Wait downstairs, please. Your friend will receive his honorarium."

"Oh, never mind that." Schubert was shocked to hear his own voice. Now, feeling everyone's full attention, he stopped dead.

"You wish to say something?" Captain Millstein stepped in with a baritone voice, *legato, pianissimo*.

Schubert staggered on. "Well, no. Yes. You see … that is … the song is still here. Music room. Unless … I mean, keep it with my com … compliments. But if you don't mind there are a few other trifling pages, which, if I might be so bold …"

"Downstairs," said the count.

Schubert bowed and backed out of the doorway. Vogl nodded formally, turned and caught up with his friend on the stairway.

Diederich followed. "You will wait here," he told them when they reached the bottom.

Schubert and Vogl again shared the chill silence of the anteroom. A few moments later Diederich returned, bearing a key with which he unlocked the music room door.

"Perhaps you will be more comfortable in here," he said ushering them in. "You may sit, of course, but otherwise touch nothing."

Diederich closed the door behind them.

Chapter Thirteen

S chubert's eyes surveyed the room nervously and filled with relief when they lighted on his precious folder, exactly where he left it, on the floor to the left of the piano chair. Vogl's face, too, showed relief, not from what he saw, but from the fact that Diederich had not locked the door, had not literally incarcerated them.

As if by instinct, Schubert headed towards the piano.

"Don't do that, Franz," Vogl said.

"I'm not going to play it," Schubert said. "I just want—"

"They said touch nothing," Vogl reminded him, and gestured to a horse-hair upholstered love seat, for his friend to sit without inviting trouble.

Reluctantly, Franz complied, muttering, "I don't see why not."

Vogl did not feel like explaining how, in an establishment like this, one might easily bore small holes in a wall or ceiling to observe or overhear conversations in the room adjacent or below. He refused to point out what, to him, was obvious: that they were virtual captives in one of the most dangerous places in the city.

Outside of certain government offices, most particularly those charged with investigating violent offenses, such as the ministry Doktor Nordwalder apparently represented, few places in Vienna contained more ruthlessness under one roof. Violence against titled citizens was a crime against the state. Thus Vogl considered himself in a virtual war zone. Having felt the oppression of a blood-thirsty atmosphere before, he had no desire to draw any attention to himself or his comrade. He seated himself in a brocade chair at a right angle to his friend, prepared to endure the wait silently.

Schubert showed no such discipline. "That was the countess wasn't it?"

Vogl just stared at him.

"She's dead, isn't she?"

"Quite dead," Vogl replied. Contemplating the world without Jennie was difficult for him.

"But how? What happened?"

"Her throat was slashed, I should say."

"You mean…?"

"She didn't do it herself, if that's what you're asking."

"Oh. I wasn't! *Gott im Himmel*…" After a moment's reflection, Schubert continued, "Was that why the captain asked you about weapons?"

Vogl sighed. "Franz, I envy you. You have neither the motive or the ability to murder Eugénie von Neulinger."

"But surely, Misha, no one thinks that you …"

"I don't know what our most senior officials, charged with

preserving order in the city, think. But be sure that they will get to the bottom of this unconscionable crime." Vogl adjusted his remarks for the benefit of possible eavesdroppers. "Now do you understand?"

The men sat in silence for a while, too long for Schubert who flashed back to a previous run-in with the police. Some two years before in the middle of the night, officers dragged him from his bed at the home of his friend, Johann Senn. That affair ended with little more than a few reprimands, but it was an experience Schubert did not wish to repeat, even in memory. Vogl's comments connected the past with his current plight.

"So much blood," he murmured.

"Characteristic of slashing wounds from a sword, I imagine," Vogl replied.

"Horrible." Schubert shivered. "But, Misha, see here. I have nothing to do with this. I need to retrieve my scene from *Alfonso*. Surely that has no bearing on … on what happened upstairs."

"Let the people above us decide that," said Vogl.

"Well, I hope they decide soon!"

"Amen."

Not long afterwards, the music room door opened, revealing Captain Millstein and the count, bearing a sealed envelope. "You may go," said the count. "Herr Schubert, this is for you. You will find yourself adequately compensated for your efforts last night."

"Danke, *mein Herr*." Schubert took the envelope but did not leave the room.

"Well?"

"Excellency," said Schubert, "I need that folder by the piano. You see, it contains part of an opera…"

"Take it and go!" said Millstein.

"Yes. Yes certainly," Schubert hastily scooped up his precious folder.

Millstein turned to von Neulinger. "Georg, I am sorry that on this, the saddest of days, you suffer the encumbrance of idiots."

The remark had an unexpected effect. The count snapped, "I do not seek sympathy, Captain."

Millstein stepped back stunned—as if slapped.

"Herr Vogl," the count continued, "you know what Eugénie was, how ... well connected ... she was to the activities of this city. I expect your complete cooperation and discretion in the coming days. I also hold you accountable for the behavior of your little friend there. You will say nothing of what has occurred here, and neither will he. As far as you both are concerned, nothing is amiss. Is that understood?"

"Nothing is amiss, Your Excellency," said Vogl.

Schubert nodded.

"Georg, we can examine them further," Millstein offered.

"Let them go. Herr Doktor Nordwalder has been alone upstairs long enough."

"That's very generous, Georg. Your restraint is exemplary."

"Captain, do not mistake me. I feel the loss of my wife tremendously. I will not abandon my duty to conduct a full inquiry. When it is known who perpetrated this outrage, rest assured that he will come to understand the full power of my displeasure." This last line was delivered in Vogl's direction, but it wasn't clear if the count intended it to apply personally.

Vogl did not inquire.

Chapter Fourteen

On the street, Vogl turned to his friend without his customary benevolent stoicism. "Well, Franz, you have your invaluable manuscript. I hope it doesn't cost you your life."

"What do you mean, Misha? You said yourself that no one suspects me of having anything to do with what went on in there."

"Walk with me a little, towards the theater."

"But I'm meeting Schober at von Schwind's."

"Just a short way. There are things you need to understand."

"Let's discuss them this evening, at the Café Lindenbaum."

"No place indoors is safe. I prefer to talk on the street. Come. Walk with me."

Sensing his friend's urgency, Schubert acquiesced.

After a few steps through partially packed snow, Vogl began, "Eugénie's murder will not go unavenged."

"I should hope not!"

"Just listen, Franz. The count demands satisfaction. He will have it."

"The shrewdest minds of the city are investigating."

"True. But who knows how clever—or lucky—the murderer is? This investigation will inevitably bear fruit. There's no guarantee that the fruit will come from the proper tree."

"Misha, are you suggesting—"

"I suggest nothing. As far as I know, von Neulinger is an honorable man. He probably won't deliberately persecute an innocent person. But he is also a man of action. If he decides, or is persuaded, that someone is culpable, he won't waste time reviewing the decision—even if he learns later that he was mistaken."

The chill Schubert felt then was greater than that brought on by the February morning. "But Misha, neither you, nor I …"

"He sent for me this morning. You appeared at the same time. Therefore, neither of us is above suspicion. No one is. Not even the officers with the count now."

"The captain who was there last night?"

"Millstein. Doktor Nordwalder, also."

"Why does last night's *soirée* matter?"

Vogl pondered this question before responding. Eugénie loved intrigue, but she tempered her love with an almost uncanny instinct for self-preservation. She always sniffed out plots against her and acted to circumvent them. No, Eugénie was taken by surprise. Eventually he said, "Franz, the authorities will solve this crime quickly. There is, therefore, a strong desire on the murderer's part to see someone other than himself punished."

"What can we do?"

"Follow von Neulinger's advice. Say nothing and stay out of the way. Do you understand, Franz?" This last was more a plea than a question.

"I understand, Misha. *Guten Tag.*"

"*Guten Tag.*"

Vogl watched his friend scurry off on treacherous sidewalks into the February chill. Then the full force of the morning's events hit him. The most compelling force in his life—his love, his hate, his obsession, his nemesis, at times his joy, more often his despair—evaporated, snuffed out in the night. It seemed impossible. What was his world without her? Only one answer came to him. Rehearsal. Rehearsal for which he was late. He trotted through the snow passing a plodding horse-drawn butcher's wagon on the way to the theater.

Chapter Fifteen

By mid-morning, Franz Schubert running late and still shaken by the hideous events at the start of the day, could not get his thoughts in proper order. The horror in that house was not his concern he knew, but the grisly images didn't pass quickly. And there was Vogl's injunction not to tell anyone.

Still he hurried. He was to meet with Franz Schober at his lodgings at von Schwind's for an important conference about the third act of their opera. They agreed to meet at eleven, and it was nearly noon. Schober hated to waste time. Already he might have abandoned Schubert to embark on another adventure. Upon reaching home, finding himself as usual without a key, he knocked on the front door with uncharacteristic vehemence. Frau Stieglitz let him in.

To his relief, Schubert saw Schober in the parlor sitting quietly, mulling over pages of their libretto.

"Have you been waiting long, Franz?" Schubert asked.

Schober responded with an expansive smile, "Ages, *mein apfelkuchen*. An eternity. However, I forgive you, for the return of the little Schwammerl into my life has obliterated the indescribable torment I have so patiently weathered just for the sake of this glorious reunion."

"Pay no attention to him, Herr Schubert," Frau Stieglitz interrupted. "He arrived not five minutes ago."

"Betrayed! Bitterly betrayed!" Schober continued, without missing a beat. "Am I fated always to fall before perfidious women?"

Frau Stieglitz left the room, and Schubert smiled for the first time that day. "I don't think she understands the meaning of 'perfidious'."

"With her intellect, probably not. In her soul, she understands perfectly."

"Franz, that's scandalous. Why do you always vilify women?"

"Forgive me. It is only because I love them so well. But who are you to talk, Schwammerl? I noticed your interest in Fraülein Schikaneder last night."

Schubert blushed. "She is charming, isn't she?"

"She'll do," Schober replied with the air of a *connoisseur*. "But now to business. I see you have the scene with you. Have you made your changes?"

"I haven't had time."

"Well, I have precious little time this afternoon." Softening his voice somewhat, Schober continued, "You see, Schwammerl, a little 'adventure' is beginning. I need my rest today."

"Franz, no adventure of yours can compare to mine of this morning."

"You haven't been slaving away at the score? That's not like you."

"How could I work? I left the music at the *soirée* and went back to retrieve it."

Schober looked amused. "Why, you little imp. That was your adventure? You wanted some time alone with the countess. Well, I certainly don't blame you. You say you have the music. Did she gratify your every whim?"

"Don't joke, Franz. She's dead."

"The devil!"

"Please lower your voice. I met Vogl there."

"They say that he and the countess were once quite close."

"Just hear me out, Franz. Vogl was summoned by Count von Neulinger. He says—"

"The count?"

"Vogl." Schubert took a deep breath. "Michael thinks that someone who was there last night killed her."

For once, Schober gave Schubert his full attention. "Killed her?"

"Cut her throat. I saw the body," said Schubert shuddering. "You know that Count von Neulinger is an associate of"—and here Schubert lowered his voice to a whisper—"Baron Hager?"

"So they say," was the hushed reply.

Now that the worst was past, Schubert continued more easily. "Michael says that a quick solution to the murder is of paramount importance. Speed matters more than the truth."

"I see," said Schober. "So who killed her?"

"I don't wish to talk about it."

"We should, though. As you say, until someone is apprehended, we're all under suspicion."

"I know nothing about it. I never wanted to go to that house in the first place," Schubert said.

"Wait a moment, Schwammerl. In my peregrinations over the planet, I have heard accounts of the beautiful countess."

"This is no joke."

"I'm not joking. I'm reviewing the people there last night. According to that greatest of all authority, the imposing god Rumor, several people resided within the circle of the Countess's s particular friends. There's Vogl himself…"

"Franz!"

"But, at his age, he's not likely to commit a crime of passion. There's that Englishman, Lord … Lord somebody … Bellingham?"

"Birmingham, I think," escaped Schubert's lips in spite of himself.

Schober smiled. "Birmingham is a city."

"Bellingham then."

"Yes, him. Now who else? Are we sure it's a man? Why not a rival? There's Zdenka Merlinbeck … or her husband …"

"You must stop this, Franz."

"And, of course, we can't rule out the immediate family, the count, his son. Is it possible that our *belle inconnue*, Fraülein Schikaneder, is actually Eugénie's illegitimate daughter."

"Enough!"

Schober stopped, finally. "You're right, Schwammerl. There are just too many. Let's return to Adolpho's confession. We know what he's done. What's wrong with the way we have it?"

Schubert accepted this invitation to return to the world of *Alfonso und Estrella* with alacrity.

Chapter Sixteen

The singers of *The Empress of the Common* endured a difficult morning. They expected a full run-through of Bildman's piece with orchestra, but Vogl's unexpected departure in the middle of the overture made for hurried re-arrangements. These did not please La Donmeyer. Just as a semblance of a run-through gained some momentum, the newest member of the corps, Fraülein Rosa, looking exhausted, stumbled during the act one dance, and knocked over the maypole, causing further delay. Assistant Manager Schmidt, universally regarded as adept at handling mishaps of this sort, was otherwise engaged, ransacking his resources in the all-too-likely event that he'd need to replace Hernando's father, should Michael Vogl become … incapacitated. Come hell or high water, *The Empress of the Common* was going before the public in eight days.

Vogl calmly walked on stage to take his part in the sextet that ended the first act, arriving in time to relieve the company's greatest anxieties, though not to save the rehearsal completely. It was already after noon, and with a different performance slated for the evening, there was no longer time to complete the run-through.

To Vogl's relief, Schmidt and the orchestra conductor decided to shorten the afternoon break to a minimum—two hours—then to finish the *Empress* as a *Sitzprobe*. That course allowed the stage hands time to set up for the evening's performance of Gluck's *Alcestis*, the piece diplomatically chosen to maintain strict and dignified neutrality in the on-going battle between Germanophiles and Italianophiles.

The impending arrival of von Weber had everyone's blood up. In short, everyone, from over-taxed musicians to under-prepared stagehands, from the put-upon management to artistically frustrated performers, felt like martyrs. With a plethora of friends with whom to commiserate, everyone was relatively happy.

Except Vogl. He chose to remain in the theater during the break, ostensibly to review his music, but his profoundly inartistic experience of the morning was hard to escape. Incredibly, his little Jennie was dead—murdered. Had he unintentionally played a role in the tragedy? Count von Neulinger suspected him. The heat of the count's suspicion still burned. Thus Vogl's vow to do anything in his power to put the count on the scent of the actual culprit was sincere.

But Vogl knew nothing. At their last meeting, Jennie accused him of "ruining everything." Inured by experience to Jennie's histrionics, Vogl didn't take her seriously, but this time her emotional smoke screen must have masked a real fire. What went wrong? What was the purpose behind all that business with Schubert's song and those letters?

Vogl forced his mind to function systematically. The previous evening, conspicuous police presence created a subtly oppressive atmosphere. What denizen of Vienna dared try anything underhanded in that situation? Only a truly desperate one; and no one, aside from Schubert, betrayed any signs of desperation.

Perhaps one of the foreigners then. Zdenka Merlinbeck's two German escorts came to mind. They appeared more mystified than moved by Schubert's music. They might not have known the formidable composition of the rest of the company. But as strangers to Jennie, why kill her? Did Merlinbeck or his wife employ assassins? Preposterous! Vogl could imagine that Zdenka hated Jennie enough to want her dead, but surely she would not resort to swords, even by proxy. Her husband seemed uninterested in everything. Even granting that such unprepossessing, professorial sorts were disguised thugs, bringing them to Jennie's attention in a social context would have been an inconceivable blunder on Zdenka's part.

What about those other foreigners, Lord Bellingham and his Russian friend, Pyotr Tagili? Bellingham had a past with Jennie, but it seemed unlikely that after almost a decade he wanted to settle an old score. Vogl reviewed his own exchange with the man. Bellingham mentioned something unusual about the strange Germans and the Balkans and the mysterious "plat'num". Bellingham's renewed contact with Jennie seemed to be only an incidental component of his government's interest in a trade matter—political, not personal, or so Vogl hoped. Bellingham's Russian companion, Pyotr Dmitrivitch Tagili, remained a complete enigma.

Jennie claimed that her marriage "permitted her to withdraw from politics," but to Jennie, truth was only a tactic. She might have involved herself in one last game, for old time's sake as it were. Perhaps her husband asked her to. Von Neulinger certainly knew his wife's talents. In 1815, brokering *sub rosa* arrangements between international competitors was the cornerstone of Jennie's repertoire.

In her heyday, she thrived during some of Europe's most delicately vicious negotiations, creating or breaking alliances between the most unlikely parties. Under a veneer of perfect civility, Jennie casually created or destroyed careers, fortunes, and even, some rumors held, a government or two. With Jennie the only certainty was that, however things turned out, she remained at the top, *natürlich*! Jennie's accomplishments as a negotiator surprised everyone. The few coups that Vogl viewed in full light showed more inventiveness than a Schiller play.

But it was a long way from ancient unsavory political maneuvering to murderous violence, especially murder by surprise. Jennie lived by subterfuge and subtlety, yet there was nothing subtle about how she died. The savagery suggested that the crime was one of impulse, not the culmination of long, deliberate planning. If so, then something happened during the *soirée* that drove someone to destroy Jennie von Neulinger.

The destroyer evidently found a way to re-enter the house or remain inside until everyone was asleep, entered Jennie's room, did the deed, and departed. None of this posed any particular difficulty for someone possessing the requisite audacity. Should anyone ask, a forgotten hat or glove creates access to the house. Once inside, the killer hides in an empty room. There's no need to smuggle in a weapon; just select one of von Neulinger's swords. Four rooms had them mounted on the walls. Locating Jennie's room might cause anxiety, but as long no one wakes up …

No one had. Jennie's killer found her and all but decapitated her. Vogl had to consider that Jennie herself left her door unlocked, expecting to meet the person. In any event, all the murderer required was a quick slash or two. Judging from her remains, Jennie had not resisted. Her killer gave her no chance to scream.

The matter of escape presented obstacles, but nothing insurmountable. The most direct egress was Jennie's bedroom window, which opened onto a small balcony with a wrought iron rail. Vogl couldn't recall the exact topography beneath the balcony, but even without special gymnastics involving tree limbs and the like, one could, with a modicum of luck, drop from the balcony to the snow-covered ground safely. New snow falling throughout the windy night obliterated any subsequent tracks. All very convenient for an impetuous murderer.

Vogl's scenario depressed him. Nothing in it prevented him from playing the murderer. Nothing in his reconstruction provided support of his innocence.

∶

The official inquiry into Eugénie von Neulinger's death echoed Vogl's speculations. A blood-smeared saber, missing from the main dining room on the ground floor, was discovered under snow beneath the countess's balcony. The weapon belonged to the count, taken from a wall in the dining room. The room had been essentially vacant after supper ended the previous night, long before the guests departed. Anyone could have gone in and remained out of sight. Outside, the snow's depth implied that at least an hour elapsed between the murder and its discovery, probably more. Ignatz Nordwalder explained everything to the count.

"The sword was discarded during a heavy snowfall, and the heaviest snow occurred during the hours just before dawn. It wasn't snowing when the countess's maid discovered her corpse. Heavy winds obliterated any hopes of tracing anyone from your garden. We can't be certain that anyone was beneath the balcony at all. But you are positive that all the downstairs doors were locked?"

"Quite positive," said the count. "Check with Diederich for confirmation."

Nordwalder nodded. "Now, Georg, we come to the painful part. We are alone; speak frankly. Do you know of any reason behind this … unspeakable atrocity?"

"No more than you know yourself, Ignatz. Our household arrangements haven't varied for months. Perhaps it was foolish to mention platinum to Eugénie, but in asking for her advice, I never dreamed that she'd take such an active interest."

"What do you mean?"

"Jennie took it upon herself to open a private platinum exchange. Diederich can tell you the exact days and times. I only recently discovered what she was up to. Adhering to our government's belief that many years would elapse before the metal, in any quantity, could be transformed into useful ordnance, I encouraged her to extract as much money as she could from the Russian broker and his various competing buyers."

"Perhaps, Georg, a matter of the heart…?"

"Please, Herr Doktor. I married Eugénie with my eyes open. We knew each other's backgrounds. We only demanded discretion of each other, not perfect fidelity, although for all of that, Eugénie was a faithful wife."

"Then …"

"I know of no one. Eugénie kept her part of the bargain."

"What of this Vogl fellow?"

"An old acquaintance. He was granted more liberty about the house than most, but I've consulted with Diederich. Whatever went on in the past, there was nothing currently going on between him and my wife. She enjoyed teasing me with their friendship, but there's no scandal."

"Perhaps he wished to rekindle the flame, and your wife denied him."

"Perhaps, but Vogl isn't stupid. He knows that we monitor our visitors, and he knows how much he stands to lose."

"Let's return to the platinum seekers."

Von Neulinger was almost amused. "Jennie's visitors? Ignatz, you saw them yourself—a laconic Russian ascetic, an aging English fop, and two German barbarians she nicknamed 'the bear and the weasel'. There's not an ounce of wit or charm among them. If Jennie 'loved' them, it was as a child loves its toys. I assure you, there were no liaisons in her recent past, or on the horizon."

"Then we must proceed to the metal itself. Hager won't like it."

"I'll see to it personally, Ignatz, that any current negotiations remain unaffected."

"Even if your wife had personal reasons to keep the 'market' open?"

"Even then."

"A thought occurs to me, Georg. Assuming that the countess tried to operate behind your back, she'd need a reliable way to receive and disseminate information outside of regular channels. Could Vogl have functioned as a courier?"

"That's a possibility. I'll investigate."

"With the utmost circumspection. Let's not incur Hager's displeasure."

"That goes without saying."

There was a knock on the door. "Come in, Millstein," Nordwalder said. "So, what do you have for us? How do we tell the city of von Neulinger's great loss?"

Millstein knew his duty, and his plan of procedure was deemed satisfactory.

Chapter Seventeen

An eloquently oracular written obituary, crafted under Millstein's supervision appeared promptly, but the fact of the death of Countess Eugénie von Neulinger already floated abroad. Rumors flew. Vogl received some of the earliest blasts, from theatrical colleagues returning from dinner. Kunegunde Rosa was among the most upset. She came into the theater fifteen minutes before she was due, alone and agitated.

"Tell me, is it true?" she asked tearfully.

"Is what true, Fraülein?"

"The von Neulingers! The fire! The family!"

Vogl chose a careful response. "There's no fire at the von Neulinger's."

"Are you sure?"

"I visited the house myself," said Vogl, still exercising caution, "not two hours ago."

"Then the count and countess are unharmed?"

"The count is well. What have you heard, Fraülein?"

"What I heard is inconsequential, since it's clearly not the truth." Kunegunde collected herself and moved up a notch in Vogl's esteem. "I now know only that you went to the house this morning."

"In that you are correct. Forgive me if I don't talk about my business there. You are better off not knowing, believe me."

"But the count and countess….?"

Vogl prevaricated no longer. "You will hear the news soon enough. Regrettably, the countess is dead. The count survives. I'll say no more."

Tears again filled Kunegunde's eyes. "That beautiful lady. She was your friend, was she not? Herr Vogl, my condolences." Kunegunde walked away.

The rest of the troupe, however, was less accommodating. "Well, Michael," a jovial Peter Thym said, "you are quite healthy for a ghost. Or was it you who vanquished the count in the affair of honor?"

"Don't talk rot, Peter."

"Von Neulinger didn't take you from us to demand satisfaction?"

"Rubbish!"

"Did you not force his wife to leap from her window and run barefoot through the snow?"

So it went. Vogl fought off falsehood after distorted falsehood. It seemed as though every returning performer accosted him for verification of disasters he had caused, prevented, or rectified.

"*Meine Damen und Herren*," Assistant Manager Schmidt said at last, "we are all assembled. Time is short. *The Empress* awaits!" Even then the company didn't settle down until rumblings of impatience from Anna-Marie Donmeyer succeeded in focusing their attention on Bildman's opus. For once, Vogl approved of the diva's self-centered professionalism.

𝄢

In one respect, the people involved with Eugénie von Neulinger were fortunate. Discussion of her death, variously reported as a murder, a suicide, an accident, even by one craven publication, "a misunderstanding," quickly subsided into a distant second place behind the all-consuming matter of von Weber's impending arrival. Despite efficient policework, people of all classes died in Vienna every day. Harbingers of impending artistic war came to town far less frequently.

Countess Eugénie died before dawn on Friday morning. News of the event was ubiquitous by Saturday afternoon. For a few hours it inspired much irresponsible speculation, but Carl Maria von Weber was supposed to arrive in Vienna on Sunday evening. Intensive *Freischütz* rehearsals would proceed for the next three weeks, with the long-anticipated performance on the first Thursday of March. What death, even a sensational murder, could compete with the artistic event of the decade (or perhaps merely the winter)?

A substantial minority believed that Weber conspired with all managers of the city's central opera house, including the Italians, to insure secrecy. The identities of the principal singers remained unknown. After the orchestra musicians received their individual parts, they assembled for only one group rehearsal, and even then they played through only the overture and chorus numbers. A few scene painters succumbed to bribes or similar cajolery, but the only enlightenment they offered was that some of the story occurred in a forest. All was going as the management wished. Everything remained in the hands of Carl Maria von Weber, with three feverish weeks to prepare his case for native German opera.

The arrangement pleased everyone. Champions of a new *Germania* rejoiced because their champion was in the ascendant. Traditionalist Italianophiles basked in the expectation of a fiasco that would solidify their status as the world's only legitimate operatic artists. Newspaper editors and pamphleteers delighted in inflated circulation caused by the controversy.

Interest in *Der Freischütz* enabled the civil authorities, oblivious to operatic concerns, to pursue their investigation through their usual means of infiltration and intimidation without attracting undue attention. Responsibility for solving the crime fell under the punctilious direction of Doktor Ignatz Nordwalder.

By inclination and necessity, Nordwalder was devoted to his mission of securing Vienna's tranquility, though he also had great passion for his avocation, chess. He saw his occupation and his pastime as highly compatible. Experience in one area often helped in the other. When determining responsibility for a crime, Nordwalder liked to think in terms of a chessboard with pieces positioned on it. His opponents were, naturally, enemies of the state, or had to be considered so. On his own side, Chancellor Metternich was his king, and (in terms of power, not gender) Baron Hager was queen. Underlings like Captain Millstein and Count von Neulinger performed as castles, knights, or (in some literal cases) bishops. His world was full of pawns, agents available for early probing of his opponents' positions, and occasional sacrifice to the greater good.

Nordwalder did not carry the analogy too far. In chess, one was acquainted with one's adversary and aware that he controlled forces equal to one's own. In his job, it was not always easy to determine who the adversary was, or what resources he had. And Nordwalder was not so foolish as to allow his allies to see themselves as pieces in his game. Still, he found it useful to think of his main objectives as to protect the Chancellor at all costs, to rely on Hager as infrequently as possible, and let other pieces fall where they may.

Unlike the majority of chess players in his era, Nordwalder won his games by patient defensive stratagems. He had a distaste for the valiant gambits others found so popular. He preferred his opponents to attack recklessly while he carefully martialed his forces for one decisive counter-thrust. Thus Ignatz Nordwalder was greatly feared in all quarters where he was known.

But Nordwalder wasn't heartless. In line with the most successful Viennese of the time, Nordwalder truly loved civil order. Unlike a number of his *confrères*, he harbored substantial respect for justice as well, although, of course, justice had to be sacrificed sometimes for the sake of expedience. He saw himself as a master player who, when the inevitable time came, would be able to abandon the game—preferably with considerable winnings—without forfeiting his life. Just results pleased him more that merely victorious results. In any event, the prospect of unearthing the Eugénie von Neulinger's killer rather exhilarated him. He believed himself more than able to undertake the challenge.

Nordwalder saw the task of narrowing the field of Eugénie von Neulinger's enemies as substantial but well within his resources. Many of the von Neulinger's guests that night worked within his ministry. All in all, that facilitated his work. The last of the count's non-ministerial guests left around midnight. Routine interrogation of servants and similar contacts proved that most of the guests went straight home and didn't stir until after the countess was dead. Nordwalder's agents aroused more than one suspect from slumber. The agents themselves delivered the tragic news. Before word of the countess's death reached the street, the number of possible suspects among the guests was under ten. The number of suspects requiring further investigation was, at most, seven.

Of these, three were quite far-fetched. Zdenka Merlinbeck claimed to have dispatched her two foreign companions towards their lodging before returning straight home. A servant remembered letting the von Merlinbecks in shortly after one. The count said he was indisposed, and the Merlinbecks retired to their chambers.

Further inquiry unearthed a housemaid who, rising to start her workday in the kitchen, saw the countess enter the house around five in the morning. Merlinbeck offered no explanation of, and had little interest in, his wife's comings and goings. So, his highly attractive wife enjoyed a significant degree of autonomy.

Nordwalder's moment of pity for his old friend became a pang of lust. Countess Zdenka seemed less desirous of withdrawing from state affairs than her husband. Nordwalder indulged himself for a moment, pondering interesting possibilities.

Then he turned his attention to Zdenka's German companions, Doktor Barenberg and Professor Himmelfarb. The keeper of the inn where they resided locked his door at midnight. When the Germans woke him "at some ungodly hour," he noticed their clothing was in disarray. Both were groggy, but the bigger one, Himmelfarb, "staggered about so" that he merited a second look. The innkeeper couldn't say whether there was any blood on either man. By then Nordwalder knew of events in "Nero's Rathskeller" that could account for Himmelfarb's condition. It was hard to imagine the Germans committing the murder, before or after the brawl, either individually or in concert. Still, one or both could have gone out again after the innkeeper left, taking a key along.

Nordwalder maintained an open mind about Zdenka and her companions, but he decided not to pursue them with undue vigor. The image of the murder weapon deterred him. The other suspects, men whose exact movements during the night were not fully accounted for, seemed far more promising. All of them knew how to wield a cavalry saber with enough skill and force to dispatch a defenseless woman.

Nordwalder remembered the Englishman, Thomas Bellingham from 1815. "If *milord* had any hand in the current business, the motive was greed, not love," Georg assured him. Other colleagues said that he played the fool to encourage his adversaries to underestimate him. Nordwalder believed the story fueled by a chance remark of Eugénie: "I find Thomas difficult to understand." Bellingham once may have come close to outmaneuvering her, before being thwarted by von

Neulinger. Like the two Germans, Bellingham returned to Vienna to purchase platinum; but since platinum was also of interest to Metternich, Nordwalder was reluctant to look in that direction.

Similar concerns prevented Nordwalder from giving Bellingham's Russian companion, Pyotr Dmitrivitch Tagili, deep consideration, although Tagili couldn't be ruled out. Like Bellingham, Tagili resided in Vienna at the British ambassador's residence. The spies there were not completely reliable. Nordwalder deeply resented Metternich's constant harping on how little he knew about the British. About the few Russians in Vienna, he knew even less. Until this platinum matter surfaced, the Ministry of the Interior showed complete indifference about them.

The two remaining suspects resided closer to home, both literally and figuratively. Not Eugenie's husband, of course, but Georg's son Heinrich merited Nordwalder's scrutiny. He spent the night traveling between taverns after his unceremonious departure from Nero's. One bar-keep in Nordwalder's employ verified that Heinrich stayed at his place until the snow abated. He left, "shortly before daybreak accompanied by two of his cronies, considerably less sober than he was." Heinrich was not a credible suspect, if the scenario of Eugenie's murderer waiting until the house was quiet, killing her, and then slipping away was accurate; this, despite the large, fresh bruise the barkeep noticed on Heinrich's cheek.

Nordwalder turned his attention away from those closest to the countess towards his own colleague, Captain Millstein.

Millstein was not ruled out by circumstances. His servants operated under a standing order never to discuss his movements or whereabouts. Nordwalder knew their loyalty to the captain, having trained some of the men himself. Nordwalder's best chance to trap Millstein came when he sent for Millstein on first hearing of the murder. Millstein was at von Neulinger's when Nordwalder arrived. With deliberate haste Millstein could have arrived before him, but Millstein might have been in the vicinity all along.

For motive: Millstein was an officer of the old school, shown not only by his living among people completely loyal to him, but also in his desire to rise through the ranks. He willingly accepted favors of women as well as men. That he was von Neulinger's underling did not mean that he intended to remain an underling forever. Nordwalder did not know of any short-cuts Millstein was attempting, but Nordwalder did not know everything. Millstein might risk some clandestine maneuvers under the noses of the ministry, and he was capable of acting decisively if they went awry. Hager preferred to employ daring, resourceful men. Millstein possessed no dominating intellect, but he was courageous.

"In addition," Nordwalder reminded himself, "there's Millstein's blunder during the preliminary investigation. Perhaps it was deliberate."

Still Nordwalder viewed the prospect of Millstein's culpability with reluctance, similar to that which he felt about the foreigners.

If any of them murdered the countess, there would be no trial. Von Neulinger would insist on a duel likely to culminate in either an undesirable international incident or the loss of at least one of Baron Hager's trusted agents. Nordwalder saw no positive outcome to his investigation if Millstein, Bellingham,

Tagili, Himmelfarb, or Barenberg were the murderer.

Fortunately, Nordwalder had another suspect. This man fit all criteria: He had not gone straight home. He had a long-standing association with the victim. By his own admission he knew the rudiments of saber fighting. Best of all, he lacked direct connection to any affairs of state. Privately acknowledging a lapse in objectivity, Nordwalder expected that the murderer of Eugénie von Neulinger would turn out to be precisely who it appeared to be—the aging, over-rated thespian, Johann Michael Vogl.

Chapter Eighteen

S aturday afternoon found Vogl fully immersed in Hofoper business, ostensibly rehearsing for *The Empress of the Common*. But he was not singing. He dispensed solace or advice as needed against the tizzy approaching panic amongst the company. Von Weber's impending arrival disconcerted them. As a senior member of the company, and veteran of more than one Grand-Opening-of-World-Changing-Significance (after all what was this *Freischütz*, compared to *Fidelio*?), Vogl dispensed opinions on matters ranging from the technique of singing German in operatic style to the technique of acquiring tickets for the *Freischütz* premier. He even comforted La Donmeyer, who for no apparent reason broke down after finishing her second act aria, weeping at the thought of "new fashions making her musical quality obsolete."

Relief finally came when Assistant Manager Schmidt announced the end of rehearsal for *The Empress of the Common*, reminding those performing in that evening's *Alcestis* to return in three hours. Hastening to leave the theater, Vogl was nonplused when Schmidt, a single-minded autocrat blind to everything except the immediate needs of the each impending Hofoper show, asked him to stay behind.

Schmidt's superiors "feared the impact of the opera across town." Sensibly, the management wasn't offering competition on the night of Weber's opening, but someone mentioned that "Bildman's *Empress* was German, too."

"What of it?" Vogl asked. "If *Der Freischütz* triumphs, the public will enjoy our foretaste of it."

"Yes, unless the Italians object, *The Empress* may then cause a riot."

"Nonsense! Our piece is a singspiel. We're not breaking new ground."

"I agree with you, Vogl, but consider the Italians. They'll press any advantage."

"True," said Vogl. Then after a moment he added, "As far as I know Domenico Barbaja is still in charge."

"Yes, he is. The most vicious dog in the pack."

"Well, why not give the dog a bone?"

"Feed his vanity?"

"No, appeal to his taste."

"We can't do anything Italian, Vogl. When aroused, Germans are even more dangerous than Italians. The directors want me to postpone *The Empress* and mount a French piece next week."

"French? No one will come."

"Precisely."

"*Der Freischütz* is on everyone's minds ..."

"And we're preparing for a mob."

"I see your difficulty, Herr Schmidt. I may have a solution."

"Anything short of armed violence."

"We won't go that far. Weber arrives in Vienna five days before we launch *The Empress*. Public attention will certainly turn from Weber's opera to Weber himself."

"So?"

"If Weber demonstrates appropriate deference to the Italians, our harmless *singspiel* may proceed in peace."

"You expect Weber to command a truce?"

"I do."

"Why? Do you know the man? Is he not in the limelight precisely because he threatens Barbaja?"

"He is. And a truce requires the blessing of an Italian."

"You're mad, Vogl. Barbaja is determined to discredit *Der Freischütz*. Remember his attack on Rossini six years ago."

Vogl shuddered. "I attended the performance. Despite that night's fiasco, *The Barber of Seville* has survived. Indeed, it thrives. Barbaja's contribution to the chaos was never proved."

He probably has agents in the field already gathering eggs to throw at the stage when the curtain opens."

"Not this time. Barbaja's too shrewd. This time, there's one man even he must respect."

"Who? Metternich? The Emperor? We can't recruit them."

Vogl permitted himself a little smile. "Have you forgotten, Schmidt, the name Salieri?"

𝄢

Moments later, hurrying homeward, Vogl felt almost

pleased with himself. He envisioned something devious enough to please Jennie von Neulinger, a final intrigue to honor her memory, as it were. Antonio Salieri, the *eminence grise* of Viennese music, though no longer producing anything of consequence, still carried symbolic weight. As much as anyone he deserved credit for Italian opera's original conquest and continuing dominance of the Viennese stage. The man was now in his seventies and determinedly *hors de combat*, but his very neutrality anchored Vogl's plan. He smiled in memory of Schmidt's reaction on the plan's unveiling.

"What are you saying? That old man hasn't touched an opera for more than twenty years."

"Yes, I know."

"He always steers clear of opera houses and their politics."

"Yes. Isn't that wonderful?"

"Nothing on earth will convince him to come anywhere near a guaranteed scandal. If by some ill star he learns of *Der Freischütz*, he'll come down on the Italian side."

"*Natürlich.*"

"So how can Salieri help?"

"Schmidt, where do we see Salieri nowadays? No answer? You should get away from the Hofoper more often. Salieri shuns the opera houses, but he goes to the court and sometimes to church."

With his influence as a theater composer waning, Salieri had turned to writing sacred pieces. When even these received little attention, Salieri redefined himself as the city's pre-eminent teacher. Although Salieri was officially retired and no longer taught regularly, he generously granted time to almost any composer desiring to make his mark in the complex, competitive musical world. One was always encountering this or that prodigy visiting the city for a "session with Salieri."

Whatever his artistic influence over his pupils, the claim that one studied with Salieri still opened doors in Vienna. No less a personage than Ludwig van Beethoven used this entrance into the city's musical circles. More relevant to the moment was that an oratorio by another of Salieri's disciples, Friedrich Schneider was to form the major part of the afternoon mass at St. Stephen's on the Sunday before the Tuesday opening of *The Empress of the Common*. Salieri would almost certainly attend. All one had to do was entice Weber to go to St. Stephen's and arrange an introduction. Better if the introduction preceded the performance. All Vienna would adore the image of the rising German star and the fading Italian star in worship together.

Schmidt saw the beauty of Vogl's scenario. "But can you make it come to pass?"

"I have hopes," said Vogl. Vogl also hoped to bring a third party to the meeting, another Salieri pupil of long ago, Franz Schubert.

Complacently, Vogl congratulated himself. According to Schubert, Salieri had already written von Weber. If the two giants met, Schmidt's singspiel was saved and Schubert would have his chance with von Weber.

Vogl's complacency evaporated at once. Among Schubert's greatest talents was his ability to squander opportunities. Anxiety on his friend's account convinced Vogl to turn his steps towards the Wipplingerstrasse.

Chapter Nineteen

With his plan of attack fully formed, Doktor Ignatz Nordwalder sent for Captain Millstein and spent the hour before his subordinate's arrival writing a series of orders, recalling some agents, dispatching others. One spy would now serve for the two Germans. They were cared for well enough by the loose network of informants housed in their inn. A larger assemblage was assigned to the artists. All was ready when Millstein appeared.

"Implement these at once," he said, presenting Millstein with the packet.

"Jawohl, Herr Doktor," Millstein responded. Then, as Nordwalder expected, the captain hesitated.

"Is something wrong?"

"Timmerich."

"Yes, Timmerich. He is in your employ, is he not?"

"Of course. But in a matter of this kind…"

"I'm sure you can find a job for him that will keep him out of trouble."

"If I must. But why Timmerich?

"We're short of personnel," said Nordwalder, knowing that Millstein wouldn't believe him. "Well, what are you waiting for?"

Millstein turned and left without saying another word, looking just as agitated as Nordwalder hoped. Sometimes over the board, it was desirable to make a purposeless move to distract one's opponents from the real object of one's attack.

Gert Timmerich was, in Nordwalder's view, just a pawn, but he realized that involving him in routine surveillance was a calculated risk. Timmerich fought in the war against Napoleon and was badly scarred by his experience, literally and figuratively. At the age of eighteen he was carried off the field at Austerlitz, unconscious because of a bit of shrapnel in his skull. When he recovered consciousness, he was missing three fingers from his left hand. From then on he carried with him a deep, permanent hatred not only of all things French, but also of his own officers, who he felt had betrayed him. Until coming under Nordwalder's care, he lived the life of a beggar. A decade of service for the Ministry of the Interior gave Nordwalder ample time to discover the most effective uses for this embittered veteran.

In the abstract, Timmerich was as loyal as a German Shepherd to the Austrian empire. As long as he didn't face any unfamiliar aristocrats, from whose class his military superiors were drawn, he reliably followed all orders with great zeal, occasionally too great zeal.

That was the danger. In action, Timmerich was fearless

and reckless. He lacked both patience and judgment. No one, not even Nordwalder himself, understood exactly what set Timmerich off or how to stop him. Twice the pawn had embarrassed the ministry by killing someone he was supposed only to frighten. Thus, Nordwalder found him most useful in extreme situations. The decidedly delicate inquiry into the death of Countess von Neulinger did not suit Timmerich's talents ideally.

But Nordwalder had his reasons. Timmerich was becoming harder to manage of late. A time-consuming, thankless task might restore his self-discipline. If he failed...well, there were other zealots in the ministry who could rectify matters.

Still, Nordwalder's primary purpose for Timmerich was to occupy Captain Millstein. Millstein had a deficient intellect. He was now asked to use a man who couldn't be trusted near any foreigner or any aristocrat. Even the slow-witted captain would eventually find the only possible deployment for this loose cannon and make the forced move.

More to the point Timmerich was the only agent Nordwalder had at his disposal who would tell him what Millstein was up to, the only double agent Nordwalder was able to plant in Millstein's stable. The captain was also a suspect, after all.

Chapter Twenty

"Are you satisfied, Schwammerl?" Franz Schober asked, lifting the blotter with authority from his newly-penned line.

"Read it again."

"'The abyss of my sorrow cannot be measured by man.'"

"Well, it's not bad, but—"

"Not bad? Listen. Weber arrives tomorrow. We must present him with a complete score. We have less than twenty-four hours."

"There's short time until the morrow, ere the score must truly scan," Schubert sang, and continued with, "The abyss of my deep sorrow cannot measured be by man." His short concert concluded, Schubert returned to speech. "D minor. Fear not me." Then he snatched the pen from Schober.

"Schwammerl."

"I'm setting that melody down before another replaces it." He grabbed a page of the score at random, turned it over and scratched out five lines to create a staff. In his haste, Schubert tipped over the inkwell by Schober's right wrist. Schober, concerned for his cuffs, jumped back. "Watch out!"

But Schubert was in another world. The pen worked feverishly for a moment then halted abruptly. "Dummkopf— six eight," he muttered, scratched out what he had written and dipped the pen in some ink on the tabletop not yet dry.

Schober recovered enough to grab the fallen ink bottle from the table. Schubert extended his pen for one more dab and looked up at his friend.

"Franz Schubert, if you don't stop this madness right now, I'll hurl this bottle at your head."

At this undignified moment, Vogl arrived. "Ah, gentlemen, business as usual, I see."

Both Franzes became all smiles. "Exactly so, Herr Vogl," said Schober.

"Thanks, Misha, for sparing me from a raging tiger," said Schubert.

"You plan to entertain von Weber with such comic interludes?"

"Tomorrow, we'll be on our best behavior," Schober assured him.

"Then there's a meeting?"

"Well, not exactly. But we do know where von Weber is staying."

"Where?" Schubert asked excitedly. Both Schober and Vogl ignored him.

"Ah. You plan to lie in ambuscade outside his lair."

"We want to approach him before he starts rehearsals for his own piece," Schubert said.

"His own piece? Franz, suppose you wanted to become acquainted with the Duke of Wellington. Would you waylay him before or after Waterloo?"

"I don't understand."

"I do," said Schober. "Herr Vogl believes that Weber is preoccupied. He won't pay any attention to us."

"But once he sees *Alfonso* …"

"If you pounce upon him, he's likely to *see* two madmen. He'll have you arrested, or worse. It has not been so long since Kotzebue's assassination. Weber's adherents may shoot you."

"Shoot us? Misha. Do you really think we're in danger?"

"Of course he doesn't," said Schober. "But I see your point, Michael. We're not going to 'waylay' von Weber. We're simply going to be present at his arrival. At an auspicious moment, we'll present ourselves."

"And if no auspicious moment presents itself?"

"We have other strings on our bow," Schober muttered.

"*Wunderbar*," said Vogl, as Schubert simultaneously sabotaged his friend by asking, "What other strings, Franz?"

Vogl seized the moment. "Please don't take offense when I tell you that I have means of enriching your arsenal."

"Bows aren't stored in arsenals," Schober said resentfully.

"Then I abandon metaphor. I propose to introduce you, Schubert, to Carl Maria von Weber under auspicious conditions."

"Misha! You can do that?"

"No. Salieri can."

"*Maestro* Antonio!" Schubert said. "Has he written Weber about me?"

Vogl replied, "Plans exist to have Salieri and Weber hear

Schneider's oratorio at St. Stephen's a week from Sunday."
Vogl did not add that the plans existed only in his own head.

"What of it?" asked Schober, never one to remain in the background too long. "Franz is ten times the composer Friedrich Schneider is."

"Talent is not the point. Salieri is going to the performance."

"And von Weber?"

"He will go also, if someone explains that the concert will benefit him. I propose to be that someone."

"How can you gain access to Weber when we cannot?"

Vogl reacted as if Schober's question was an insult.

"Unlike you, I am welcome at the Theater an der Wien …"

"Where *Der Freischütz* is being staged." Schubert's re-entry into the discussion diffused the incipient quarrel. "Brilliant, Misha."

"I forgot. We are in the presence of one who, in his day, was not unknown to the fabled Mozart," said Schober with less than perfect grace, "but Mozart's time has passed." Vogl did not rise to the bait, so Schober continued, more calmly, "We can't afford to distract von Weber once rehearsals start."

"Oh stop it, Franz," Schubert said. "Weber will accept us, and then we'll want Michael to play Adolfo."

"Assuming my own day hasn't passed," said Vogl.

"No more pessimism from my two best friends," said Schubert with unusual sincerity.

"Quite right, Schwammerl," Schober responded. "Optimism is our watchword tonight. I feel confident that *Alfonso und Estrella* rests, at the moment, in your capable hands. I now embark on an adventure in another venue where promised pleasure awaits. Gentlemen, please excuse me. *Guten abend.*" Schober finished with a distinctly old-fashioned bow towards Vogl and was gone.

Schubert confided to his friend, "I believe the hair of this 'adventure' is darker than her predecessor's."

"Let's talk of something else," said Vogl.

"Very well. I didn't expect to see you again today, Misha. Franz chose this spot for a secret rendezvous. How did you find us?"

"I asked at von Schwind's. He hadn't seen you, so you must have avoided the Café Lindenbaum for someplace more remote."

"Quite clever, Michael. You have the makings of a first class investigative scholar."

For the second time that evening, Vogl looked vaguely insulted. "That title I dream not of," he responded. "Have you eaten, Franz?"

"Not since breakfast, now that you mention it. What about you?"

Vogl went through the customary charade of claiming he was famished and ordering enough for both of them. Schubert, as always, appreciated the repast. As they reached dessert, Schubert said, "Thanks for your willingness to communicate with Weber, Misha, but we probably won't need you. Schober is quite resourceful."

"I don't question his resourcefulness. I question his professionalism. Meeting von Weber means nothing if he sees you as street urchins."

"One look at *Alfonso* will convince him that we are professional."

"This?" said Vogl, indicating the chaotic debris of blotted pages, spilled ink, crossed out words and measures.

"I mean, once it's copied. I'm doing that tomorrow."

"Well, I wish you every success—and Schober," Vogl added lamely. "Shall we go, Franz?"

"One more pipe for me. Don't worry, Misha. Everything will be all right."

"I hope so. Good night, Franz."

Chapter Twenty-one

Exactly twenty-one hours later, at 7:30 on the cold, starry evening of Sunday, February 17, a coach pulled up outside the home of Frau Helena Stahl. For once, the streets of Vienna were as calm and orderly as the authorities liked to claim they were. The day of devotion, the bitterness of the weather, and the early onset of darkness apparently quelled the sort of burning passions that produced the various human excesses the authorities fought to tamp down. All was quiet, as most citizens huddled indoors, or, if they had no shelter, in parks around whatever sources of fire they could muster, where authorities customarily turned a blind eye.

Frau Stahl's home, rather more brightly lit than most at that hour, emerged as a beacon. It was a well-respected refuge for visitors to Vienna, situated advantageously near the Theater an der Wien. Many theatrical artists stayed there. Thus ,the two blazing torches at the doorway and the large number of candles still burning in the windows caused little curiosity. Nor was the one unfortunate ministry minion assigned to patrol the streets particularly surprised by the gathering of nearly a dozen souls across the street. These hearty souls resembled others of their kind: the males outnumbered the females; several eager hands held sketch pads and pencils.

Nordwalder's pawn paid no special attention to the two young men at the back of the pack. One was somewhat taller than common with an aristocratic bearing including a rakish moustache. The other was uncommonly short, wearing a frayed coat and standing alone in the crowd, without hat or scarf. The shorter man held a thick portfolio and frequently tugged at the sleeve of the taller man. The little man occasionally rose to his toes, but whether to get a better look at the street or to combat the chill was uncertain. Even in conservative Vienna, going onto *relevé* in public was not a crime. The ministry employee paid more attention to the arriving coach.

When the coach stopped, excitement grew, and several people moved at once. A servant coming from the house almost collided with the man jumping down from the seat next to the driver. Both apparently intended to open the passenger door. The driver's companion arrived first, allowing the servant to confront the small mass of people crossing the street seeking a better look at the coach's inhabitants. "Stay back," he ordered.

The gaggle obeyed. A cloaked, hooded figure emerged from behind the coach, inspiring whispers among the onlookers. Is it he? Is it he? It was only the driver, descended from his perch to help two additional servants from the house unload three or four trunks and two crates. Next from the coach descended a stout man, wearing a somewhat daring fur coat with a yellowish tint and a hat too tall for the current fashion. As soon as his foot hit the ground, he marched down the street and around the corner. Clearly he was not the long-expected one.

Almost a full minute passed. Someone murmured a profane oath. Then another figure stepped from the carriage, far less imposing than the first. Not even the black greatcoat of the most ordinary cut and fabric concealed its wearer's gaunt frame. He relied on a walking stick and moved slowly, with a perceptible limp. At the foot of Madame Stahl's staircase, he paused for a moment, emitting an audible cough.

As if taking the cough for a cue, the crowd reacted, but not in unison. Along with the refrain, "Is it he?" could be heard the counter strains, "That's the man! That's our savior!" Two female voices began chanting, not quite in tune, "*Heil dir in Siegerkranz*", that most patriotic statement of pro-German sentiments set, ironically enough, to the tune of the English "God Save the King". Several in the crowd moved forward, although a few held back, seizing the moment to write or sketch in their notebooks.

As those in the surge reached the coach they heard again the cry, "Stand back!" This time, they did not comply. Two or three men continued forward, as the limping figure, with the help of a servant, mounted the front steps. The crowd looked up and saw Frau Stahl herself, standing with still more servants behind her.

"Are you Viennese, or are you jackals?" Frau Stahl asked, in a strident voice. "Control your curiosity and go home. This man is exhausted. Herr von Weber, welcome to my home," she continued more kindly.

Nordwalder's minion heeded every word, but saw no cause for action.

Weber apparently understood what the onlookers wanted. The phenomenon of artist-worship was not new to him. Rising to the occasion, he turned in the doorway and delivered a wan smile and modest bow to the crowd before being whisked inside.

The solid thunk of Frau Stahl's closing front door effectively signaled the crowd to disperse. Docilely, they obliged.

Such was the arrival of Carl Maria von Weber into Vienna.

By and large, the onlookers disbanding in the cold night, seemed surprisingly cheerful. Scraps of conversation revealed how close some had come to von Weber, or how "heroic" the composer seemed. The champion of German opera would be among them for several weeks—there was ample time to hound him.

Two, however—the tall aristocratic young man and his short, bare-headed, portfolio-bearing friend—hung back. They withdrew more slowly than the rest and were two of the last three to leave.

Following established procedure, Nordwalder's man had remained aloof, never participating in any of the crowd's activity. He said nothing to anyone during the entire hour he was there. He had not moved or been moved when the coach arrived. His employers had no interest in von Weber or the fate of opera in Vienna, so neither did he. Following dictated instructions, Nordwalder's man stayed unobtrusively in the shadows across the street from Frau Stahl's until he was alone.

This man tarried only a moment. Unhurriedly, he hunched

his overcoat over his shoulders and ambled after the two parting friends. At the now deserted corner, he glanced once at the back of the taller man before proceeding, at a judicious distance a few yards behind, along the path of the shorter, hatless man.

The next morning Doktor Ignatz Nordwalder, through his subordinate, Captain Millstein, properly briefed by his agent, Gert Timmerich, received a full, albeit unenlightening, account of Franz Schubert's movements between 7:30 and 9:00 on the evening of Sunday, February 17, 1822.

Chapter Twenty-two

The week following Weber's arrival produced constant, virtually ubiquitous frustration. Mid-winter conditions put dampers on everything, from commerce to crime, and the Interior Ministry faced the fewest challenges to its authority of any week in the year. This meant that incidents of intra-ministry maneuvering, such as back-biting and blame-shifting, increased alarmingly. Little poses more danger to a hierarchical society than bureaucrats with too much time on their hands.

Private citizens with both pure and impure motives were stymied. Consider the activities of Franz Schober.

The librettist of *Alfonso und Estrella*, Schober strove with intermittent valor to introduce himself and his work to von Weber. On Monday, Tuesday, and Thursday, Schober appeared at the Theater an der Wien, libretto in hand. Early Monday afternoon, Weber passed within six feet of him, but was so deep in consultation with a *repetiteur* that interruption was impossible. On Tuesday afternoon, just before the company's dinner break, Schober bribed one of the theater's employees to let him into the building apart from Weber's supporters, who were congregated outside the theater. But Schober was brusquely pushed aside moments later by that same employee whose duty was "to protect Weber from all unsolicited encounters."

Had the stars been in a different alignment or the temperature a few degrees warmer Tuesday night, the case of Eugénie von Neulinger would have been over, and Schober would not have seen Wednesday at all.

It all began naturally enough, with Schober deciding to drown Tuesday's sorrows in a place of high revelry but low reputation, a place in a part of the city not far from St. Stephen's Cathedral that featured several temples to Aphrodite. Worshipers of all sorts, from all strata of society, found their way there every day of the week at all hours of the day and night.

Schober was rather well known in his chosen temple, by sight as well as by a wide variety of assumed names, and felt comfortable there, especially after imbibing a quantity of spirits. A frequent visitor, he traveled among men of his own class who engaged in similar pursuits. He rarely considered his sporting ground as the home to many destitute souls who, for various reasons, could not find refuge elsewhere. When such ideas crossed his mind, he congratulated himself for his charity, for dispersing sums liberally among the more comely members of the class of the deserving poor.

Occasionally, men received his *largesse* as well. Men such as the one he bumped into in the doorway of #19 on the Annagasse.

Schober got the worst of the collision with the shabbily dressed man. He was knocked back a couple of steps. Nevertheless, he offered an apology and planned to continue inside. He was stopped by a hand to his chest.

"Your apology means nothing, *mein Herr*," the shabby man snarled.

Schober took a moment to collect himself. There was no mistaking the malice of his new acquaintance, but Schober responded with good humor, "Then allow me to buy you a drink."

The shabby man's gaze modulated from rage to suspicion. "A drink."

"A gentleman can do no more. If you will just let me pass …" Schober glanced down at the hand still resting on his chest and felt a spasm of horror. It was only a thumb and forefinger. The remaining digits were scarred irregular stubs. Coarse dirty brown wool covered the rest of the palm. Nonetheless he rallied. "Please accompany me as the guest of Herbert Hummel" (Schober's hastily selected *nom de guerre* for the evening—it pleased him that rather than an outright lie, his self-introduction could be construed as an invitation to a co-conspirator.).

The shabby man responded still suspiciously but without subtlety, "Gert Timmerich."

Gert Timmerich visited #19 on the Annagasse for different reasons than Schober. He disliked the sort of revelry practiced there and loathed the men and women who indulged in it. But one of his associates, Captain Millstein's personal valet to be precise, often chose that address as a place to share information with Timmerich. Timmerich lived nearby and didn't object. He would meet the valet at the appointed hour, give or take what he needed, and leave.

This evening Timmerich, having received new instructions, was in a bad mood. More surveillance. More lurking in doorways, rapidly averting his gaze, wandering all over the city for no reason. If they wanted to dispose of someone, why waste time? All this following and reporting made his blood boil.

The collision with the man wearing the maroon coat just increased his disaffection. Timmerich didn't recognize the smirking fool as the person standing with Franz Schubert outside Frau Stahl's house two evenings before. Schober meant nothing to him. All he saw was a self-centered, self-satisfied aristocrat, and Timmerich wanted nothing more than to wipe the stupid smirk off the man's face, preferably with a carving tool.

With the offer of a drink, Timmerich's brain began to spin. Since receiving his head-wound at Austerlitz, alcohol had little effect on him, certainly less effect than the condescending aristocrat offering it. The white teeth, the nicely waxed moustache. Timmerich felt the urge to grab its two points and twist the rich man's head off. Nonetheless, he let his left hand fall to his side and stepped out of the doorway.

As the maroon coat preceded him inside, Timmerich's right hand went into his coat pocket and curled its fingers lovingly over the whalebone handle of his favorite weapon. How nicely that maroon coat would mask any blood that happened to spill on it.

The two men found an empty table in an alcove. "Wine or Schnapps?" Schober asked jovially.

"Schnapps," Timmerich grunted, the first word he'd said since entering.

"Wait here, my good man," said Schober patting the man on his left shoulder.

Timmerich could barely contain himself, but he formed a plan: create a diversion—throwing over the table would serve—and in the ensuing scramble insert his knife between Herr Hummel's ribs. Unless he was caught red-handed, there'd be no reason to connect him to the deed. One less snob in the world wouldn't bother anyone. Dr. Nordwalder often paid him for this sort of activity. This service he'd perform for free. In fact, it would make up for the frustrations of the evening. But when he looked up, the maroon coat was out of sight. Timmerich slammed his damaged left hand down on the table in increased frustration.

Schober's life was saved by a charming young woman he thought he recognized, but whose name he couldn't recall. She was standing in conversation with a female friend near a doorway at the back of the hall that led up a flight of stairs. Schober, with glasses of brandy in each hand, and the contents of two more inside him, altered his course and approached the women. "How lovely to see you again, my dear," he said.

Neither woman seemed to recognize Schober, but one of them answered, "Are those drinks for us, *mein Herr?*" sparing him the need to apologize.

A somewhat confused colloquy ensued, the upshot of which was that the girl Schober thought he recognized went towards Timmerich's table carrying both glasses of brandy while Schober followed her companion carrying an unopened bottle through the door and up the stairs.

The danger passed. Timmerich decided that dispatching the aristocrat was not worth the wait. He gulped down the brandy the strange girl gave him, dashed the empty glass on the floor, shoved the startled waitress aside, and stormed out. The remaining glass of brandy was her tip, and she downed it at once.

𝄢

Schober spent most of Wednesday recuperating from Tuesday's adventures and avoided the Theater an der Wein. By evening, he recovered enough to dine at the home of a friend of his own station, Franz Bruchmann, whose sister Justina he found quite fascinating. Schober, in fact, had cast her as the heroine of an ambitious "adventure." That evening his hopes for Justina remained unfulfilled, so Schober returned to his post outside the theater on Thursday morning. There, another day-long wait in the cold proved futile.

Thus by Thursday evening, Schober was desperate. He said as much to his friend and collaborator, Franz Schubert. "Tomorrow, you must accompany me, Schwammerl."

"On whose piano?" Schubert said grumpily. He'd spent the first three days of the week in bed, recovering from a cold occasioned by staying out hatless in Sunday's frigid air. Thursday evening was the first time Frau Stieglitz allowed him to leave the house.

"You know what I mean," said Schober. "At the very least, give me the score. Weber needs to see the music."

"We agreed, Franz. The score remains in my hands until it passes to von Weber."

"Then bring it to the theater tomorrow."

"I shall do no such thing."

"Why?"

"I'm busy."

Schober was taken aback. "What business is more important than *Alfonso*?"

Schubert looked a little sheepish, almost embarrassed. "An adventure," he said.

"Delightful!" said Schober, his mood changing instantly. "Fraülein Rosa?"

"It's nothing like that," Schubert began. "My time in bed this week started me thinking."

"I, too, have had some of my best thoughts in bed."

"Alone?"

"No. Not usually."

"Then hear me out, Franz. Monday and Tuesday I was too ill to work, but I thought about my profession, of those who really succeed at it."

"No greater way to make a mess than seeking to create success," Schober improvised.

"I'm serious, Franz."

"You're also successful enough, or you will be once *Alfonso* reaches the stage."

"Perhaps. I've achieved a little, it's true, but only on a small scale. The truly great composers, the Beethovens of this world, create on a grand scale. I manufacture cottages, they construct cathedrals."

"Our opera is that cathedral."

"Not mine. The glory goes to the singers presenting your words. I want my music to speak for itself. In any case, that's what I thought about, and in the process, a notion for a piano piece struck me."

"And did you jot it down?"

"That's just it, Franz. For two days, I couldn't 'jot down' anything. But this piece has taken root in my mind and seems to be developing in gargantuan proportions."

"What of it?"

"I must write it. I'm starting tomorrow."

"So you mean to abandon *Alfonso und Estrella*? To leave your creation, our child, the fruit of the union of two faithful lovers, to the cruel machinations of fate, to …"

A sneeze from Schubert ended Schober's flight into melodrama. He reverted to a more direct approach. "Will you at least join me tomorrow evening at Frau Stahl's?"

"No one's admitted over there. You told me that yourself."

"Well, Schwammerl, we must try something."

"All right—no, wait. I'm performing with Vogl tomorrow, I just remembered."

"Where?"

"I don't know. Misha arranged it."

"But you won't forget *Alfonso*."

"Of course not, Franz. Arrange the meeting with von Weber, and *Alfonso* and I will go."

"I tell you, I need your help to arrange the meeting."

"Not tomorrow. In a week or two."

"Schwammerl!"

"Don't worry, Franz. Things will work out."

Schober sighed, accepting his defeat in the skirmish. "So, what is this monumental piano construction?"

"I have you to thank for it, actually," Schubert said. "You

remember that page you ripped at … at the *soirée*?"

"I thought we agreed not to mention that evening."

"Yes. But you tore a page of "*Der Wanderer*". During my lassitude, I sat down to repair the page, and the oddest things started happening. The notes took on a life of their own."

"Ah, now I see," said Schober. "This great and noble enterprise, this excuse to abandon your greatest creation, emerges from delirium. How wise you are, Schwammerl. Should I supply you with opium? They say it does wonders for headaches, and it accelerates the hallucinatory process almost as well as absinthe."

"Thanks all the same," Schubert said with a noise halfway between a cough and laugh. "Both my monument and I are perfectly healthy now. You'll hear it first, I promise."

"Then let's toast to the success of the enterprise. Wait here, Franz, I'll get us a bottle." Setbacks never stymied Schober for long.

Chapter Twenty-three

Countess Eugénie von Neulinger's funeral took place on the morning of Tuesday, February 19. Her husband oversaw her internment in his family vault. It was a sign of the times that Eugénie became the vault's first occupant. Her husband, like so many others, attained his place in society through valorous service in the Napoleonic wars. His ancestors were negligible. The funeral was well attended for reasons similar to those that governed the von Neulingers' previous formal gathering. No one dared attract the authorities attention by signs of disrespect. Few members of the funeral party displayed any actual feelings. Perhaps they took their cue from the count, who observed the obsequies with unwavering stoicism.

Ignatz Nordwalder noted these reactions carefully, but if he hoped for any incriminating display, he experienced frustration. Most of his suspects, all but three of the foreigners, were present. The bewitching Zdenka Merlinbeck was there, lacking her German escort. She stood dutifully beside her apathetic husband, occasionally letting her eyes wander over the crowd, but otherwise observing perfect decorum. When her eyes lighted on Nordwalder, he caught a gleam of recognition, nothing else.

Another *Auslander*, the Russian Tagili, was absent, but the foppish Englishman Bellingham was there with two other officials of the British Embassy. Bellingham seemed more invested in the proceedings than his companions. If the stories about his adventures of 1815 were true, he had reason to be. Nordwalder saw only one quiver disturb the "stiff upper lip" of which the British were so proud. Moreover, Bellingham's gaze remained fixed on the casket as long as it was in his view.

Captain Millstein formed part of the honor guard escorting the countess to her final resting place, and he performed with proper soldierly *sang-froid*.

Only two members of the funeral gathering gave public vent to their feelings, but in neither case did the reactions seem inappropriate to the occasion. The countess's stepson Heinrich wept openly and, at times, volubly into a handkerchief of black crepe. The fashion of youth apparently was to wear its heart on its sleeve. Nordwalder was a little surprised to see Heinrich's display of emotion, but if there were an ulterior motive in Heinrich's indulgence, it was probably to disconcert his father. Perhaps Heinrich used his handkerchief only to hide his face, which still showed the traces of a diminishing bruise. Even in that case, Nordwalder saw no evidence of guilt. From that, Heinrich, through unimpeachable sources, was virtually exonerated.

Careful tracing of young von Neulinger's movements revealed that he visited two unlicensed taverns on the night of the murder, coming to the second after the brawl involving Himmelfarb and Barenberg. Nordwalder still smarted because descriptions of who hit whom, when, with what, and for what reason, varied even among the trained observers present on the scene. Yet all sources agreed that a violin shattered, along with numerous bottles and glasses, and that several pieces of furniture received minor abrasions. The mayhem explained Himmelfarb's blood and Heinrich's bruise.

After being tossed from the tavern, the Germans disappeared into the night. Their scent was picked up at their inn. Not so Heinrich. He returned to the cellar with two companions, intent on making reparations. The proprietor accepted some of Heinrich's money on behalf of the Italian violinist, who suffered the greatest economic loss, but he refused Heinrich and his cronies permission to stay. More confrontational chatter ensued until Heinrich—or one of the others—huffily announced that they would "take their custom elsewhere."

They remained elsewhere, actually unaccounted for, for approximately an hour before Heinrich and his friends appeared at another establishment presided over by an agent of Nordwalder. There they remained until some time after sunrise. At that time, Heinrich, stirring from a doze, was overheard saying, "I can't be late." He left with his two companions in pursuit. The trio strayed towards Heinrich's parents' house, but at the last minute, they veered off in another direction. Since the countess had died before dawn, Heinrich's morning decisions were irrelevant.

There remained the slimmest possibility that during the interval between taverns, or at some time during the night with his friends asleep, Heinrich had slipped home and slain his stepmother, but his companions swore—under some duress to be sure—that he'd stayed in their company all night.

"With that shiner on his cheek, he didn't want his father to see him," one pointed out. Upon hearing that logical remark, Nordwalder repositioned Heinrich in the back ranks of his inquiry.

Nordwalder's attention settled longer on one more mourner, Michael Vogl, who seemed genuinely moved as the countess passed by him. Like Heinrich, Vogl dabbed his eyes with a handkerchief, but unlike the younger man, Vogl did nothing to attract attention. He stood far back in the crowd apparently lost in his own thoughts. That Vogl was such a well-respected actor, Nordwalder admitted grudgingly, suggested innocence. If his dignified grief was an act, Vogl would plant himself in view of an audience. Instead, Vogl isolated himself. Then, unexpectedly, he left before the final prayers were read.

Nordwalder concluded that Vogl's sense of loss was real. Yet he consoled himself. The countess's murder sprang from the murky depths of passion, profit, or politics. Vogl would not be the first to dispose of a friend or lover only to suffer pangs of regret from the sacrifice of his victim.

Nordwalder watched the *cortège* march away from the tomb, contemplating his next move. Already his network flooded him with information. He needed to narrow, not expand, the field of inquiry. This required direct interrogations. First, Captain Millstein, whom he would send for as soon as they returned to the ministry.

Chapter Twenty-four

"Admit it, old man," Michael Vogl ordered himself upon returning from Jennie's funeral, "Thomas Bellingham is right." A confirmed stoic, Vogl welcomed advancing age, time's natural contribution towards mastery of the passions. His fortification against the morning's ordeal was a strong dose of the Meditations of Marcus Aurelius, but the medicine proved insufficient. He set down the volume and sighed.

Seeing Jennie pass out of his life this final time pained him almost as much as her first exit with Lord Bellingham. In the privacy of his study, he didn't hold back tears. It was all he could do to fight down the urge to sob. But more than his immediate loss troubled him.

Jennie brought him nothing but anguish. From the earliest torments of burning, too temporary love, through the ravages of rage and self-harming jealousy, through bitterness, hypocritical expressions of unfelt resignation and cynicism, to his current sense of dread, Jennie functioned, in a callous, insouciant way, as his muse. Vogl felt all his emotions travel with her to her tomb. With pangs of self-mockery, he admitted he was weeping for himself as much as for his long-lost love.

The torment became subtler still. Jennie showed the world how to change with circumstances. In her manners, public and private, she always stayed in vogue. Her father's cellar, her various *chevaliers'* conveyances and opera boxes, the homes she maintained and visited, right down to this last one, all became enchanted for a moment by her presence. When she was borne into her final resting place, Vogl became utterly disoriented. He felt unbearably alone. The dignified band, the expressionless faces, the absolute stillness—these were not part of Jennie's world.

For a moment Vogl was transported to another time, another cold funeral. There was the multitude, there were the musicians, there had even been then, as now, flakes of swirling snow, but that ceremony lacked similar solemnity. Vienna incurred lasting, immeasurable shame at the burial of one of its brightest lights, extinguished before its time. Vogl could almost hear the echo of wailing, those hurried formalities and the race to get away from the burial of Wolfgang Amadeus Mozart, as if the city felt chagrin for letting the great man get away from them.

Now they couldn't even find his grave. How different Jennie's memorial would be. The von Neulinger mausoleum was a permanent eyesore. Even after death, Jennie forced Vogl to consider how distant his theater-driven life was from her worldly reality.

"A featureless entity in an unfathomable world," Vogl muttered as he reached the nadir of his unhappiness. He felt drained, dried up.

Nonetheless, duty called him to the Hopfoper, the long-awaited full run-through of *The Empress of the Common.* "Perhaps casual chaos will do us good," Vogl declared to his hangdog face in the mirror. He forced himself to change to less funereal garb and leave the house. Vogl walked quickly and arrived five minutes ahead of time. While hanging up his hat, coat, and scarf in the men's cloakroom, he felt the presence of someone behind him—Kunegunde Rosa.

"Herr Vogl, will you please wait for me after rehearsal?" she asked.

Before Vogl could frame a response, Schmidt called the cast to the stage, and Kunegunde hurried away.

The girl's effect on Vogl was extraordinary. All through the rehearsal, through Schmidt's ill-tempered corrections of miscues and dropped lines, through Anna-Marie Donmeyer's melodramatic complaints about false *tempi* and obnoxious woodwinds, Vogl navigated with studied grace and equanimity. He contributed his portion to the enterprise without qualm or mishap, almost without effort. Only one question interested him: what on earth could young Fraülein Rosa want with a has-been like him?

As the others left, Vogl found Kunegunde along with his hat, coat, and scarf. "May I escort you home, Fraülein?" he said for the benefit of any onlookers. They left the theater together.

"Now, Fraülein, what is troubling you?"

"Father wants me to be a sprite," Kunegunde said. "In *Der Freischütz.*"

"Congratulations. You will be the envy of Vienna."

"But I want to stay here."

"Your loyalty is commendable, Fraülein, but, in all honesty, your career would be better served by joining the Theater an der Wien on this occasion."

"I don't care about my career. Only father does. I want to work with my friends here."

Vogl took a moment to frame comments about the capricious nature of the performing arts, the importance of seizing every opportunity, the value among friends that came from any one of a group advancing. But before he began his little homily, Kunegunde spoke again. "Father has invited von Weber to the gallery for Friday evening."

"Really!"

"Yes. To view the paintings. Then," she added with a little tremor, "I am supposed to sing for him."

"You are to be envied."

"Don't make fun of me, Herr Vogl."

"I'm serious. I envy you myself."

"Then you misunderstand. You see, I was wondering … I must obey father, but may I ask a favor?"

"Of what sort?"

"I want to sing some of the songs you sang last week."

"You mean Schubert's?"

"Yes, but I don't have any. Can you get me copies?"

"I expect so, Fraulein, but is it wise?" In her artless way, Kunegunde sent Vogl's mind spinning every time they spoke. He sifted rapidly through a slew of conflicting possibilities. For Kunegunde, auditioning with songs she had not sung before, songs designed for the salon, not the stage, seemed foolhardy.

However, Schubert might benefit if Weber heard his music.

"I don't know, and I don't care. Schubert's songs are so fresh and lovely. My repertoire is old, and it's all Italian."

"Ah. I'll look around," Vogl said noncommittally.

"Oh, thank you. Herr Vogl, one more thing … about these songs … do you play the piano?"

"Of course, and if I may say so—"

"I can manage the singing all right, if someone keeps the beat."

"My dear, I'd be delighted to help." Help she clearly needed. Vogl had no false modesty about his interpretative talents. No one was more suited to the task of guiding this foolhardy young singer through the nuances of Schubert's melodies than he. He began with, "There is a great deal more to a Schubert song than …"

"That takes care of rehearsal, but who'll accompany the performance?"

She'd stung him again. Vogl often played piano in public. True, his appearance in an unaccustomed role on a noteworthy occasion might cause comment and distract from the girl. Perhaps she had a point. But before he said anything, Kunegunde went on, "Can you recommend someone?"

"Why not Schubert himself?" Vogl blurted out. In for a pfennig, in for a krone.

Kunegunde blushed. "Do you … do you think he might?" she said, grabbing his arm eagerly.

Things clarified. Fraulein Rosa was not guileless after all. Vogl appreciated the trap into which she lured him. "He might," he said, adding, "if I asked him," applying salve to his bruised ego.

"Will you?"

"Yes, I'll talk to Schubert." Vogl sighed.

After depositing Kunegunde at the Oberes Belvedere Gallerie, Vogl set out to track down Schubert, feeling oddly uplifted.

Even entombed, Eugénie's mischievous spirit lived on in the unlikely form of a headstrong, impulsive young woman's interest in a young composer and his own willingness to channel that interest in the composer's direction. Maybe some harmony existed in the universe after all. Weber wanted to see some paintings. Schubert wanted to see Weber. Kunegunde wanted to sing with Schubert. Kunegunde's father, who controlled access to the paintings, wanted the *cachet* of associating with Weber, the genius *du jour*. This convergence resonated in Vogl like a C major chord. Everyone gets their heart's desire—*natürlich*.

The moment of euphoria passed. Jennie's contributions to the music of the spheres usually produced more dissonance than harmony. Having Weber, Schubert, and Kunegunde in the same place at the same time was no guarantee that Weber would consider Schubert's opera, or that Schubert would fall for Kunegunde. This meeting, far from making dreams come true, might cause them to collapse. Vogl landed back on the solid earth of modern-day Vienna on a cold February afternoon. He started toward the von Schwind's, the preliminary to a chase through some coffee houses, or worse if Schober found Schubert first.

Before he reached the Wipplingerstrasse, a firm hand fell on his shoulder. It belonged to Diederich, Count von Neulinger's servant. When Vogl turned, Diederich assumed a more formal manner.

"Herr Vogl, will you please come with me?"

"With pleasure," Vogl said, insincerely. Von Neulinger's unwelcome summons could not be denied. Schubert, Kunegunde, and Weber had to wait.

Chapter Twenty-five

For most, life after Eugénie von Neulinger's funeral quickly returned to normal. Activities in coffee houses and offices regained their accustomed rhythms. There was no notable change in the rates at which pastry, sausages, beer, and wine were produced or procured or consumed. Aside from employing a few additional broomsmen to remove the snow from the thoroughfares, the ministries had little to do.

Yet a calm exterior did not always mean that calmness reigned within.

At the von Merlinbeck's, for instance, that very afternoon, as the count napped upstairs, the Countess Zdenka had an intense colloquy with her two German metallurgists. Their conversation was not sentimental.

"With Eugénie out of the way," Zdenka insisted, "you can make the Russians another, less costly offer."

"We can," Jurgen Himmelfarb replied, "but we won't. My

colleague's mania for platinum is nonsense. I'm going home."

Zdenka, unruffled, turned to Barenberg. "You do not share this opinion, Johannes?"

"Platinum will transform modern warfare. There has never been enough of it available to make a difference until now. We must gain control of this vital resource before the Russians realize its value."

"We'll never get their platinum," Himmelfarb snapped back. "We're begging for mining rights, which the Russians will rescind as soon as they understand what they have."

Barenberg, mildly exasperated, waited patiently for the last reverberations of Himmelfarb's defeatism to subside. He then continued. "You reinforce my argument that we must act quickly, Jurgen. Tagili thinks we're chasing lead. The Russians need money. We can get in and get the platinum out before the czar catches on. If we don't, the English will. Give me a little time for calculation, and I think another attempt—"

"Attempt it without me. We know they want too much money. With no von Neulinger to help us, we are powerless."

Himmelfarb's remark energized Zdenka. "Perhaps I can act in Eugénie's stead," she said, placing a hand lightly on the big man's shoulder, to forestall his next outburst. She rose from her sofa and languidly paced the room. The two men were mesmerized. When she stopped and turned to speak, they hung in suspense, like members of an audience watching William Tell lift his crossbow. "Doktor Barenberg, how much time do you need?"

"A couple of days," Barenberg said, but seeing Jurgen's look of impatience mirrored in the countess's face, he finished, "but I can give you a rough idea in under an hour. It's merely a matter of calculating—"

Zdenka cut him off with a disarming smile. "Will you do so now?"

"With pen and paper, peace and quiet."

"We can supply all of that," said Zdenka, still smiling.

"I require some papers from the inn."

"I'll send for them."

"They're private," Barenberg snapped, but facing more scowls he added, "but I can manage a rough estimate without them." Under the countess's spell, Barenberg soon found himself ensconced in a well-appointed study with an ample supply of writing materials.

"Now, Jurgen," said Zdenka, resuming her seat on the sofa, "what shall we do while Johannes is occupied?"

Zdenka rejoiced in having cleared a significant hurdle in her quest to return to the front of Vienna's political battles, despite the fools she had to manage. With polished grace, she pressed the advantage provided by her practiced method for dealing with men in tandem: divide and conquer.

𝄢

While the Germans hammered out platinum dreams at the Merlinbeck's, Ignatz Nordwalder moved on the murder investigation.

"That explanation will not do, Millstein. You committed a grievous blunder."

"Yes, Herr Doktor."

"Explain this lapse of judgment."

"I cannot, Herr Doktor."

"Captain Millstein, I ask again: why did you let those papers out of the house?"

Ignatz Nordwalder displayed his impatience consciously. Far more important than Millstein's explanation was the manner in which he delivered it. Nordwalder respected the Captain's loyalty while doubting his intellect. Allowing Vogl and his friend to leave the house with some scraps of music was not so much a grievous blunder as a foolish one, merely a weak move, not a catastrophic error. Nordwalder sought proof that his colleague was merely a fool.

Millstein began slowly. "I thought that the papers had no bearing on the situation."

"And who are you to make that assessment?"

"I asked Georg first."

"The count, at the height of his grief, in the throes of his loss?"

"Well, you were otherwise occupied."

Nordwalder simply glared at the captain, who sniveled, "What could some nobody's music have to do with what happened upstairs?"

"Yes, Captain, that is the question. Now that you've let the music go, we may never know the answer."

Millstein shifted his feet.

Nordwalder let the silence linger. Eventually he said, "Perhaps the situation can be salvaged. Perhaps we can retrieve the music."

"I'll send for the composer right away," said Millstein.

"No, you won't." Nordwalder felt quite relaxed. "Think Captain. Think like a criminal. If you have in your possession papers implicating you in a murder, and someone asked you to produce them, might you not burn them or slip in some alterations or substitutions?"

Millstein said nothing.

"We will get the music back, if it still exists, without alerting our quarry. Do you have a man capable of such an undertaking?" Nordwalder was indulging himself. Millstein's minions were as good as any in the ministry in getting what they needed from ordinary citizens.

"Of course, Herr Doktor."

"I expect the music here tomorrow before noon."

"You will have it."

"Keep Schubert under observation until you get it."

"Timmerich is watching him now."

"*Danke.* You're dismissed."

With a bow and click of the heels Captain Millstein left the room.

Nordwalder felt satisfied with his interview with Millstein. He contemplated his next endeavor—taking on the English. Might as well eliminate all the fools first.

♪

Eugénie's decorous funeral rankles. She deserved to be thrown to the dogs. But etiquette requires that the world give the guttersnipe her final triumph. That situation could not be rectified. But her evil survives her. Her last machinations, thwarted or not, must never come to light. The source was stopped, true, but all vestiges of her doings must be eliminated, root and branch. Until that is done, Honor cannot rest.

All is safe for the moment. Why not let time take care of the rest? Too risky. What, then? Whose memories must be stilled before they triggered the realization of Eugénie's unspeakable desires? Not many. Only one or two. Just a couple more sacrifices to Eugénie's perfidious nature. Nothing too difficult to manage. All will soon be well.

Chapter Twenty-six

"A most attractive offer," Zdenka Merlinbeck said, assuming a most studious expression, one capable of transforming bookworms into lapdogs. Johannes Barenberg rewarded her with a modest bow.

"I'll submit it to the Russians without alerting the English," Zdenka continued.

"I'll prepare a more thorough proposal tonight," Barenberg said.

"Wonderful! Now, Johannes, please stay for some refreshment with me before you go."

"Jurgen expects me at the inn."

"He can wait. He left because he has no interest in your new proposal. Therefore, he has no reason to complain while we review it." As always, when she set out to impress Barenberg, the countess's logic was impeccable. "Nor would he begrudge you a cup of coffee. I always take some at this time of the afternoon."

"Very well, I accept, Countess."

"Jurgen concerns me," the countess said once the servants finished delivering the coffee. "Why has he lost heart? I barely persuaded him to give us another week."

"Homesickness," said Barenberg.

"Of course he's homesick. He's also impatient. Bavaria's mountains will be there when he returns."

"Jurgen doesn't understand the ways of the city."

"I admire his bluntness," said the countess, "but bluntness rarely works here. Paradoxically, when a great number of people trample the straightest path, the person taking a more circuitous route often wins the race."

"Quite so," said Barenberg, impressed.

"On the other hand, with only a week to work with, our plan must infuse subtlety with audacity."

In terms of logic, the countess was correct, but she was already too late. That very afternoon, Pyotr Dmitrovitch Tagili, took advantage of certain lapses in his host/captors' attention entailed by Eugénie von Neulinger's funeral and slipped away from the British embassy. He presented himself before the French ambassador, determined to arrange safe passage back to the Urals. Having seen his soaring, avaricious scheme for selling mineral rights he didn't actually possess return to earth with Eugénie von Neulinger's interment, he felt the need to abandon Vienna with haste. In his own way he, too, was homesick.

Chapter Twenty-seven

"Y ou're no fool, Vogl," Count von Neulinger said, presenting the singer with a glass of wine, "and you mustn't take me for one. That is why I've arranged this private discussion. We will speak frankly."

"I understand, your Excellency."

The two men sat in the anteroom in von Neulinger's house where Vogl last saw Jennie. Vogl occupied the chair in which Eugénie sat; the count remained standing. Vogl appreciated the count's conscientious calculation. This "frank" discussion would not be an exchange between equals, at least not for awhile. The count towered over Vogl, asserting his command.

"I doubt you do," said von Neulinger. "This is not part of the official investigation. Doktor Nordwalder is responsible for that. Of course, if anything we say becomes relevant, I will pass it on to Nordwalder. Otherwise, this discussion stays just between us."

"What are we discussing?"

"Suppose we begin with platinum."

"Platinum?"

"It's a metal with properties similar to gold. Until quite recently, it was considered so rare as to be of no practical use. But some Russians apparently have discovered a vast quantity of platinum in the Urals. Whoever masters platinum's practical difficulties will gain huge strategic advantages, or so our government believes. As laymen, our only interest, Herr Vogl, is that several governments covet platinum in large quantities. I know this, and my wife knew this."

"That explains the presence of some incongruous guests last Thursday evening," said Vogl.

"Precisely."

"The two Germans?"

"Himmelfarb's a Bavarian mining engineer; Barenberg's a prominent metallurgist. We know less about the Englishman, but the Russian, Tagili, is being courted by several embassies. He came under English 'protection' that night."

"But your Excellency, what has this to do with me?"

"You talked to an Englishman."

"Lord Bellingham."

"Yes. Did he say anything about platinum?"

"Come to think of it, he did mention something strange. He associated it with a Lord …Wallace or some such."

"Wollaston?"

"Perhaps."

"Wollaston is Barenberg's counterpart in England, a professor of metallurgy."

"I see. Please inform Doktor Nordwalder with my

compliments." Vogl could not resist the moment to remind the count that they were having a casual discussion.

"He'll be informed. Now, about your commission."

"Commission, Excellency?"

A flash of anger crossed von Neulinger's eyes. "Your commission from my wife for a new song."

"Of course. Forgive me."

"Tell me about it."

"There's not much to tell. Eugénie requested a fresh song for her *soirée*. She supplied the text. I had my accompanist, Franz Schubert, set it to music."

"When did she give you this text?"

"Two days before I sang it."

"That didn't give your composer friend much time."

"Schubert was up to the task."

"As were you. You sang from memory, I recall."

"I'm a quick study," said Vogl.

"Indeed. Did you work on the words while Schubert wrote the music?"

"I did not."

"Why not?"

"Franz doesn't allow it," said Vogl with a slight smile. "He insists that all material is exclusively his until we rehearse it."

"So you never saw the original?"

"No, I didn't. Is that important?"

The count paused for a moment. Then he said, "You saw the effect the song had on Eugénie."

"She fainted. At the time I thought it remarkable."

"I did, too, Herr Vogl. Alarming, in fact, not at all like Eugénie. When she recovered, she sent for you."

"That's correct."

"Was that not odd, Herr Vogl?"

It was Vogl's turn to pause briefly. "I suppose so. Now. I sang the song as Schubert set it. I have no idea what upset her."

"You've already told me that nothing of importance passed between you and my wife when you last spoke with her. Do you still stand by that?"

"I can't think of anything substantial. Eugénie expressed her displeasure, but aside from giving me the letter to leave on the sideboard, which you know about, she did nothing else. I apologized. She was quite brusque with me."

"How like my wife," said the count almost to himself. Both men knew how Jennie managed to accomplish a great deal while revealing almost nothing. For the first time during the conversation, Vogl sipped his wine. The count, seemingly in no hurry to end the interview, observed him in silence. Eventually, Vogl put down his half-empty glass. "Herr Count, I have some other engagements this evening. You know I am always at your disposal …"

"One more thing, Herr Vogl."

Vogl, half-risen, sat back in his chair, realizing that he had overplayed his hand. The count was calling his bluff. Thus, he was not altogether blindsided by the question he dreaded most, "Who is Fraülein Schikaneder?"

Vogl began, "The lady who came with Schubert and me to your home last Thursday," carefully balancing his inflection so that the remark could be interpreted as an innocent question or a plausibly responsive answer. He wouldn't appear uncooperative.

"No one has seen her since she left my home in your company," the count continued smoothly, without rancor.

Nonetheless Vogl sensed the threat. To circumvent a lot of unpleasantness, he said "I can produce her, if I must. But will you accept my word, Count, that she has no significant knowledge of anything that went on here?"

"I might, if I knew more about her. I assure you, Vogl, that I protect young women's reputations as well as the next man, but from Eugénie's letter, I assumed that Fraülein Schikaneder was her acquaintance, not yours."

Vogl confessed, "There is no such person. At my behest, one of my theatrical colleagues assumed the name 'Schikaneder' for the evening. She was eager to meet the countess."

"What wonderful colleagues to have, Herr Vogl. How did my wife come to accept this one?"

"She didn't. She wrote the name 'Schikaneder' on the envelope, and I persuaded the lady in question to play the part."

"That was foolish."

Vogl caught a trace of amusement in von Neulinger's assessment; he played to it. "I don't improvise well. I delude people only with the aid of a script."

"If you say so." The count did not sound convinced. "But why did my wife address a letter to a total stranger?"

"Our—my 'Fraulein Schikaneder' was not the intended recipient."

"Then who was?"

When Vogl paused this time, it was for conscious effect. With a hint of a sigh he said, "I can't tell you."

"Can't or won't?" von Neulinger did not disguise his

impatience. If Vogl intended to withhold information, the count had both the means and the resolve to change his mind.

This Vogl knew well. He continued, uncomfortably. "I can't. I thought I knew. If anyone but Eugénie had given me the charge, I could answer you, but … I can't."

"Explain!"

"The name on the envelope was a ruse, Excellency. I took the letter to the home of a family von Schwind. I am always admitted there, because my accompanist, Franz Schubert lives there. The missive was to go directly to Schubert. I thought Eugénie was just being playful."

"Franz Schubert?"

"So I thought. He wasn't in, so I left the letter on a sideboard. You will remember, Herr Count, that I asked Eugénie to give Schubert an honorarium?"

"I paid him myself."

"Precisely. Some time afterwards. Until then, I assumed that the letter contained the payment. Obviously, it did not."

"Obviously?"

"Herr Count, Franz Schubert is utterly without guile. Had he received any money he'd have spent it. Had the countess written anything interesting to him, he'd have told me."

"But you left the letter for him at von Schwind's."

"I left it there, but I don't know who picked it up. Others enjoy free admittance to the house. There is, for instance, von Schwind himself, a painter. Frequently, I encounter Schubert's friend, the playwright Franz Schober, there. The von Schwinds adore the arts, though they lack the wherewithal and taste of the von Neulingers," Vogl finished diplomatically.

"Schober. I've met him."

"He attended the *soirée*. Schubert wanted him. I believe they are working on a project together. Schober came along as Schubert's page turner." What else Schober was and did, the count could discover for himself.

"I remember him now. He talked with Heinrich."

"That's the man. He and your son both aspire to make marks in the theater."

"Thank you, Vogl. You've been most helpful," said von Neulinger, at last condescending to let Vogl go. He stepped back from the chair, permitting the actor to rise. As Vogl reached the doorway, the count spoke again. "Vogl."

"Your Excellency?"

"I speak now as a father." This apparently was not easy for the count. "What do you know of my son's theatrical aspirations?"

"I believe he has a manuscript he wants to show me."

"*Natürlich.*" Jennie's favorite word again. The count didn't pronounce it with Jennie's enthusiasm.

"So far he hasn't shown me anything."

"If he does, do all you can to discourage him."

"I've promised him an honest critique. Usually that suffices."

"Thank you for your cooperation, Herr Vogl."

"Think nothing of it, Herr Count."

9:

On the street Vogl reviewed his performance. The more he reviewed, the more chilled he felt—not because of the ambient cold, from which his greatcoat protected him. But rather because one of his worst suspicions was realized. Jennie prevented her husband from seeing the poem that Schubert set. Loyally, until his interview, he had not divulged Jennie's method of getting her text to Schubert. Vogl hoped that he had adequately deflected attention from his friend, whose only connection to the crime came through the song. Without a direct connection between the composer and the countess, Schubert was safe—unless someone found it convenient to forge that connection. Vogl shuddered.

Somewhat more comforting was that Fraülein Rosa remained out of sight from the officials—for the moment, and possibly forever. Count von Neulinger himself promised to protect her as long as she had no involvement in the murder. If he deemed Kunegunde innocent, Nordwalder would probably not overrule him. As for stretching the investigative web to include Schober, well Schober could take care of himself. At least he possessed resources far greater than either Schubert's or Kunegunde's.

Vogl's instincts about Jennie and the song were correct. *"Die Sonne und das Veilchen"* caused an unexpected upheaval. What went wrong? He sang what Schubert gave him. Unless Schubert altered the text somehow, which was highly unlikely, what disturbed Jennie? Perhaps she noted a response from one of the other auditors. If so, why castigate me? Vogl thought.

"I didn't say anything, *mein herr,*" a puzzled street sweeper responded.

Vogle hurried on. It was all too much. He simply had to await developments. Amidst much anxiety, he, too, suffered the throes of a frustrating week.

Thursday morning Vogl's luck began to change. He found

Schubert at von Schwind's and told him about the engagement at the Belvedere Gallerie on Friday. He purposely did not tell Schubert any details, except that he would be paid. Vogl then tried half-heartedly to persuade Schubert to come to the Hofoper to rehearse that afternoon. He withheld the name of the person Schubert was to accompany. If Schubert knew that Kunegunde, a female whose singing voice was unfamiliar to him, was involved, he'd refuse instantly.

Schubert pleaded his new piano enterprise and begged off anyway. Vogl was not disappointed. He took his personal copies of Schubert's songs to the Hofoper, and accompanied Kunegunde himself.

In an abandoned rehearsal room, after the day's labors on *The Empress*, Kunegunde ran through a gamut of emotions: delight that Schubert had agreed to play the following evening, disappointment that Schubert was not present, gratitude that Vogl had Schubert's songs for her to practice, amazement that Vogl could play the piano parts himself.

"I thought you were a singer. I never guessed that you were also a musician."

Vogl, too, experienced an array of emotions, but unlike Kunegunde's progression, his were amalgamated. Amusement, envy, self-satisfaction, and despair, all utterly beyond reason, ebbed and flowed like voices in a Bach fugue. While inordinately entertained by Kunegunde's enthusiasm, Vogl felt irrational jealousy because she expressed more interest in Schubert than in him. His despair grew from his as yet unfulfilled desire to receive an unqualified compliment from her. All in all, the sensations exhilarated him.

Artistically, the session went reasonably well. "*Gretchen am*

Spinnrade" proved too difficult to prepare on short notice, so they concentrated on the lighter, less demanding *"Die Forelle"*. By the end, Vogl determined that even in the presence of exceptionally discerning auditors, Kunegunde would not disgrace herself. Her voice was not completely trained, but she understood what she sang about, the essential quality when attempting Schubert's *lieder*, and treated the music with commendable respect for both pitch and rhythm. While she lacked the power to engross a large theater full of strangers, in her father's house, among friends expected to be kind, she could produce a modest success. Everyone in the room would have experienced far worse performances and the attendant burden of having to say nice things about them. Such were the hazards of Viennese cultural life. If disaster loomed he would be there himself to save the situation. Vogl felt sufficiently prepared.

Chapter Twenty-eight

Friday evening, the forces of chaos still flourished, but the spirit of futility passed. A pivotal moment occurred at shortly before seven o'clock that evening, when Schubert's path literally crossed von Weber's.

It happened this way: Schubert, running slightly behind schedule, met Vogl at the head of the Belvederegasse. Together, they started towards the palace.

"So Misha, what are we singing tonight?"

"We are not singing."

"Very well. What are you singing?"

"I am not singing. You are playing for someone else. Have no fear, the young lady is quite proficient."

Schubert stopped walking. "Young lady? Misha, have you gone mad? I don't play for strangers."

"This girl is no stranger. You know her as Juliet Schikaneder."

Schubert's face grew red—either anger or bashfulness.

"Misha, I won't do it." He turned back, but Vogl blocked his path.

"Her real name is Kunegunde Rosa. Her father is hosting this little affair."

"Misha, get out of my way. I will not help you pursue that girl. Find some other way to pull the wool over her parents' eyes. I never suspected anything like this from you."

"Don't talk rot, Franz. This doesn't concern Fraülein Rosa or myself. Among her father's guests tonight is a German, Carl Maria von … someone."

"Von Weber? Why didn't you say so? How did you manage it?"

"I'll tell you some other time"—as soon as he found a few minutes to construct a suitable fiction. "You must prepare yourself, Franz. Fraülein Rosa has agreed to sing "*Die Forelle*" as part of the program. I assume you have it with you."

As Schubert struggled to dig the music out of his folder, a slim man hobbled past going in the other direction. "Misha isn't that …?"

"I think so."

"Where is he going?"

"I don't know."

By the time Schubert realized that the limping man was indeed von Weber, the moment to initiate conversation with him was gone.

At the gallery things were in a mild uproar. Weber had not been told that after the viewing a reception and a recital were part of his host's agenda. He stayed only to see the paintings. He expressed regret that he could not stay because of a looming rehearsal and hurried off. For Kunegunde, his departure produced relief. The feverish intensity in von Weber's large brown eyes utterly disconcerted her.

"I could never sing for him," she told Vogl later. The rumor persisted that Rosa wanted to induce Weber to find a place for his daughter in *Der Freischütz*, but Rosa was too busy playing host to show any unhappiness. His guests were equally diplomatic about having to stay past the guest of honor's departure.

Vogl, too, was gracious. When Herr Rosa explained to him with great earnestness, "Weber's time for social events is very limited," Vogl nodded his own earnest understanding to mask his private embarrassment. In spite of his thwarted desire to arrange (and claim credit for) a meeting between Schubert and Weber, he merely let events take their course.

The frustration of this near-miss was alleviated by Rosa's next sentence. "He's attending Mass at St. Stephen's on Sunday. Until then he's devoting all his time to his opera."

Vogl vowed to make the most of his reprieve. Schubert, too, would go to St. Stephen's on Sunday. Vogl hoped to bask in unearned gratitude then.

Schubert's excitement at being within a foot of his quarry dissipated with the disappointment of missing him. He muttered resentment against Vogl for dragging him away on "a fool's errand." This, in turn was superseded by the realization that the red-headed Fraülein Schikaneder, rechristened "my daughter, Kunegunde," was extending her hand to him. The smile that so dazzled Vogl galvanized Schubert, who dropped his music folder. She knelt down with him to retrieve it, and their formal introduction was concluded at knee height.

"I'm so glad you're playing for me, Herr Schubert" she said. "Danke."

"The thanks belong to Vogl," Schubert muttered, then added to his own surprise, "but the honor is entirely mine." He meant it. A few minutes later, he and Kunegunde huddled in conference by the piano. From the rubicundity of Schubert's face, Vogl concluded that Schubert was engrossed by his current companion and no longer worried about von Weber.

To a person, Rosa's dozen invited guests, having met von Weber earlier, found the rest of the evening most enjoyable. To begin with, they rarely saw anything as comical as Schubert's unceremonious entrance. When the music started, Kunegunde's singing proved to be entirely respectable. Accompanied by Schubert, she sang her Italian and French selections with confidence and correctness. Her performance of "*Die Forelle*" seemed to please the listeners, all friends of Rosa liberal enough to tolerate the innovative German piece. Schubert adjusted easily to Kunegunde's interpretation, which was not unlike Vogl's own. At the end of the evening, Schubert received satisfactory payment from Herr Rosa and even more generous thanks from his daughter.

"I cannot tell you, Herr Schubert, what a treat it is to sing with one of Vienna's greatest musicians."

Schubert was unused to such praise. Vogl overheard his clumsy attempt to respond gallantly,

"You sing quite nicely, too, Fraülein."

"I hope we perform together again sometime."

Confused, Schubert then said, "Herr Vogl's waiting," and quickly withdrew.

9:

All in all, Schubert experienced a very pleasant evening. On his solo walk back to von Schwind's, he entertained himself with bittersweet memories of seeing von Weber and performing with Kunegunde. He recalled in no particular order her earnest singing, her entrancing red hair, and her apparent desire to see him again.

Twenty paces behind him, Gert Timmerich entertained different ideas, mostly obscenities at memories of his two superiors, Captain Millstein and Doktor Nordwalder, but Schubert figured prominently in them as well. Separately, Nordwalder and Millstein denied his request to be relieved of surveillance duty. Furthermore, when Timmerich offered to "toss the rat into the sewer at once," Nordwalder vetoed the proposal. "Just tell Millstein where he goes," Nordwalder counseled, "and tell me what Millstein says. If anything more is required, you will be given every consideration."

Timmerich suspected that Nordwalder scoffed at him. Dark thoughts formed around the theme that he brooked no disrespect from anyone, of any rank. His temperament and training as a special agent forbad him from telling Millstein how Nordwalder had planted a traitor in his camp, but Timmerich longed to rebel. His right hand twitched in his pocket around the bone-handled knife.

What if he killed the little twit anyway? The plump little piglet didn't even know that he was being shadowed, after three days. Subconsciously, Timmerich, trained to hold back exactly twenty paces behind his subject, sped up and gained three paces on the oblivious Schubert. Would Nordwalder really mind if this nonentity ended up face down in the gutter? Timmerich's unrefined philosophy about hunting murderers was literally to eliminate all the suspects. Surely one of them was guilty, and thus the murder would be solved.

As he always did, Schubert led Timmerich to the Wipplingerstrasse where he entered the same abode he always entered. Timmerich returned to routine—a ten minute wait in the shadows before heading off to report to Captain Millstein. Millstein always accepted his reports at face value. Why didn't he request evidence, say a tooth or even a finger?

Such were the fancies with which Timmerich satisfied himself as he made his way back to base through the cold.

Chapter Twenty-nine

D oktor Ignatz Nordwalder felt a different kind of satisfaction that Friday night, after an inauspicious beginning. The British Embassy informed him that Lord Bellingham was away on business but would receive the Doktor early the following week. Thus Nordwalder turned his attention to Zdenka Merlinbeck. He sent word to her husband's home, where he was received at once. He entered a ground floor sitting room to discover Zdenka sitting on a settee. The count stood beside her.

Some women rely on mobility to emphasize their charms. Perpetual motion of the facial features or subtle gesticulation can produce marvelous effects. Zdenka Merlinbeck's beauty was of another kind. Her strong, chiseled features beneath a coiffure of jet-black hair, enhanced by glints of strategically placed jewelry, begged for the kind of perusal given to statuary. Her eyes were a dusky violet. Alone they had inspired at least two poets to paroxysms of ecstasy. Zdenka was aware of the impression she made. When she moved at all, she moved languidly. At the moment Nordwalder entered the room, she sat quite still.

"Please sit down, Herr Doktor," Merlinbeck offered.

"No thank you, Excellency. This is not a social call. I'm here to discuss the von Neulingers."

"A horrible business," said the count.

Zdenka, motionless until this moment, lifted her gaze to Nordwalder's face and said with velvet voice, "My husband speaks for both of us. Yet the tragedy there has nothing to do with us."

"*Contessa*," said Nordwalder, unmoved, "please tell me about your two companions that evening."

"Himmelfarb and Barenberg? They are more my husband's associates than mine."

"But your husband did not sit with them at the *soirée*, you did."

"That's right. I had one of my headaches," the count volunteered.

"I remember that evening quite well, Kurt," said Zdenka with surprising force. "I know all about your headaches, but the Germans' business was with you, and I assume that Doktor Nordwalder is inquiring about the Germans' business."

When the count offered no reply, Nordwalder stepped in. "Perhaps, Count, we can talk later. At the moment I'm piecing together the events of that evening. Did either of you notice anything unusual about either of the men or about anyone at all, for that matter?"

Zdenka, in complete repose, took a moment to consider. Nordwalder waited, his stillness matching hers. Though not completely experienced in the matter, he had competed with women in the past, at least in chess. At last the countess said with a little sigh, "Alas, I noticed nothing. In terms of conversation, the Germans were rather dull. They said little, and when they did speak, all they spoke about was platinum."

"Platinum?"

"That's right. Doktor Barenberg seemed fascinated by the differences between platinum and gold."

Doktor Nordwalder brightened a little. "That is most interesting, *Contessa*. What precisely did he say?"

As decorum demanded, Count Merlinbeck remained with his wife, but as the discussion devolved to an intricate exploration of the potential utility of platinum, he found an excuse to leave the room.

"We won't see much more of him this evening," Zdenka said casually. "He spends a lot of time these days with his collection."

"His collection?"

"Bottles. Brandy bottles."

"I see," said Nordwalder. Zdenka's alteration of her position on the board was one to consider carefully.

"In any case, we won't be disturbed. Please have a seat, Herr Doktor." This time Nordwalder accepted. "May I offer you some refreshment? Coffee, perhaps."

"No thank you, *Contessa*. As I've said, this is not a social call."

"Some other time, then." For the first time Zdenka gave a slight smile. Few women of her age dared such a gesture, but she still had a complete set of perfect, nearly white teeth, which she used to her great advantage.

"Perhaps," Nordwalder said. "This evening I must perform my painful duty. Frau Merlinbeck, it is well-known that you and the Countess von Neulinger did not get along."

"I wouldn't put it that way, Herr Doktor. In earlier days a certain rivalry developed between us, but as one matures, one puts these matters aside. Eugénie and I were not intimates by any means, but there is… was … no longer any bad blood between us."

"Nonetheless, I understand that last Thursday was the first time you were invited to her home."

"That is not strictly true, Herr Doktor." Again Zdenka permitted herself another slight smile.

"You were invited before?"

Zdenka emitted a small laugh. It betrayed a hint of her upbringing, at the hands of Hungarian peasants—a little wildness beneath her hard-won veneer of aristocracy. "I wasn't invited last week either. Eugénie invited my husband and his two German associates. Kurt … feared … expected … one of his headaches. He arranged for me to join them."

"Why should the Germans be invited, but not you?"

"From their limited range of interest, I suggest that the cause was platinum."

"Their presence at the musicale concerned platinum?"

Zdenka again took a moment for motionless reflection, the perfect stillness of the tigress. Then she began slowly, "I hope you won't think ill of me when I tell you this, Doktor Nordwalder. I rarely speak conjecturally, but I now see some events of that evening in a different light. Will you keep what I tell you in strictest confidence?"

"You have my assurance, *Contessa*."

"Just before the music began, I noticed Eugénie in deep conversation with Thomas Bellingham."

"Thomas Bellingham?"

"Thomas, Lord Bellingham."

"Ah, one of the Englishmen."

"At the time, I thought nothing of it. Thomas and Eugénie were old friends, and I supposed they wanted to reminisce. At any rate, she did. In fact, it amused me to see Eugénie struggling to maintain his attention. His eyes kept wandering towards me."

"How flattering."

Zdenka again emitted her almost feral laugh. "Nonsense, Herr Doktor. Thomas is no great student of chivalry, but he knows better than that. I realize now that he was only interested in what I was doing."

"And that was…"

"Tending to my charges. You see, I know a smattering of Russian. Herr Himmelfarb asked me to help him."

"Help him in what manner?"

"Communicate with Pyotr Tagili. He's Russian, you understand. Tagili has some French along with his native tongue, but Himmelfarb speaks only German. They discovered their difficulties only when they introduced themselves to each other, using up every bit of the English they knew. It was most diverting. You men! Utterly helpless without us."

Nordwalder let the comment pass. "And did you help?"

"As much as I could. Himmelfarb wanted to discuss numbers. He kept asking 'how much, how much?' I kept telling him 'how much', but the concert began before they came to any agreement."

"And you don't know what the numbers referred to?"

"I don't. I wasn't interested," said Zdenka. "Perhaps they were discussing prices. I presume that platinum, like everything else, can be bought." This last remark was punctuated with one of Zdenka's most devastating smiles, a particular display employed only when absolutely necessary.

"Quite so, *Contessa*."

"Now that I have answered your questions, Herr Doktor, will you answer one for me?"

"If I can."

"Do you know how I can get a hold of the composer who was there that night, the little pianist?"

"Franz Schubert?"

"Yes, that's his name. You see, I found some of his tunes rather pleasant, and I may host a gathering here one of these days."

"His current abode is certainly listed at the ministry. I'll send it home with your husband the next time he stops by."

"I'd prefer that my husband know nothing about it," said Zdenka. "Don't look so shocked, Doktor. He will turn fifty next month and I want to surprise him. That's all."

Nordwalder permitted his face to relax to show the countess that he understood, but Zdenka had made a serious miscalculation. Nordwalder's current position at Hager's right hand depended on his thorough knowledge of all the people he dealt with, not merely those whose activities excited the attention of the ministry. He, too, cared to remain informed about his own associates and subordinates. Kurt Merlinbeck's forty-eighth birthday occurred last November.

Suavely, Nordwalder offered, "I see. The matter requires

some discretion. Perhaps I could bring Schubert's address over to you myself."

"I'd like that," Zdenka said, offering another glimpse of her perfect teeth. "May I not persuade you to have some refreshment before you go?"

"The offer is most tempting, *Contessa*, but tonight I must decline. I'll return soon enough."

"I hope so," said the countess, extending her arm in order to ring for a servant.

Alone in the salon, Zdenka languidly poured herself another cup of coffee and reflected. Until Nordwalder's visit, her clearest course for a return to power was through control of one of the two Germans, Himmelfarb or Barenberg. Deciding that as a pair they were permanently ineffectual, she planned to latch onto one, whoever proved to be the stronger, and groom him for her purposes. Now, however, such tedious and possibly fruitless effort might not be necessary. She relaxed on her settee, entertaining visions of receiving Doktor Nordwalder in the future—and of learning more of the unimposing, but perhaps vitally important, little composer.

Chapter Thirty

Shortly after noon on Saturday, Schubert put down his quill to exchange weary gazes with Franz Schober, who had stopped by von Schwind's on his way home. Schubert tried to summon the energy to go out. For reasons of his own, each had passed a virtually sleepless night. Schober was accustomed to nocturnal wanderings and looked better, but Schubert felt better. Three hours of intense, productive work on his new piano piece obscured his inner glow. Schober simply felt the last vestiges of some strongly fortified spirits.

"So, Schwammerl, your masterpiece progresses?"

Schubert stifled a yawn and nodded.

"Mine too, but like yours, it is unfinished. Behold Ulysses!" With a swing of his arm across his breast, Schober struck a noble pose.

"What's that, Franz?"

"Last night I drifted by the home of my Penelope. Amidst

feasting and revelry, I was turned away betimes and forced to seek the solace of sirens. Now, though exhausted by my labors I, in service to King *Alfonso*, prepare to set out on the perilous voyage to the unknown land of *Theatricus Wiennius*, where the giant Carlissimus von Weberississimus resides. Will my loyal crewmates Franzl, Petra, Bertel, Butschel, and the irreplaceable Volker the Minstrel join me on the perilous voyage?"

"We all refuse!" said Schubert with a laugh at the catalogue of his nicknames.

"All?"

"Every one of me," said Schubert.

"'*Et tu*, Schwammerl? Then fall Schober'. I'm going home to sleep."

"Very wise of you, Franz."

Schober, despite his reprieve from another day in the cold, balked at his friend's casual surrender in the fight for *Alfonso*. "Do you mean to let our opportunity pass?"

"On the contrary, gallant Ulysses. I have succeeded where you have failed."

Such an event was rare in Schober's experience. "*Pardonnez moi?*"

"I have seen the great *Weberissimus*, and …"

"*Weberississimus*," said Schober.

"He *iss* not as big as all that," said Schubert, enjoying his friend's ill humor." He limps, as you know. So please, don't interrupt. I saw the man last night, and—"

"What did he say?"

"To me, nothing. Stop interrupting me, Franz. Von Weber only passed me in the street. We didn't exchange a single word."

"Then—"

"Ein moment, Franz. I came back here crestfallen, as you can imagine, only to discover on the sideboard a letter from Salieri. We are going to St. Stephen's tomorrow," Schubert announced with pride.

"What of it?"

"We, along with von Weber, are going to hear a new composition of Friedrich Schneider. I'm not sure if it's a traditional Mass or an oratorio. So you see, I have outdone both you and Vogl. I tossed and turned half the night, wondering what to say to him."

"I can help you there," said Schober.

"I must do this *solo*," Schubert responded, "considering how Salieri is now."

"You've told me many times."

"He won't remember you, so he won't receive you."

"At least I can go to the concert."

"Tomorrow afternoon at four."

"Look for me in the left portion of the transept."

"*Danke*, Franz." On that note Schubert rose from his seat, and after his usual series of fits and starts, headed out to spend the afternoon working in the more congenial surroundings of the Café Lindenbaum.

Gert Timmerich picked Schubert up as he left the house and dutifully followed him. This time his routine varied slightly. At the end of the street, Timmerich stopped and clapped his hands together twice. Any uninvited observer would suppose that he was acting against the cold. But the one who was waiting for the gesture understood.

Five minutes after the composer and Schober parted, a second functionary knocked on the rear door of Schubert's abode. A couple of florins passed from this man's hand to the kitchen maid who opened the door, and, by her shy smile, seemed to recognize him. By the time Schubert arrived at the coffee house and Timmerich positioned himself outside, Schubert's room and papers had been searched thoroughly. The mysterious man left the house empty-handed, looking glum, without so much as a word to the kitchen maid.

Chapter Thirty-one

Clouds dissipated, causing the temperature to drop precipitously during the afternoon, and Saturday evening was bitter cold. Nowhere was the chill more pronounced than in the dining room of the inn housing Jurgen Himmelfarb and Johannes Barenberg. The two metallurgists glared at each other across a table. Cups of chocolate lay untouched in front of them.

"So, where were you, Jurgen?" Barenberg asked, his voice not masking his malice.

"I am not accountable to you," Himmelfarb said, with greater volume and equal malice.

"I worry about your well-being," Barenberg lied. "When a man leaves his lodgings at an ungodly hour, he must be in trouble."

"You were sleeping. I wasn't going to wake you." This was true. Himmelfarb didn't want Barenberg to know anything about his journey. "If you must know, I needed time alone to think. I hate it here."

"The situation will resolve itself soon." Barenberg adopted a low, mellow tone, presumably meant to sooth. "But Jurgen, we must work together. Neither of us will succeed without the other."

"When it comes to platinum, I agree," said Himmelfarb, "but I don't need to consult you before taking a walk."

"A walk in the cold before dawn?"

"What about it? I'm accustomed to the cold of Silesia. I'm trying to reconcile myself to staying in this horrible city. I like it better with fewer strangers about." This remark was true to some extent, but Himmelfarb was withholding some key information. His travels had a specific destination, as Barenberg suspected. "I hope you're satisfied, Johannes."

"My satisfaction is not relevant. I'm concerned for your safety, Jurgen, and for Prussia's faith in us."

"Safety? Pah! I can break any Austrian dog in half."

"Dogs sometimes travel in packs," Barenberg said quietly.

"Then the next time I go out, follow me."

Barenberg planned to do just that but temporized with, "Before doing anything rash, take precautions."

"It's you who should be careful, Johannes. If I catch you behind me, I may break you in half."

Silence reigned for a considerable time. Finally Barenberg said, "I'm going upstairs to work out our final estimate. Meet me for breakfast."

"*Jawohl, Mein Kapitan!*" Himmelfarb mocked.

"Oh, stop it, Jurgen. We're stuck here, so we might as well be civil. Don't forget, tomorrow we go to St. Stephen's."

"St. Stephen's?"

"The concert."

"Of course. In this stupid city music trumps everything. Why can't the Viennese just keep quiet?"

The two Germans retired upstairs. Both had been less than candid. Barenberg went to his room, but only to change coats. Ten minutes later, stopping only to listen for his partner's snoring, he slid out of the inn for his own private walk. Himmelfarb stopped his feigned snoring and saw Barenberg through the window of his room, traveling in a direction he expected. He chose not to follow. He knew where Barenberg was going. All he cared about was when Johannes came back, which was gratifyingly soon.

The Germans had a new experience in common. Both felt the sting of the same unsuccessful mission to the home of Zdenka von Merlinbeck for a hoped-for tryst. On his sortie, Himmelfarb was told at the front door that the count was indisposed and would receive no one. Later, Barenberg went to the door Zdenka suggested only to find it locked. After circling the house twice, he sullenly trudged back to the inn.

Through all the Germans' comings and goings, Zdenka kept to her room. She hadn't slept so soundly in years.

Chapter Thirty-two

The only aspect of his preparation for meeting Carl Maria von Weber that did not cause Schubert anxiety was the decision what to wear. Aside from selecting the cleaner shirt, the better trousers and the less frayed coat, he had no choice. On the way down the stairs his friend and host, Moritz von Schwind, accosted him.

"Surely, Franz, you're not going to meet the master looking like that."

"What do you mean, Moritz?" Instinctively, Schubert's hand went to his face. Did his receding cold make his nose too red?

"That brown neckerchief—hardly appropriate for the composer of grand opera. Besides, there's a spot on it." Von Schwind the artist had a true painter's eye.

"But it's all I have. My white ones are even dirtier, and the black has a hole in it."

Von Schwind proposed a solution. "Here. Take mine."

"I wouldn't dream of taking—" but before Schubert could complete the protest, von Schwind removed his pale blue neckerchief and grabbed for Schubert's throat.

Schubert stepped back and almost fell on the stairs. "Well, if you insist," he said.

During the ensuing exchange von Schwind explained. "Brown is the color of earth, good for laborers and builders, good in the summer when you walk in the forest. Artists receive inspiration out of the ether. To show you're an artist, use ethereal colors. Here, take this too."

Von Schwind extended his hat. It was two inches taller than Schubert's and showed less wear.

Schubert didn't complain this time. "You're very kind, Moritz."

"Just make sure to invite me to the premier of *Alfonso*."

They left the house together.

𝄢

Gert Timmerich hated standing around doing nothing while his quarry did nothing. He hated the reason they gave him—to help solve the murder of a useless countess he had never met. He feared Count von Neulinger as much as he hated him because of his title and only grudgingly accepted Doktor Nordwalder's assurance that the man had value to the Austrian state. As far as Timmerich was concerned the count belonged in hell with all the rest of them. Actually, thought Timmerich, the fires of hell would be too good for them.

Timmerich hated the cold, which reminded him of Austerlitz. Nearly every day of every winter evoked in his mind that one foul morning when he excitedly embarked on his patriotic duty, only to be sent in one direction after another without ever seeing the French enemy.

In the afternoon, however, pieces of shrapnel found him as he was marching away from the fighting. When he regained consciousness, they advised him sardonically to start learning French.

After weeks essentially on his own in the cold, he found himself back in Vienna, a changed man. Still eager to strike decisive blows for the empire, he responded eagerly to the attention of certain officers who offered him the chance. So what if the people he bludgeoned or stabbed weren't in any army? They were enemies of the homeland. Death to all of Austria's enemies!

When he killed the first of the three Austrians assigned to him, a veteran of the Napoleonic wars like himself, his political understanding intensified. Everyone was a potential enemy. There were loyal Austrians and disloyal Austrians. Timmerich knew himself to be a loyal Austrian. Anyone who opposed him was, therefore, a traitor, including the fat little bug who apparently had nothing better to do but walk between his lodging and coffee houses, keeping him outside in frigid air for nearly a week now. Timmerich now hated Franz Schubert.

Killing the simpleton would be so easy—stab him through the ribs with the bone-handled knife, an homage to the bayonet he never had the chance to use. His prey was oblivious to his presence and suspected no danger. It would be simple and so satisfying, no more difficult than killing a woman. The only challenge was where and when. Millstein and Nordwalder did not like their orders countermanded.

He would have to act when he could deny responsibility, perhaps right at the end of his shift, or just before his shift was to start, maybe this very moment, the instant Schubert came out the door. Timmerich could claim he saw the attack and rushed to Schubert's rescue too late.

Schubert's emerging from the house with a companion pushed Timmerich from his reverie. With more energy than he had used in a while, he slid between two houses as the two men turned, as always to the right, and headed up the street.

Three paces before passing Timmerich in his aerie, Schubert stopped abruptly.

"Did you forget something, Schwammerl?" Schubert's companion, Moritz von Schwind asked. Timmerich knew the man, and although he knew nothing about him, aside from his name, he despised him.

"My pipe."

"You left it behind on purpose. Salieri doesn't allow smoking in his presence, you said."

"Salieri doesn't like much of anything anymore."

"He likes you. Otherwise he wouldn't let you join him this afternoon."

"He tolerates me, but I don't know why. He doesn't even like my music."

"Nonsense."

"It's true. He calls it decadent. 'Too many modulations, not enough counterpoint. You don't need so many melodies. Make them work with each other, not just one after the next'." Schubert gave a passable impression of a crotchety old man whose Austrian speech featured vestiges of an Italian accent. The strange sound piqued Timmerich's interest for a moment, although the substance of the conversation meant nothing to him.

"Yet he always treats you kindly."

"Underneath his complaints, he's actually very kind, and I do appreciate his attention. He has opened several doors for me over the years."

"Then don't keep him waiting. What's that under your arm?" von Schwind gestured to a pair of portfolios.

"The music I'm going to show von Weber."

"You're carrying the opera with you?" Von Schwind's voice carried disapproval.

"I thought, Moritz, just in case…"

"It's a mistake. Von Weber isn't going to look at any manuscripts today. Just show him your published works." Von Schwind indicated the other portfolio. "We've already been through this. You want von Weber to see you as a fellow artist, almost as eminent and in demand as himself. Imply that accepting your opera is an opportunity for him, as much as it is for you. You're only showing him a small sample of your output to give him a sense of your skill."

"But I am not in Weber's class. His operas are the talk of Europe."

"And yours will be, too, once Weber agrees to take it on. But you mustn't appear desperate."

"Perhaps you're right."

Von Schwind became peremptory. He stepped directly in front of Schubert and extended his hand. "Give it here."

For a moment, Timmerich almost respected von Schwind. He watched as Schubert reluctantly held out the folder with his precious manuscript.

Von Schwind took it and said, "I'll take it back to the house."

"I'll take it back and stay home."

"Don't be a fool. Weber is in Vienna for a month. If you don't meet him today, you may never get another chance. Now get going. Salieri is waiting."

Schubert started down the Herrengasse at a pace showing more resolve than he felt.

For the second time in the week Timmerich missed the chance to alter the course of events. From his doorway, he overheard all the meaningless gabble as he stepped from foot to foot impatiently battling the cold. When the two men at last separated, Timmerich, aware that he couldn't avoid being seen by von Schwind hurrying back down the street, adopted the ruse of dropping a coin on the ground and stooping to retrieve it. The man never got a look at his face, even though Timmerich's nose came within inches of the portfolio he carried. In this portfolio were the only manuscript copies of Schubert's two most recently completed pieces, the opera *Alfonso und Estrella* and a little song, "*"Die Sonne und das Veilchen"*."

Aside from the occasional military march, Timmerich didn't care for music. In any case, his instructions were clear —keep track of Schubert—his, not to reason why. Thus he let von Schwind march right past him, and the Ministry of the Interior lost its opportunity to get its hands on the material it coveted. All Timmerich felt was a twinge of relief that his quarry walked a little faster than usual. The pace helped counteract the effects of the cold.

Chapter Thirty-three

The crowd making its way to St. Stephen's Cathedral represented what most Viennese worshipped most—not so much the formal liturgical doctrine as the music to which it was set. Any reverence held for Saint Stephen, or any other canonized personage paled in light of reverence for Saint Franz-Joseph (Haydn), or Saint Wolfgang (Mozart—whose middle name, aptly enough was Amadeus), the true proof that the Almighty smiled on Austria.

In the ranks of the artistically beatified stood Ludwig van Beethoven and Antonio Salieri, and perhaps the young Gioachino Rossini, three Auslanders, a German, and two Italians. No matter that in life they often made life difficult for the Viennese. Places in heaven awaited them whenever they showed the good sense to shed their earthly mantles. Other composers formed their own unacknowledged hierarchy of aspirants, cardinals, bishops, and priests—complete with all the trappings of maneuvering for advancement, longing for prestige, and all too frequent poverty, found among churchmen, especially the most devout.

In 1822, Salieri seemed closer to ascension than his acerbic German counterpart. Neither was producing much in the way of fresh music, although continual rumors asserted that Beethoven was still working—in defiance of his deafness and diminishing public interest in him. From a musical perspective, Salieri's influence nowadays truly meant little. But even when Schubert studied under him five years before, Salieri already was maneuvering his way out of his position as Vienna's musical czar to become (only) the city's most prestigious teacher. Now Salieri was, by consensus and reputation, the Grand Old Man of Viennese music, a venerable deity one could worship comfortably from afar. In reality, he was just an old man.

It was prudent to maintain cordial relations with him, but that was all. People listened graciously to his ancient opinions and outmoded musical preferences, then promptly ignored them. Weber's agreeing to go to a concert with him was mere diplomatic courtesy. In such circumstances, Schubert's intrusion might be an annoyance, but "For *Alfonso*! For *Estrella*!" Schubert forced himself to knock on Salieri's door.

Schubert was ushered straight into Salieri's Grand Salon, with its three pianos and multitudes of chairs easily moved to provide for any number of players and auditors in any combination. Salieri sat in the center of the room, flanked by two attendants. He was a relic in a hollow well. Once, Salieri loomed as a giant commanding a sea of imaginative sound.

Now, the effect that Schubert thought so awesome in the old days seemed pathetic.

But on Salieri's right, next to one other guest, stood Carl Maria von Weber. A generation ago, Weber would have dreaded losing Salieri's favor; now he looked somewhat restless, even bored.

"Come closer, please," said the erstwhile giant. "My eyes are not what they once were."

Instinctively, Schubert's hand moved toward his glasses, which sat where they belonged. He edged forward. "Maestro, it is I—"

"Yes, Schubert, I see you now. Come in. Come in. Have you learned to stay in one key yet?" Salieri often brought out this old pleasantry in reference to Schubert's fondness for modulations.

Schubert gave his habitual smiling response, "Not yet, Maestro."

"Well, I forgive you. Meet the rest of the assemblage." There were only two guests. "Signor Hertzl and Signor di Weber."

Schubert had concentrated solely on Weber. He was completely thrown by Hertzl. He meant to deliver a little encomium about the honor of encountering a stirring modern force, but couldn't give the speech to two people. To whom should he speak first? To Hertzl, about whom he knew nothing, or to Weber, the object of feverish preparation? Would either man be offended?

Schubert's sweating hands resolved the matter for him by dropping von Schwind's hat to the floor. "Oh, excuse me," he said to no one in particular, as he knelt to retrieve it. "It's borrowed, you see."

Weber smiled. "Think nothing of it, Herr Schubert. My host tells me that you are one of the greatest composers of the age."

Again Schubert was thrown, more by the timbre of Weber's voice than by his unexpected words. Though the tone was polished, the voice itself was raspy, as though someone had stuffed cotton into the bell of a clarinet.

Hertzl saved the moment by seconding Weber. "I heard you play last month at Madame Sonnleithner's. I'm delighted to meet you in person."

"The pleasure is mine, entirely," Schubert finally responded to both men, "and, Herr von Weber, it is I who am honored to …"

Salieri interrupted with, "We don't want to be late, but we do have time for some coffee and cake before we go." On cue, a servant rolled in a cart. The squeak of its wheels drowned out Schubert's prepared remarks once and for all.

This was the way Salieri's meetings went these days. He followed a carefully prepared script leaving little time for others' contributions. Of course, both the cake and coffee were excellent. All of Salieri's guests said so. Schubert contented himself with savoring his portion and following the conversation.

"Do you know, Signor Weber, that little Franz here studied with me?"

"So I've been told," Weber responded in that odd voice with the velvety rasp. Tactfully, he did not add that Salieri told him not ten minutes before.

"Not very successfully," Salieri added, smiling. "He

was dutiful enough, but he had a hard time hearing two overlapping melodies. He was a soprano, you understand." Again Salieri smiled, and his guests responded in kind. The vagaries of singers, especially those with strong high registers, who tended to equate all music with the unrestrained sounds of their own instruments, were a well-known bane to them all.

Weber laughed. "I suppose we all pass through that stage. I sang in my youth." The rasp in Weber's voice made this hard for Schubert to imagine.

"And who taught you counterpoint?" Salieri asked.

"No one, formally, Maestro. I picked some up along the way."

"Then I think you'll find the piece we hear today quite interesting. Schneider has included a fugue at the end of his *Gloria* that is quite magnificent."

"I look forward to it."

"Schneider is a pure craftsman, unlike this little fellow here," Salieri said, indicating Schubert. "He's a melodist—a modulating melodist," he added, not unkindly. "I did what I could for him ..."

"Oh, no, Maestro. You taught me a great deal," Schubert protested.

"I know you tried, Franzl, but you never put your heart into the tasks I set you. Now I'll tell you a secret. I'm glad you followed your own way. Your songs persuaded me to accept you as a pupil in the first place. Your melodies provided quite a relief from the usual fare. I hadn't heard the like since the passing of Mozart. Are you familiar with the work of Mozart, Signor Weber?"

"I've heard some pieces, of course, but I don't claim deep familiarity."

"He became somewhat too fanciful for my taste, but his technique with *opera seria* is unsurpassed. Is your work *opera seria?*"

"I wouldn't call it that."

Salieri sighed. "I feared as much. What is your subject?"

"It's rather hard to explain, but of course, you shall attend the performance as my guest."

"Thank you for the offer, Signor, but I rarely go to the opera now. I find the bustle of the evening too tiring. I may still venture out of an afternoon, but I leave night life to the young, like this fellow here. I understand that you, too, Franz, have written something."

"Yes, that's right! It's..." At that moment a servant emerged to remove the cart. Again the squeak of the wheels took precedence over whatever Schubert had in mind.

"Now we must go to St. Stephen's," said Salieri. "Signor Weber, will you explain your opera to me as we go?"

The journey to St. Stephen's was not long, but given Salieri's infirmities, rather complicated. By the time the maestro was properly wrapped and transported into his coach and the others properly positioned around him, fatigue overtook the desire for conversation. During the ride, Weber explained that his opera centered around a shooting contest—that was all. At the cathedral, the fuss made over Salieri, escorting him to his position of honor in the front row, unwrapping him and allowing him time to acknowledge the polite overtures of those who recognized him moving ponderously to his seat, precluded any furthering of Schubert's plans.

Chapter Thirty-four

Schneider's opus served its purpose, providing three hours of harmonious devotion for the devout, sufficient musical craft for the secular aesthetes, and sufficient opportunities to be seen and heard for the performers on the altar and in the audience. Schneider conducted with correctness, if not imagination.

Throughout the performance Schubert's attention wandered. Before the piece began he located many friends in the crowd. As promised, Schober sat prominently at the left of the transept, among a group including von Schwind and many others, ready and willing to act or react as circumstances dictated. Circumstances dictated nothing, so they remained quiet and polite. A few rows behind him, Schubert saw Vogl sitting with Fraülein Rosa and her parents. Periodically ,Kunegunde turned her head and whispered animatedly to one the adults, but of course nothing said was audible to Schubert.

Other faces struck chords in Schubert's memory—

aristocrats and wealthy citizens in whose homes he played, various fellow musicians and the like. To his great disappointment, Ludwig van Beethoven was not present, but Beethoven rarely appeared in public now. If rumors about his deafness were true, his absence was understandable. In any case, Beethoven was Beethoven, unlike most Viennese, and his failing to appear at some concert or other wouldn't affect him or his reputation.

Among Schubert's immediate party, Hertzl followed the performance with the most attention. He was a factotum for the Theater an der Wien, currently assigned to assist Weber. Since his charge had no immediate needs, he competently assessed Schneider and his performers, seeking out those of unusual mettle.

Weber himself sat stiffly throughout the performance, but frequent drumming of his fingers on his knees—drumming not always reflective of the tempo of the oratorio's music—suggested restlessness.

Salieri sat with his head bowed and his eyes closed. Charitably, Schubert assumed that he was listening with both care and reverence. Since he wasn't snoring, the hypothesis was sustainable. However, when Schneider's fugue began at the end of the oratorio's second section, Salieri's head snapped up and his eyes focused. When it was over, his head bowed again.

After the fugue, during the third part of the oratorio, Schubert became aware of Count von Neulinger, standing far back in the audience, in an understated dress uniform alongside his son, dressed in simple black. Next to them, Schubert recognized Captain Millstein and Doktor Nordwalder, the Justice ministry officials who confronted him that terrible

Monday morning. None of them displayed discernable interest in the music, not even Heinrich, despite his self-definition as an artist. Their eyes scanned the crowd incessantly.

𝄢

Nordwalder also scanned the audience. He attended the concert as part of his investigation, both of potential murderers and of their pursuers. All his spies had their subjects well in hand. Most were here, at St. Stephen's, receiving some complimentary musical edification along with their charges. He often found himself observing Zdenka Merlinbeck's elegant form as she listened with seemingly rapt attention, in contrast to her husband who valiantly waged a losing battle to keep his eyes open. Next to the count sat the two Germans, Himmelfarb and Barenberg. Neither metallurgist seemed lost in the realms of aesthetic bliss. Himmelfarb's head kept swiveling, as if looking for an escape route. Barenberg fixed his gaze on his partner. Periodically both their heads turned towards Zdenka, only to encounter the somnolent count. It was all very amusing. Nordwalder considered discussing these matters with the countess in the future.

Because of the sacredness of the occasion, the oratorio received no applause. All in all, it was a typically quiet Sunday afternoon in Vienna, until everyone rose to go. Great flurries of activity began. Some people rushed to beat the crowd out of the cathedral. Others struggled to capture positions from which to expostulate in regard to the "great event" that just transpired. Still others jostled for access to acquaintances to share some private conference.

Such was the behavior of Himmelfarb and Barenberg. They weren't trying to confer with each other. Although they still operated in tandem, each German sought for a private moment with Zdenka von Merlinbeck. Each had the same tripartite agenda. First, each wanted to find out why, despite following specific instructions to the letter, Zdenka was not available for their clandestine visits. Second, each planned to ascertain when he could try again. Third, each was desperate to learn whether Zdenka favored one of them over the other.

Count von Merlinbeck presented a significant obstacle. Barenberg, who sat next to the count during the performance, tried to push past him. He slid his wiry frame in front of the count. Although he achieved the position he wanted—next to the countess with no one between them—he did not achieve the object of his desire. The countess reached past him to help her husband onto his feet.

Himmelfarb, now in the spot next to the count and deserted by his partner, helped Zdenka with the count by lifting him up and pushing past him. Now he stood facing Zdenka directly, but with surprising agility, she ducked under Himmelfarb's arm and led her husband out in the other direction. Himmelfarb and Barenberg confronted each other.

Doktor Nordwalder observed all these maneuvers as he maneuvered himself nearer to the action. While the countess escaped without him, Nordwalder heard Himmelfarb snarl, "Out of my way, Johannes."

Barenberg gave a more controlled, but equally acrimonious response. "We will not let the sun set on this, Johannes."

𝄢

Salieri's party was among the last to leave St. Stephen's. While his attendants wrapped him up and offered other forms of support, Schubert spoke to the guest of honor.

"Have you written religious works, Herr Weber?"

"Not for a long time. The theater is my profession now."

Weber punctuated this comment with a small cough. Schubert noticed how frail the man was.

Though a head taller than Schubert, he probably weighed less. He limped, and he had trouble amplifying his voice above a whisper. Even crotchety Salieri, wrestling with his servants and his coverings, seemed to have more physical vitality. Yet Weber currently enthralled all of Vienna. Schubert was no stranger to infirmity himself. He understood the sheer strength of will that propelled the true artist through the world. As von Schwind foretold, he felt himself in the presence of a kindred spirit. However, spiritual kinship did not lead to easy conversation.

Schubert next tried, "I'm sure the stage is a demanding mistress."

The remark produced a perceptible reaction from von Weber—a wry grimace. "I don't find it so. The theater consumes me, it is true, but not in that way. Neither stage nor *paramour* demands as much as a wife and child."

"I'll remember that advice."

"Oh," said Weber with a more congenial smile, "if you want my advice, become a banker. Bankers lead comfortable lives."

"But hardly fulfilling."

"Not for the banker, maybe. But artists need money like all the rest, and a banker with the right sensibilities could enrich us all."

"I see," said Schubert, smiling himself, "you advise me for

your benefit, not mine."

"Why the devil do you seek advice from me? Herr Salieri says that you write beautifully."

"That he does," Salieri interrupted, "but not correctly. There is much to glean from Schneider's work, little Franzl. I hope you paid attention."

"Of course, Maestro," Schubert lied, but Salieri was now ready to leave the church and turned his mind to other matters.

"*Vieni, Signori.* My coachman needs his supper."

Both Salieri and Weber encountered and responded graciously to waiting stragglers. Schubert lagged behind ignored, until Schober whispered from behind him, "Have you done it, Franz?"

When Schubert turned, Schober pushed past him and accosted von Weber on his own. "Herr Weber, it is an honor to know you."

"Thank you," Weber said, as he received a similar compliment simultaneously from someone else. The exodus from St. Stephen's was in full flight.

Schober snapped to attention and said sharply, "Franz Schober. Schwammerl's librettist."

"*Enchanté,*" Weber said hollowly, just as Salieri called him to hurry. Weber, despite his frailty and his limp, moved with great energy, though the effort cost him a cough or two.

"Meet me tomorrow at Café Lindenbaum," Schober whispered as Schubert passed. Schubert gave his librettist a nod of acknowledgement.

During the coach ride back, Salieri again expressed an interest in Weber's opera. Again the ride was too short for Schubert to accomplish much, despite an additional stop to let Hertzl out. The story of *Der Freischütz* perplexed Salieri. "A magic bullet, you say? Extraordinary. Does it sing?" were the Grand Old Man's actual last words on the subject. His coach pulled up to his door. All three passengers disembarked; Salieri took a hurried leave and was trundled inside.

On the street Schubert and Weber stood, each in his own way lost. Schubert felt the relief that the cessation of formalities always gave him, but he also felt vaguely embarrassed by how his two associates treated von Weber. He still wanted to broach the subject of his opera, and reached inside himself for the courage to do so. His opportunity was slipping away. At that point Weber expressed his own anxiety.

"Herr Schubert, am I near the Theater an der Wien?"

"Not far. Come with me. I'm headed that way myself."

As they started walking, Schubert ventured, "I'm impressed, Herr Weber, that after such a long day you are going back to work."

"Actually, I'm not. I must get back to my lodgings. I don't know the city well, but I can find my way home from the theater."

"But Frau Stahl's is nearby. You don't have to go via the theater. We can save time by cutting through the Volksgarten. With your permission, I'll guide you."

"How do you know where I'm staying?"

For a moment, Schubert ran out of words, but Weber smiled at him. "Does the knowledge come from that man who called himself your librettist?"

Schubert nodded.

"I thought I'd seen him before. I feared that he was an

Italian spy."

Schubert looked shocked. "You're not serious!"

"No, I'm not," said von Weber, "but I've seen a lot of that man. He didn't seem to know who you were."

"What do you mean?"

"He mispronounced your name."

Schubert understood. "Oh. Schober is who he says he is. He called me by an old schoolboy nickname."

"*Schauspiel?*"

"Schwammerl.'"

"And why does a mushroom need a librettist?" Weber asked with amusement.

The moment had come. "You see, mein Herr, I—that is to say we, Schober and I—have written an opera."

"A finished work?"

"Yes. That is, the writing is finished. The piece has not been produced."

"Now I begin to understand," said Weber. His manner changed subtly.

Schubert found himself facing the moment von Schwind had foreseen. Weber's enlightenment was giving way to suspicion. After a searching glance at his companion, he asked wearily, "Is that what you have in your hand?"

"This?" Schubert looked down at the folder, carried faithfully throughout the afternoon, and framed silent thanks to Von Schwind. "No, Maestro. These are just some of my published pieces. I … I happened to have them on me," he finished weakly. The moment to show von Weber his collection did not seem right.

"So where is the opera?"

"That? Oh, I left it with a friend. I could get it for you, but I don't want to impose. Your work is so important; you don't have time for mine."

Weber apparently abandoned his suspicions. "Well, I won't promise you anything," he said, "I don't have a lot of time for new projects. But I may be able to look at the work."

"I wouldn't dream of such a thing!" some reflex in Schubert responded. But then he realized what Weber said. "Really?"

For an agonizing moment, Weber said nothing. Then he asked, "What is its title?"

"*Alfonso und Estrella.* It's a romance."

"Interesting," Weber said.

For one of very few times in his life, Schubert felt that his reputation as a composer might be exuding influence.

"We were inspired to write it after hearing about *Der Freischütz* in Berlin last year. In Vienna, opera has been the province of the Italians."

"So they say," said Weber, "but that can change. Is this *Alfonso* piece your first opera?"

"Oh no. One was produced two years ago. *Die Zwillings-brüder,*" Schubert added with a trace of nostalgia.

"Was it well received?"

"I don't know," said Schubert. "Much was written about it at the time. But the more I read, the more confused I became. My friends liked it. In any case, it was a mere trifle—a one-act farce."

"All opera becomes farce once the critics weigh in on it," said Weber with a cough. "Your experience didn't embitter you, I gather."

"Well, I wasn't keen on starting another, until Schober

told me of your success."

"Schober, your librettist."

"Yes. He convinced me to attempt something really significant. We rejoin the road here for Frau Stahl's."

There was a wine shop on the corner. "Yes," said von Weber, "I know where I am now. Will you partake of a glass with me before you head off?"

"Well, I—" Schubert said before halting abruptly. He was in an all-too-familiar quandary. As much as he liked talking with von Weber, and as much as he'd enjoy the refreshment, he couldn't pay his share. Among those who knew him, Schubert was so well-liked that few begrudged buying for him, but Weber was a stranger and a potential business associate. Reluctantly, Schubert continued, "I shouldn't take up any more of your time."

"Not at all," said Weber. "I insist."

Miserably Schubert countered, "I have no money."

"Neither have I," said Weber. "But I've taken two meals here this week. The proprietor will advance us a little credit." With that, Weber entered the wine shop, and Schubert followed.

Weber's celebrity *du jour* status, reinforced by a long-standing compact between Frau Stahl and the tavern keeper in which she agreed to indemnify half the costs of any bad debts her guests incurred, assured the men prompt, polite service. They were ushered to a table near the back of the establishment and supplied with tumblers of palatable Rhenish.

Excited by his unusual good fortune, Schubert proposed a toast: "To opera!"

Before drinking, Weber did an odd thing: he touched the

wine with his finger then touched the finger to his tongue. Only then did he lift his glass, responding in his best rasp, "To *German* opera!" Both composers sipped carefully, Schubert out of parsimony as he was accustomed to making one glass last several hours.

Schubert, after sipping, attempting to act The Perfect Host, touched his finger in his wine, as he'd seen Weber do.

Weber noted the gesture and smiled. "I should apologize for my behavior."

"You were not indulging in an old Saxon ritual?"

"Hardly." Weber laughed without coughing. "But I never drink in a strange place without first testing the waters."

"Oh?"

"Please allow me to explain my 'Old Saxon' behavior. When I was a young man, I did my own engraving. Late one night, I gulped down what I thought was some leftover wine. It turned out to be etching acid. Suffice it to say that when I regained consciousness, my chance to portray Don Ottavio was gone for good."

"Terrible!"

"On the contrary. Wonderful. I have devoted my time to conception rather than to performance ever since."

"You find this a good thing?"

"It's a necessary thing. Look about you, Herr Schubert. Too many musicians today rely on pure virtuosity for their livelihood. The damage they do to the art is two-fold: They create effects devoid of substance. Worse, they write things that few can play, things only other virtuosi can reproduce. Music and drama are advancing into new realms. Today composers must create new forms for common citizens to appreciate in a conscientious, playable, professional manner, not for musical athletes who perform professionally but create amateurishly. That is why I stopped writing concerti," said Weber, pausing to take another sip of wine. "Van Beethoven showed us the way." A flush rising in Schubert's face caused Weber to continue. "You have met Beethoven?"

"I have been in his presence on numerous occasions," Schubert responded, "but we're not formally acquainted. He wouldn't bother with the likes of me."

"He didn't respond to my request to visit him. I hear that he keeps mostly to himself nowadays."

"That's true. Deafness is a terrible affliction."

"Yet I'm told he continues to produce."

"I hear that also, but there has been little actual music lately."

"Sometimes I think that God smites the great with infirmities just so they can rise above them." As if to reinforce his point, Weber coughed again.

"Are you familiar with Beethoven's symphonies?"

"I led orchestras through two of them."

Schubert became excited. "Really? How exhilarating."

"Terrifying is closer to the mark. Particularly the one they call *Eroica.*"

Schubert confessed. "I once convinced the publisher to show me the score, but to hear it in an actual concert—"

"Very challenging, yet inexpressibly rewarding, and most instructive. The way he manages the French horns alone validates the effort. But tell me more about yourself. Have you written any symphonies?"

"Six, when I first chose the life of a composer."

"When you roamed the world as Schwammerl?"

It was Schubert's turn to laugh. "Not quite so long ago as that. I was a schoolmaster at the time and had students to play my compositions. Since I stopped teaching, I can't afford decent musicians."

"I haven't tried my hand at a symphony since my own salad days," said Weber. "I lack the time and solitude the act requires."

"I sympathize," said Schubert. "I started a symphony last year, but worldly concerns forced me to abandon it. But you write operas; surely they take even more time."

"I create dramas," said Weber, "dramas enhanced by music. I add or subtract music as the drama demands. Much of that work occurs during the heat of battle, as it were. I no longer have the energy to work out the extended structure of a purely orchestral work."

The men sipped their wine. Weber broke the silence by saying, "Krautsalat."

"I beg your pardon?"

"*Krautsalat.*"

"No thank you. I've already eaten today."

"No, no. You reminded me of my own schoolboy nickname. You were Schwammerl. I was Krautsalat. Thanks for the fillip to my memory, Schwammerl. Have your opera sent to me at Frau Stahl's, not the theater, and I will do what I can for you."

Weber's tumbler was empty. Schubert hurriedly drained his. Both men feeling, for reasons of their own, the inadvisability of having another, exchanged a few more pleasantries and left the wine shop. Cordially, they bade each other good night outside Frau Stahl's establishment.

The night was over for Weber but not for Schubert. His excursion through the Volksgarten was considerably out of his way. Given the results of his efforts, however, he undertook the long walk to von Schwind's in high spirits.

𝄢

Eugénie's exit should have ended everything, but life is never that simple. Prudence demands the cleaning up of loose ends. The inconvenience is unexpected, but hardly serious. Just perform a few simple actions to eradicate the last traces of dishonor, irrecoverable with the demise of their bearers.

There is little danger. Certainly none from the unsuspecting victims, as long as they remain unaware of what they have. They must never find out. Take care of them with quick, decisive action. Just exercise modest caution. Avoid being observed.

The victims are socially negligible, easily replaceable cogs in the mill of society, unlikely to generate much interest among the authorities. Few will mourn them. None will take up their causes.

Here at last looms the prospect of peace and freedom, freedom from torment, freedom from doubt, freedom from shame. If Eugénie must rest in peace, let it be peace and oblivion.

never specified the means. "I give you an hour to come up with a pistol," Himmelfarb continued.

"I won't do it, Jurgen. This will be a fair fight."

"What's unfair about pistols?"

"You're a large man, Jurgen, a much more imposing target."

"I will take my chances."

"I can't allow that. Honor demands. Get yourself a saber. There are several inside the inn."

"Nonsense. I've never handled a saber. Pistols."

"It's too dark for pistols now."

This time Barenberg was right. Both Germans noticed an alarming number of staring faces. One or two twitched as they desperately tried to suppress bursts of laughter. Then Barenberg, emotionally drained and physically exhausted, noticed something else.

"It's cold."

"It is," Himmelfarb agreed.

The two Germans stared at each other, ignoring the onlookers. Finally, Himmelfarb muttered, "We've been here too long." He tossed his pistol on the ground. It did not discharge.

"We have indeed," Barenberg admitted, dropping his saber.

The conflict was over. Within twenty-four hours, Barenberg and Himmelfarb left Vienna, in separate coaches. Barenberg headed for his home and colleagues in Munich, Himmelfarb headed for the mountains of his beloved Silesia. Members of the Ministry of the Interior congratulated themselves, and a legend was born.

𝄢

Monitoring foreigners was only one of many duties of the ministry. Its tentacles extended throughout Vienna, and not all their machinations resolved as nicely as those that had prevented bloodshed between two lovesick German metallurgists. While that conflict was playing out, Gert Timmerich, tired and infuriated by his continued shadowing of Franz Schubert, experienced something quite different.

After leaving St. Michael's he tracked his quarry through the park without difficulty, but when Schubert and the thin man entered a *weinstube*, there were too few people inside for him to dare entering. He'd been trailing Schubert for days, and though the pudgy man never noticed him, Timmerich professionally avoided taking unnecessary chances. One of Millstein's other agents might see him and report him. So while Schubert tarried with a glass of wine, Timmerich used the time to make other plans. It was time to finish the job.

An hour later, as Schubert parted ways with the thin man, Timmerich knew where he was going. He had half a mind to hire a carriage, drive to his charge's lodging on the Wipplingerstrasse, and start back for him from there. There was a nice dark side street on Schubert's route, not far from his lodgings. Maybe wait in its shade, grab the little fool as he walked by, and cut his throat. Fear of his superiors had kept him from this sensible action for a long time, but Timmerich was now beyond fear. Cold and boredom had drained all fear out of him. Besides, he assured himself, the ministry had always taken care of him, and no doubt would continue to do so, however grudgingly. He could tell too many embarrassing stories if they turned on him.

Timmerich decided that riding ahead was more trouble than it was worth. He'd simply adhere to his absurd instructions, follow Schubert one last time, overtake him at the alley, and finish his self-imposed assignment there. Timmerich trudged slowly, paying little attention to Schubert, anticipating with great pleasure the moment ahead. Thus the hand on his shoulder caught him by surprise. He turned, and seeing who it was, smiled.

"I've come to relieve you, mein Herr."

"Just in time," Timmerich added with semi-conscious irony. The fat little musician would live another day.

"Come. You must be cold."

"You have no idea."

"This way."

"Would you like my report?"

"It can wait."

"Of course. I've said all along I was on a fool's errand. Will you permit me one question?"

"Questions are dangerous. But go ahead."

"Why are you here?"

"Events have reached a critical stage. The time has come for decisive action."

"I am at your service for anything," Timmerich said with enthusiasm. Now they stood at the water's edge.

"Gert, your services are no longer required. *Auf wiederseh'n.*"

Timmerich never saw the pistol, much less heard its discharge. Mortally wounded, his last sensation was of the almost polite hand between his shoulder blades propelling him into the Donaukanal.

Finale: Allegro, ma non troppo

Chapter Thirty-six

"Herr Schubert, what's wrong?" Frau Stieglitz had never seen her tenant awake so early or look so agitated.

"My room," Schubert said brusquely.

He received a brusque reply. "It's still there, isn't it?" Six o'clock on a Monday morning was no time for games.

"Have you been in my room?"

"Not since yesterday's cleaning."

"Well, someone has."

"Nonsense!"

"Come upstairs and see for yourself."

Frau Stieglitz, wiping her hands on her apron, marched up the stairs.

"See?" said Schubert.

What Frau Stieglitz saw did not disturb her. The room looked like it often did: some candle ends mixed with bits of bedding, and a couple items of clothing on the floor amidst papers strewn everywhere. Schubert's small tobacco jar lay overturned on the table with some of its contents spilled out, but that was all. The mattress on the bed lay half out of its frame; that was the worst.

She shrugged. "You had a rough night."

"The room was like this when I came in last night," Schubert said.

"Is anything missing?"

"Everything is out of order. My manuscripts—"

"Now, Herr Schubert, I've never known you to be tidy …"

"Unless you disturbed my manuscripts, someone else has been here, I tell you."

"Herr Schubert," said Frau Stieglitz. "I run a respectable household. No one here would do such things as you imply. There must be some other explanation."

"I'd like to hear it. I haven't slept a wink all night, I've been so upset."

Frau Stieglitz asked, "When did you leave here yesterday?"

"Around three."

"And you returned…?"

"Around eleven."

"Was the window open when you returned?"

"I don't remember."

Frau Stieglitz had her explanation. She would confront Marie, the housemaid, but she wouldn't chastise the girl too severely for neglecting a room that hadn't been available for cleaning until late Sunday afternoon.

She asked gently, "Did you leave the window open?" Sunday's weather had been blustery.

Schubert's memory for such details was never good.

Under Frau Stieglitz's prompting he admitted the possibility. It was closed now, but during the night he felt hot and cold by turns and couldn't account for all of his actions. He had moved around the dark room frequently during his restless night, stumbling over items on the floor, taking off and putting on his coat and things of that nature. Her most telling point began with a question.

"Herr Schubert, what do you own that anyone wants? All of us here know how little you possess. What stranger passes up the rest of the house to rummage around in this wasteland?"

Schubert succumbed to her logic. All that contradicted her was that the pages of his piano fantasie, set out for work before he left for Salieri's, were no longer on the table—an island of order amidst the general chaos. They were scattered about the room intermixed with other papers, some of which he hadn't touched for months. After anxious searching, all the pages of the piece, now clearly derived from *"Der Wanderer"* emerged from various locations at first light.

When Frau Stieglitz left him, Schubert accepted the unlikely scenario that one of his friends—maybe a disgruntled Franz Schober—had played some idiotic trick on him. Frau Stieglitz replaced the mattress, restored the bedding, and prevailed upon him to "sleep a little," until his normal breakfast hour.

More than the disorder of his room or his disarranged fantasie, Schubert fretted over the fate of his opera. Before going to bed the night before, Moritz von Schwind, to whom he had entrusted the score, promised to send the music directly to Frau Stahl's the first thing in the morning. The way the night had gone, Schubert wished he had kept the score himself. Nonetheless, he drifted off into exhausted slumber.

Ironically, when he came down the stairs in a more civilized manner three and a half hours later, Frau Stieglitz accosted him. "Moritz asked me to give you this, Herr Schubert, from von Weber."

Schubert's heart skipped a beat as he received a few sheets of paper. When he saw the pages were not his *Alfonso*, his fear abated. What he held was his setting of *"Die Sonne und das Veilchen"*, accompanied by a terse note explaining that the sheets had been included in error with the opera score.

Thoroughly disconcerted by this *faux pas*, Schubert raced upstairs to his room, grabbed his piano fantasie and attendant paraphernalia and set out at once for the Café Lindenbaum.

"Herr Schubert, your breakfast!" Frau Stieglitz shouted after him as he disappeared into the cold. She closed the door just as a tall figure shrouded in a large cloak passed by— Schubert's morning shadow.

Chapter Thirty-seven

A ct I scene ix: *Phaedrus and Marcellus enter the town. There is bustle on the street. A church bell chimes in the background. A beggar approaches.*

Beggar: Alms! Alms! Your assistance sirs, I pray.

Marcellus: Be off with you! (Marcellus moves to strike the beggar.)

Phaedrus: No, Marcellus, wait.

Marcellus: Prince Phaedrus, you cannot allow this upstart, this vagabond, this vile mendicant to interrupt your day.

Beggar: I mean no offense, sirs. If not for necessity…

Marcellus: Silence, mooncalf! Do not speak first to a prince.

Phaedrus: I prithee, no more, Marcellus! We must never forget the unfortunate.

Marcellus (Unsheathing his sword): At least permit me to teach this dog a lesson. A drop of blood so that next time he will not whimper at his betters.

Phaedrus (Grabbing Marcellus's arm): Put up your blade, I

say! We do not know the torments this man has undergone, what causes him to prowl the desperate streets. (Phaedrus produces a coin from his vest.) My friend. My worthy, destitute friend. I do not know the cause of your distress, but I would fain alleviate it. (Phaedrus gives the coin to the beggar.) May your fortunes improve from this hour.

Beggar: O, thank you, most munificent sir! Your kindness shall not soon be forgotten. (Exit).

Marcellus: Prince Phaedrus, was that wise?

Phaedrus: What matters wisdom in a case like this, Marcellus? Suffering provides us wisdom of its own. A kindred spirit is as vital as a member of a kindred class.

Marcellus: I see. I see at last! You have made the man happy. Also, you have given me cause for reflection. Oh, Phaedrus, you are good! Come, they await us at the palace.

Phaedrus: Go along. I'll join you in a moment. (Marcellus exits)

Michael Vogl sighed and put down Heinrich von Neulinger's beautifully-penned, utterly dreadful manuscript. A Turkish prince with a Latin name viewed every moment of his existence as a chance for complaint. Less than half way through the first act, ebullitions of Prince Phaedrus' *weltschmertz* disrupted his dressing for the day, his breakfast, the arrival of a companion, and his first excursion into society. Undoubtedly, more doleful meditations lay ahead. Vogl comforted himself with the thought that he could honor the father's request to discourage the son without a qualm.

For form's sake, Vogl thumbed through the remaining pages, pausing briefly at the end of each act to assure himself that Prince Phaedrus' Ordeal took no unexpected turns. The author himself was due in an hour to hear Vogl's verdict, and Vogl did not want to be caught in a lie.

Predictably, young Phaedrus rejoiced at the end of the act, having received attention from—what was her name? Julianna!—and suitably despaired at the end of Act Two when she slighted him. All that remained (after forty-two more pages) was to discover how Phaedrus decided to "end it all!" There it was, "from the highest spire of the palace" with dozens of people, the horror/grief/or remorse-stricken Julianna among them, no doubt, observing from below.

Vogl imagined Schultz's reaction to "the highest spire," after the scenes in Phaedrus's dressing and dining rooms, the village square, the steps and ceremonial hall of the Royal Palace, the harbor, "the water's edge", and, of course, "the apothecary's shop with three skeletons hanging from the rafters." Vogl read the scene, and yes, these three "representations of man's true essence" (to use Prince Phaedrus's turgid words) served as the prince's audience. A creative manager might have the bones applaud the end of the soliloquy. After indulging himself in this reverie, Vogl put the manuscript down—just another trite, grandiose, unproducible play by yet another man who would be Schiller.

When Heinrich was announced, Vogl reminded himself to be tactful. Heinrich's script meant a lot to him. The exquisitely legible handwriting alone proved that. Heinrich also showed some acquaintance with some works of the masters, Shakespeare and Goethe along with Schiller. More importantly, despite the impossibly magniloquent sufferings of his protagonist, Heinrich was a creature of real flesh and blood, who showed every sign of true suffering himself. His important father had wanted his son discouraged but presumably not crushed into permanent debilitating despair.

Heinrich's earnest unhappiness did not translate into viable stagecraft. Breaking this news required finesse.

Heinrich entered Vogl's sitting room. Vogl expected him to be attired all in black, if for no other reason than continued mourning for his stepmother, but here Vogl received his first surprise. The coat and trousers were black, sure enough, but his neckerchief was a surprising pale green. He held a pair of tan deerskin gloves. Perhaps underneath the Hamlet-esque forms and fashions of the day's youth, Heinrich possessed a mind of his own.

"Herr Vogl, *Guten Morgen*," Heinrich began. Too impatient to receive Vogl's formal reply, went on eagerly, "What do you think of it?"

Vogl, himself forgoing formal greeting, began, "You have written some wonderful speeches—" but got no further before Heinrich interrupted him.

"Before we proceed, please return the manuscript."

"Very well." Vogl handed over the pages with alacrity.

"The ending is far too morbid. Julianna must take pity on our hero at the last moment."

"That's less conventional," Vogl offered, but it was becoming clear that, like Phaedrus, his creator preferred monologue to dialogue.

"It's not a matter of convention, it's a matter of truth. Over the past few days I've come to realize that there are catastrophes greater than disappointment in love."

A cynic might offer that success in love is the greater catastrophe, Vogl thought, but did not say.

"Phaedrus must be truly heroic. Is it not more courageous to absorb rejection than to succumb to it?"

"It is. But in your new scenario, the heroine no longer rejects the hero."

"She takes pity on him, but does not agree to marry him," Heinrich continued with excitement. "I don't want anything immoral. I must find a mechanism to demonstrate that her love is pure. Phaedrus will live inspired by its purity. She must get him down from that tower!"

"Why not have *him* get *her* down?" Vogl suggested, half in jest.

"Herr Vogl, that's brilliant!" said Heinrich. "You understand. We see Julianna preparing to throw herself to her doom because ... because ... I'll think of something. And then, casting aside all bitterness, Phaedrus scales the spire to catch her just before she falls. Phaedrus? What a hideous name. I rechristen my protagonist Flamminius. It will create a sensation. I'm going now. I must commit these thoughts to paper while they are still fresh. *Guten Tag.*" A hurried bow, and Heinrich, green neckerchief, deerskin gloves, and Flamminius *né* Phaedrus were gone.

The painful scene Vogl anticipated passed without compromising his good standing with the playwright or his father. Heinrich's play remained unproducible, no matter how the plot resolved. Vogl imagined presenting the script to Schmidt just to hear him rant about its scenic demands, not to mention the search for an actress brave enough to throw herself from a high tower into the waiting arms of a precariously perched "hero," more likely to drop her than endure the threat to his own well being. In Vogl's experience, few actors were heroes when not reciting from their scripts.

Vogl speculated further about Heinrich's new vision. Creating a reason for Julianna, currently no more than a cipher in the script—the insipid inspiration for cascades of self-pity, to drag herself up the highest tower might take months. During that time any number of events might cause him to abandon *Phaedrus* altogether. In fact, if Heinrich's attitude of the morning remained in effect, Phaedrus's—Flamminius's — disappearance altogether was the likely outcome.

For Vogl, to his great surprise, had encountered a cheerful man. In their previous encounters, Heinrich seemed morose, tormented. His manuscript conveyed unalloyed gloom. What had brought him such relief during the last few days? The aftermath of his stepmother's funeral, which tormented the rest of Vogl's acquaintances, evidently served as a tonic for young Heinrich.

Enough on Heinrich the erstwhile playwright. With his critical duties behind him, Vogl directed his thoughts toward the rest of the day: a rehearsal at the Hofoper and an appointment with Schubert, ostensibly to plan recitals for the spring, but in reality, to assure himself that his friend had at least one reasonable meal that day.

♪:

The first obstacle is out of the way. The path becomes less dangerous. No one "on the list" has the late Timmerich's training, or the capacity to defend himself. The others will offer no resistance, will have no chance to resist, certainly not the man I follow in Timmerich's stead.

Still, haste is required. No shame has yet come to light. It must never come to light. Thus … disguise.

No one has paid any heed so far. The disguise holds. Cleverness has its place in the modern world. To be remembered as someone else, if anyone remembered at all, that is reassurance enough.

The victim a mere thirty paces ahead, walks so casually, so obliviously. Easy to track. Easy to kill. If the poor little fellow has composed a requiem, perhaps we'll hear it at his funeral. Maybe he, Timmerich, and Eugénie will enjoy it together. All is prepared. All will be well. Exit Franz Schubert.

Chapter Thirty-eight

"The papers, Millstein?" Ignatz Nordwalder asked. To disconcert his subordinate more, Nordwalder smiled.

Despite his military training, Millstein shifted his weight uneasily from foot to foot. "I don't have them."

"You mean twenty-four hours were not enough?"

"I thought ..."

"Ah, that's our difficulty, Millstein. Don't think. Act."

"But I did, Herr Doktor. Badenauer searched Schubert's home yesterday.

"Not Timmerich?"

"I chose Badenauer because he understands music."

"I see. Continue."

"He found nothing called '*"Die Sonne und das Veilchen"*.' I therefore assume that all papers on the subject no longer exist."

"Of course that's what you assume," Nordwalder said,

adding just enough emphasis to imply that he tried unsuccessfully to mask a sneer.

"What more can I do?"

Nordwalder, enjoying himself now, allowed a small sigh to escape. "Where was our subject during Badenauer's search?"

"Where we all were, at St. Stephen's."

"Oh yes. I saw him there. He wasn't empty-handed."

Millstein remained speechless, permitting Nordwalder a chance to smile at him again. "Don't feel downhearted, Millstein. You unwittingly followed my advice not to think. I'll enlighten you. Herr Schubert held a large folder."

"Did he? I will find out about it. Timmerich is following Schubert as we speak. When he reports tonight, I will inquire."

"Good idea, Millstein," said Nordwalder sarcastically. "You're dismissed."

Millstein clicked his heels and left. Nordwalder moved on to the next item on his agenda, one even more pleasurable: drafting a letter ordering Count Merlinbeck to the town of Graz. Merlinbeck might not appreciate the summons, but Nordwalder had a powerful contact in the Ministry of the Interior under whose implacable seal the letter would be sent. The Count would be out of Vienna for several weeks, leaving his wife behind. Zdenka would have nothing to do in Graz. She would be much happier in Vienna.

Nordwalder was considering whether Merlinbeck's talents better suited the region's ironworks or timberlands when the morning reports arrived and jarred him out of his complacency. The discovery of Gert Timmerich's body, washed up on a bank near the Aspernbrücke, was utterly disconcerting, as well as infuriating.

Chapter Thirty-nine

The fate of Eugénie von Neulinger's murderer was sealed at noon, although many hours passed before the actual *dénouement*. At midday, a grotesque, limping figure, clad in a long ragged cloak approached a waiter with a simple request. After receiving a perfectly appropriate tip, the waiter delivered a glass of wine to Schubert's table.

During these actions Schubert worked feverishly on his Wanderer Fantasie. He had ordered nothing. He did not look up when the waiter put the glass down. Had he looked up to discover his benefactor, he would have been disappointed, for the figure in the ragged cloak was no longer present. Had he ever been aware of the authorities' interest in him, he would have been astonished to learn that for the first time in over a week, he was actually alone. No one lurked in the shadows watching him. No one searched his rooms. No one paid the slightest attention to him.

♩:

Across town at that hour, at the Hofoper, many hostile eyes focused on Kunegunde Rosa. Again she had stumbled into the maypole. Herr Schmidt shouted, "This is a dress rehearsal, Fräulein. You are supposed to know the steps!"

"I do," Kunegunde protested.

"So the pole fell on its own accord?"

"Oh, no. I …" Kunegunde began,

"Just missed crushing my skull," the maiden three places to the right chimed in.

"Frau Pászny, please allow me to handle this," said Schmidt. "Fräulein Rosa, if you've caused structural damage to the scenery …"

"Shouldn't Hernando's father be entering now?" came sweetly, yet stridently, from upstage center. "Katarina," becoming impatient, fired a warning shot.

"*Ein moment*, Frau Donmeyer; after I assess the damage here."

"Scenery can wait. I will not. The dance is unimportant."

Anne Marie Donmeyer had overstepped a boundary. Two or three of the village maidens lifted voices in protest. The line that became audible was "only someone past dancing utters such tripe!"

"Ladies!" Schmidt barked, "and gentlemen," he added quickly although no male member of the company was on stage at that time, "we will present this spectacle with all of its components, scenic, vocal and kinetic, in their proper places. No more bickering. Once I determine the extent of Fräulein Rosa's damage, we will proceed."

"Then you will proceed without me," Frau Donmeyer decreed and turned for a grand exit off right. The effect of the gesture was lost because Frau Donmeyer almost collided with Johann Michael Vogl.

"Anne-Marie, you are right," he said. "It is time for my entrance."

"You wish to contribute something, Herr Vogl?" Schmidt asked, sarcasm masking his gratitude.

"Only that I saw how the maypole came to topple, and I assure you it was not Fraulein Rosa's fault."

"But we all saw—" one of the maidens began, only to be silenced by Schmidt's glare.

"We all saw Fraülein Rosa stumble," Vogl went on smoothly, "but only I saw who pushed her."

"Why would anyone do that?" Frau Pászny asked.

"Jealousy, perhaps?" said Vogl softly, attracting all the maidens' attention. Schmidt took advantage of the diversion to study the damaged scenery.

"Of me?" Frau Pászny asked, half flattered.

"Not this time," said Vogl with some gallantry.

"But the damned thing nearly fell on my head."

"An unintended consequence," said Vogl. "Physical harm was not the object."

"But no one's jealous of her," Anne-Marie Donmeyer said, indicating an embarrassed Kunegunde.

"As usual, Frau Donmeyer, you are correct. The target of the attack was you."

"Me? Nonsense! I am not a dancer."

"No. You are Katarina. Your role is essential to the success of our enterprise, so essential that if you are unable … or unwilling to perform, an understudy takes your place."

Two of the dancing maidens were capable of taking on the role. One of them had played Katarina before; the other was preparing the role in a production in Salzburg the following month. These women glared at each other as La Donmeyer glared at them.

"If you left the theater now," Vogl said, recapturing the company's attention, "Herr Schmidt would carry on without you."

"But which one…?" Frau Donmeyer began.

"Come, we have wasted enough time. The shove was probably accidental. No harm resulted, and Herr Schmidt is ready."

And so he was. Rehearsal went on without further displays of temperament. But beneath some calm exteriors, minds churned. Frau Donmeyer was now aware of how she had almost been duped. Outwardly she maintained her best behavior while inwardly contemplating ways to unmask her rival and gain revenge.

Fraülein Rosa put her energy into her performance, determined not to cause her castmates any further trouble. Inside, she burned. She didn't enjoy this first-time, first-hand exposure to backstage backstabbing.

Both possible understudies felt conflicted. Each vacillated between shock at the effrontery and respect for the audacity of the other's plan; each mentally catalogued the maneuver for possible future employment; each woman believed that the other had pushed Kunegunde.

Vogl carried on with aplomb, inwardly satisfied. As far as he could tell, Kunegunde had stumbled on her own accord. He invented the alternative scenario to do precisely what it did, save the rehearsal. Such little services to theatrical art kept him on the boards. Consummate professionalism, he told himself. And then, a little guiltily, he wondered if his actual motive was to rescue Kunegunde. If she discussed the incident with him afterwards, he admitted he would not be disappointed. Rarely in the days since Jennie's murder, had he felt so comfortable. Most of the time he wrestled with the feeling that his troubles were far from over.

He received the desired outcome from Kunegunde more or less. According to his hopes, she confronted him as soon as the first act ended. "Herr Vogl, nobody pushed me."

"I know my dear," Vogl said and smugly awaited an outpouring of gratitude.

"You lied!" she said.

"Well, yes, but—"

"I abhor all such unscrupulous behavior. I never thought you capable of such a thing." She turned and walked away.

"*Meine Damen und Herren*, Act Two," Schmidt announced. Vogl made a hasty, embarrassed exit to the wings. His little psychological homage to Jennie, ended as most others did, with increased misgivings alloyed with guilt.

𝄢

Doktor Nordwalder and Captain Millstein had waited almost an hour for Count von Neulinger to join them; thus the investigation into the death of Gert Timmerich began slowly. Now, in the early afternoon, Nordwalder laid out the essential facts.

"Timmerich's body was discovered at dawn by a thirteen

year old boy and his grandfather, calling themselves fishermen. In reality they were scavengers who knew the places where flotsam comes ashore. They sent for us 'at once' presumably after searching the body for anything of value that we couldn't trace."

The convenient notion that the two murdered Timmerich in the course of a robbery became insupportable when it was discovered that Timmerich was shot in the chest at close range before falling into the canal. No one heard the shot. Timmerich lived alone and kept irregular hours. He was never noticed at his lodgings, present or absent. Only the happy coincidence that an officer called to the scene recognized the body allowed a speedy identification.

"And that, gentlemen, is all we have," Nordwalder concluded.

"Why have you sent for me?" the count asked.

Nordwalder deferred to Millstein. "Timmerich was operating on my instructions."

"To do what?"

"To keep track of Franz Schubert."

"I see. Does this Schubert own a pistol?"

"Like our fishermen, he's too poor," Nordwalder said.

"Perhaps he borrowed or stole one."

"Perhaps, but we don't think so, do we, Captain? Millstein, why were you shadowing Schubert?"

"Well," Millstein began uncomfortably, "we thought that Schubert could shed some light on … on what happened to the your wife, Count." Both Nordwalder and von Neulinger paid close attention. "There was a song sung that evening, written specifically for that occasion, and—"

"Now I understand," said the count to Millstein's relief. "You think Timmerich possessed this song when he was shot."

"No. We haven't found the song yet," said Millstein. "Timmerich watched Schubert to see if he tried to dispose of it. Perhaps the song has been destroyed in spite of our efforts. Schubert may still have it somewhere."

Von Neulinger shook his head. "The music is unimportant."

"What do you mean?" asked Millstein.

"We don't need to see the notes. We need the words."

"How do you know this, Herr Count?"

"Millstein," Nordwalder interrupted with a hint of exasperation, "are you adept in the science of harmony?"

"I know nothing about it," Millstein answered.

"Nor does any other guest at the *soirée* awaiting a special song. But we all speak German, don't we?"

Millstein nodded. Nordwalder thought, with satisfaction, that he perceived a slight blush.

"Please continue, Count."

"I know Michael Vogl, the man who sang the song. Let me ask him what he sang."

"That may not be the wisest course," said Nordwalder.

"Vogl won't lie to me. He wouldn't dare. We all heard him sing. If anything clashes with our memories ..."

"I see your point," said Nordwalder, "but do we want to alert Vogl at this stage? I suggest a less confrontational approach."

"As you wish, Herr Doktor. Still the song probably has little relevance. Why not clear this matter up?"

Nordwalder thought for a moment. "Come back at four. I am meeting with the English before that. Let's wait until we hear what they say. If nothing comes from the meeting, summon Herr Vogl. Now back to Timmerich. Aside from his work, what do we know about him? How does he stand in regard to the ladies?"

9:

Unconcerned with Timmerich's reputation, as the dress rehearsal for *The Empress of the Common* came to a close, Michael Vogl attempted to salvage his own in the eyes of one lady. He rejected the stratagem of direct apology to Kunegunde or a straight-forward explanation of his actions, selecting instead indirect flattery.

"I think the finale went rather well, don't you?" Since the third act finale was all choral, Vogl thought himself on safe ground.

"I don't know," the girl replied. "I always slur the words in the *vivace* section."

"'Warmth and comfort shall reside / With Hernando's lovely bride?'"

"I sang 'loving bride'."

"Ah, so. Well, that is what rehearsals are for. You'll be perfect tomorrow. In any event, the chorus sounded glorious to me."

"Can I believe that?" Kunegunde said, without a trace of humor. It had the effect of a much longer soliloquy, and Vogl responded carefully.

"Why not? I don't lie for pleasure."

"But this morning…?"

"This morning, I was thinking of the greater good."

"Mine?" Kunegunde started to blush, but she did not look pleased.

"To some extent, but …"

"Herr Vogl," Kunegunde interrupted angrily, "Don't patronize me. I am responsible for myself. I was perfectly prepared to accept the consequences of my failings this morning."

"But I wasn't!" Vogl sought to stem the tirade.

He succeeded. Kunegunde let Vogl continue.

"In the normal course of events, Schmidt assesses a small fine."

"Then I'll pay it. Herr Schmidt can dismiss me from the company, if he likes. I won't object."

"But someone else might."

"Who? You? I reject any special protection from you."

"I was thinking of La Donmeyer."

"Frau Donmeyer? Why should she care what happens to me?"

"I daresay Anne-Marie is utterly indifferent to you, but consider the incident from her point of view."

Kunegunde became attentive.

"La Donmeyer has performed in *The Empress of the Common* many times, as have most other members of the company. She doesn't need another dress rehearsal. She lives for attention. Who knows how long she might have prolonged the incident this morning without my intervention? Others might have egged her on. By speaking as I did, I made her reconsider. The others followed her lead. *Natürlich*."

"But you blamed someone else for my transgression."

"Actually, I blamed no one, Fräulein. Two alternative

Katarinas, each suspects the other. Now, to escape suspicion, they'll behave like perfect angels throughout the run of the show."

"This is all too subtle for me, Herr Vogl. I guess you knew what you were doing, but I don't approve of it."

Vogl wasn't sure he fully approved of his behavior either— then or now. But he was in too deep to admit as much. "Let's say no more about it." Vogl hoped that he had accomplished as much as he could with Kunegunde, but he added, "I am off to meet Franz Schubert. Would you like to join me?"

"Schubert?" Kunegunde's blush resurfaced in full glory. Vogl felt that he could write a small monograph on the variety and expressiveness of Kunegunde's blushes. "He won't mind?"

"Why should he mind?"

"He seems so wrapped up in his music."

"Thus it falls to his friends to distract him."

"I don't distract him. He never talks to me."

"He is always shy around women, but he likes you well enough."

"Well, if I'm not imposing …"

"Fraülein, we'd both enjoy your company."

With that, Vogl offered his arm. To his great relief, Kunegunde took it.

Chapter Forty

B efore his interview with Thomas Bellingham, Nordwalder formed a plan to squeeze out more information than the tight-lipped English usually divulged. It required delicate maneuvers within various ministries and the nerve-wracking business of keeping Baron Hager in the dark. But the upshot was that he, Nordwalder, surrounded by a cadre of ill- and mis-informed technocrats, bureaucrats, flunkeys, spies, and counterspies, now posed as a potential platinum "merchant."

Like Tagili the departed Russian, he had enough scientific and economic information to make credible offers to buy or to sell, as circumstances suggested, without being made privy to any real negotiations.

Nordwalder carried a letter requesting a personal interview with Bellingham. It implied that English commercial interests were affected by Eugénie von Neulinger's death. Bellingham was the Englishman in whom she was most likely to confide.

When informed of the letter, the English planned a counter strategy of their own, which from their perspective was also ingenious. Pyotr Tagili's untimely departure essentially ended the attempt to gain control of Russian platinum. With the Germans out of the way, there was less urgency to compete in the platinum market. Lord Wollaston had what he needed for experimental purposes. Neither Russia nor France possessed the immediate capacity to turn platinum into the force Wollaston predicted. Since the "Avenue von Neulinger," to use the ambassador's words, had come literally to a dead end, there was no one in Austria whom they could trust.

Nonetheless, if the Austrians wanted to prolong the negotiations, there might be some benefit for the Crown. Austrians were always up to something. The British needed someone to feel them out, and Lord Bellingham would serve their purposes admirably. "Since B. knows nothing of value, he'll tell them nothing of value," the ambassador recorded in his journal.

Thus, for the meeting, they provided Bellingham with two clerks and one interpreter. Bellingham appeared as their lone empowered negotiator. Both clerks were expert in German. One was an expert in financial dealings, the other an expert in military matters.

The session began auspiciously. After the initial formalities, Nordwalder left most of his entourage outside, while he and one clerk and one interpreter sat closeted in a room with Bellingham and his reduced forces.

The discussion soon slowed to a crawl. An unexpected language barrier impeded almost every step. For example, Bellingham opened with, "You want to know about that evening at Jennie von Neulinger's. Deuced unpleasant business."

Nordwalder's interpreter, unfamiliar with the word "deuced," told his boss, "He remembers two nasty transactions."

Several minutes passed before the confusion was resolved.

The eventual translation of Bellingham's "He's to hang fire for a bit, I understand" told Nordwalder what he already knew. The Russian Tagili was presumably back in Moscow. Since Tagili left Vienna three days before, he could not have shot Timmerich. Nordwalder's interest in Tagili, never very serious, dwindled into extinction.

Still Nordwalder persisted. In the end, he received the information he sought—a sufficient explanation of how Schubert's music fit into "the platinum muddle."

"I suppose there's no harm in telling you," Lord Bellingham said, "since the whole affair has been knocked into a cocked hat."

The last phrase came to Nordwalder through his interpreter as "this poorly-dressed affair," but Nordwalder had learned by then to ignore the most non-sensical portions of Bellingham's discourse.

"You see, it all boils down to Tagili. He's the only one who knows how quickly the platinum can be extracted and shipped abroad. But Tagili's a hard-nosed chap, probably with unclean hands."

Nordwalder restrained himself from asking about the Russian's scratched, smutty nose.

"The czarists wouldn't throw in with us unless we—not to put too fine a point on it—tossed them a sop. Since the entire show is speculative, we refused to advance Tagili a farthing. Instead we offered a share of future profits. Of course, my superiors required completely clean hands in the matter and instructed me to leave them entirely in the dark. That's when I asked Jennie to tender our offer."

"And how much did you offer?"

"One fifth of all proceeds for the first year, but Jennie overplayed our hand. I should have known she'd want to get her own fingers in the pie."

"The countess purveyed your offer through Herr Tagili's food?"

"Good heavens no!" said Bellingham. "Whatever gave you that idea?"

Eventually, an understanding of all the hands, and their hygiene and of "fingers in the pie" emerged. Before the session was over, the Austrian and British interpreters were well on the way to becoming close friends.

"Now where were we? Ah! Jennie's idea—I don't know why—was to present our offer in a song. But, in the event, she offered Tagili only an eighth of the profits. I suppose she expected the Russian to haggle, but he merely became huffy. Then Jennie was found dead the next day. With her killer still at large, poor Tagili got the wind up, and immediately set sail for Moscow."

Nordwalder lost a moment trying to envisage a water route from Vienna to Moscow before determining that Bellingham's statement was the result of either deep Russian duplicity or pure English idiocy. In either case, Tagili had gone, propelled in some manner by Schubert's song. "*Danke, mein Herr,*" he said. "I now have a great deal to consider."

The contest between the Austrian investigators and English diplomats resolved into a spirited stalemate, a result which satisfied Nordwalder.

Nordwalder's deliberations on his bigger game began on the coach ride back to the ministry, manifested by the redistribution of his retinue. Against protocol, he sent all his English speakers in one coach and ordered them "without delay" to explore the nuances of Lord Bellingham's remarks.

The session with Bellingham yielded positive results. Everything in Bellingham's manner, everything Nordwalder gleaned from their conversation, suggested that the struggle for platinum led to abandoning the negotiations, not to murder. Nordwalder's strategem had produced the desired result without having to include Baron Hager in the game.

With platinum off his plate, association with Zdenka Merlinbeck lost the taint of unwanted political repercussions. Back in his office, he drafted a series of letters to the effect that the timberland around Graz required Count Merlinbeck's constant attention throughout the coming spring.

𝄢

Delay, delay, delay! Why this intolerable delay? There is there no word of disturbance, yet Schubert's demise should have occurred hours ago. Is he still alive? Impossible! But think: imagine the worst. The toad, the slug survives the pruning of the garden. What then?

There is still time to tie up the loose end. This inconvenience is not insuperable. But no more subtlety. This evening, or tomorrow morning, one can provide something along the lines of Timmerich's treatment.

David W. Frank

You survive my venom, Herr Schubert? Very well. How will you withstand a pistol ball in your heart? All will be well.

Chapter Forty-one

At the Café Lindenbaum Franz Schubert worked incessantly through the morning into the middle of the afternoon on his piano fantasie without noticing the tumbler of wine on his table. He didn't notice it when he put down his pen and stood up to stretch, as it was hidden from his view by mounds of paper. Myriad musical notions for his composition asserted themselves in his head with such insistency that they collided. He needed time to assimilate them, to designate them to proper places. He looked around the dark room for someone to talk to, but he saw no one he knew.

Unwilling to pass time idly, Schubert decided to take on the onerous task of drawing staff lines on blank foolscap. The task was pure drudgery, but over time it saved a significant amount of money. Usually he waited until necessity forced him to draw the lines and chose a time when he had no energy for anything else, but his fantasie pressed him. He'd be grateful for the extra sheaves then.

When he sat down, his eye fell on *"Die Sonne und das Veilchen"*, which had come back from von Weber. Why not prepare a copy of the song for a publisher? This task, too, was laborious, but the song wasn't very long, and copying it wouldn't interfere with the permutations of *"Der Wanderer"*. Only when preparation for this task neared completion did Schubert notice the tumbler.

He didn't remember ordering it, but that didn't surprise him; nor did the wine's odd color disturb him. More than once he had mistaken a beverage cup for his inkwell, though never vice versa. The results were never catastrophic to his health or taste. He vaguely remembered leaving von Schwind's without money, but he could have been mistaken. He ran his hands over his pockets. The gesture convinced him that he had started out with a few coins, ordered and paid for the wine, and forgot about it. At last he picked up the tumbler. Muttering *"An die Musik"* to the empty place across from him, he brought it to his lips.

"Starting without me, Schwammerl?" boomed the cheerful voice of Franz Schober.

"Ah, Franz! Just in time to join me," Schubert said placing the glass back on the table, untasted.

"I thought you'd never ask. What do you have for money?" This was one of Schober's standing jokes. It had its customary effect. Schubert brushed his hands futilely over his pockets and shrugged.

"No matter," Schober continued insouciantly, "I'll find a waiter. No, not that one, he knows me. I passed a fellow on my way back here who looks like a novice. Wait for me."

Schober had plenty of money, but as he often explained to Schubert, there were principles involved. According to Schober, "Artists experience life more intensely than the common man, and we deserve respect and admiration on that account. The petty customs of the unenlightened branches of mankind do not bind us. If money must pass from artists to ordinary men and women, it should go to pleasures greater than alcohol." According to this reasoning, Schober concluded that every free drink validated his beliefs.

Whenever Schubert attempted to act according to Schober's philosophy, the results were regrettable. For instance, the coffee house two doors down no longer admitted Schubert unless he showed them cash in hand. He thus concluded that Schober was the greater artist.

But today, Schober's greatness did not prevail. He returned empty handed, looking grim. "He's coming," he said bitterly, seating himself across from Schubert, producing florins from his pocket. The waiter arrived. Schubert was amused at the way he hovered and eventually extorted his tip from Schober.

"Our novice waiter is an artist in his own right," Schubert commented. "Lord knows, wangling *weh-weh* from you is an art."

"Such are the trials of the man misunderstood," said Schober, affecting an air of gloom before dispelling it with, "so how did you find von Weber?"

"There was no difficulty. He was waiting for me at Salieri's."

"My friends insist on tormenting me," Schober complained theatrically.

Schubert relented. "He's remarkable. One sees the mark of his genius at every turn."

"I followed him for a week, around countless turns, and I saw no such mark."

"You prove my point," said Schubert with a laugh. "Only the true genius can distinguish the notesmith from the wordsmith at first glance. Weber is both."

"You really did speak with him." Schober sounded impressed.

"For a long time."

"May I hear about this colloquy? Or is it beyond the scope of us poor mortals?"

"Not a bit. Von Weber is quite down to earth. He knows not only what German opera is about, but also how to present it."

Finally Schober asked the essential question. "How then, stands *Alfonso*?"

It was a moment to savor. Leaning back in his chair, hooking a thumb into his vest, counterfeiting an air of complacency he never felt, Schubert said, "Oh, that. I sent him the score—at his request."

"Schwammerl, we've done it!" said Schober with gratifying excitement.

"Well, he has only agreed to look at it."

"And to look at it is to worship it. Schwammerl, this is cause for celebration. Drink up!" Schober lifted his tumbler.

"*Ein Moment*," said Schubert. "If we drink to von Weber, we must drink in von Weber's manner. Lower your glass, Franz."

Schober obliged.

"Now observe," said Schubert, lifting his right index finger. "I learned this from the master yesterday."

"The gesture of genius?" Schober mocked.

"Just observe."

Several things happened at once. As Schubert lowered his finger towards his tumbler, Michael Vogl entered the Café Lindenbaum with Kunegunde Rosa on his arm. Although they were backlit by the setting sun, Schober recognized the pair of silhouettes and rose, grabbing Schubert's arm in the process. As Schober was saying, "Isn't that Fraülein Schikaneder?" Schubert's finger touched his wine. He let out a small "*Ach!*" and as he pulled his arm back from Schober's grasp, the wine sloshed all over the table.

"Oh, bad luck, Schwammerl," Schober exclaimed as Schubert hastily snatched his music from the spreading reddish stain. The flurry of activity subsided. By then Vogl and Kunegunde stood at Schubert's table, and Schober began re-establishing social order.

"*Guten Tag,* Herr Vogl, *und* Fraülein Schikaneder."

The pair returned the greeting with polite nods before turning to Schubert, who stammered, "I've burned my finger."

A pungent aroma reminiscent of burnt almonds came from Schubert's place, prompting Vogl to ask, "Franz, what are you drinking?"

"Franz and I were commemorating von Weber's acceptance of our opera when this happened," Schubert said, with a vague gesture at the mess on the table, "but please join us, Misha. We'll have to hurry. There's a Schubertiad at Mohr's and…" When Schubert turned to indicate Schober, he noticed Kunegunde for the first time, and stopped in confusion.

"*Es freut mich zu gehen,* Herr Schubert," said Kunegunde.

"Fraülein Rosa," Schubert stammered, prompting Schober to correct him.

"It's Fraülein Schikaneder, is it not? Juliet, if I am not mistaken."

"No, Rosa—Kunegunde Rosa."

"I see," said Schober, not comprehending. "Franz, does she not resemble…?"

"I chose the name Juliet Schikaneder for a harmless masquerade, but things did not turn out that way."

Vogl felt the reproach implied by Kunegunde's remark and stepped in. "We all want to put that unfortunate evening behind us," he said. "I daresay, none of us had anything to do with the aftermath. Franz, you have not answered me. What were you drinking?"

"Wine, but I never touched a drop. Misha, what's the matter?"

Vogl's glance turned to Schober. "I know nothing, Michael. The wine was here when I arrived."

"That's right," said Schubert. "Why all the fuss?"

"What sort of wine burns holes in cloth?" said Vogl.

"Cheap wine, I expect," said Schubert. "I always order the cheapest."

The smell of bitter almonds had dissipated, but Vogl hadn't forgotten it. "You ordered this wine?" he asked.

"I must have," said Schubert. "I worked alone here all day."

"Worked on what?" asked Kunegunde, who wasn't interested in Schubert's drinking habits.

"Just a little piano piece," Schubert muttered.

"Fraülein Schik … Rosa, never ask an artist about a work in progress. It's the same as asking a vintner about his wine before it comes to market."

"Oh, forgive me, Herr Schubert," said Kunegunde, blushing.

"There's nothing to forgive," said Schubert. "Franz is just being difficult. I've stopped working for the day anyway," he finished lamely under Kunegunde's smile of encouragement.

"About the wine," Vogl said half to himself but loud enough to capture the others' attention.

"Honestly, Misha, you're rarely this tiresome," Schubert said. "Schober and I were celebrating the safe conveyance of *Alfonso* into the hands of von Weber. I was demonstrating a most extraordinary mannerism of von Weber's—he touches his wine before sipping it. Said he accidentally drank etching fluid once. Franz saw you, the wine spilled. Now you know all about it."

"Franz," Vogl said, "Is something the matter with your hand?"

Schubert had been rubbing his index finger distractedly during his explanation. Now he noticed the red spot.

"Herr Schubert, you were almost poisoned!"

Both Franzes simultaneously said something inelegant to the effect that such a thing was impossible. Kunegunde gasped.

Schubert recovered his wits first. "Nonsense, Misha," he said. "I have no enemies." His eyes darted about the coffee house, seeking out a more likely candidate for poisoning. As before, Schubert recognized no one.

Schober spoke next. "Someone could be after me, I suppose." He probably imagined a string of men in his wake, viewing him as a threat to the honor of a fiancée, sister, or, in one case, wife, not to mention the multitudes whom Schober saw as envious of his artistic abilities. "But no. The wine was already here."

"Perhaps a lunatic?" said Kunegunde.

"Good thought, Fräulein," Schober responded. "Perhaps some fiend wants to test his methods on Schwammerl before applying them elsewhere."

"I assume for the moment that Franz was the intended victim," said Vogl, again capturing everyone's attention, "and I may know why. Franz, have you done anything out of the ordinary lately?"

"Nothing but write music, as always."

"Has anything unusual happened to you?"

Schubert remembered the scene of the night before. "Now that you mention it, I came home last night to discover my room ransacked. Frau Stieglitz convinced me that the wind did it."

"Reconsider," said Vogl, unaccustomedly direct.

"Well, my papers were in disarray. My piano fantasie was scattered about the room, but I found all the pages. Nothing was missing."

"What about *Alfonso*?" Schober asked.

"That must be it!" said Schubert excitedly. "I was going to take *Alfonso und Estrella* with me to the concert yesterday, but Moritz convinced me at the last minute to abandon that idea. I gave him the manuscript. He took it to von Weber this morning. *Mein Gott*! We must warn him!"

"That won't be necessary," said Vogl. He looked at the sheets of music on the table.

Schubert followed Vogl's glance. "Oh, 'Die Sonne'? That's nothing."

"What is it doing here?" Vogl asked.

"An accident. It went with *Alfonso* to von Weber by

mistake. He sent it back. I was about to make a fair copy when Franz came along. Ach! Look, some of that blasted wine spilled on it." There was a tiny hole surrounded by a purplish stain near the bottom of the song's last page. "No matter. I can reconstruct it."

"Is that the only copy of the song?"

"Of course. Misha, you're becoming tiresome again."

Vogl remained inflexible. "Music and words?"

"Of course."

"Where's the original poem?"

"I have no idea. Wait a minute." Then he reached in his right hand pocket, producing first his pipe then a crumpled folded, tobacco-stained piece of note paper. He unfolded it. "No that's the invitation to Mohr's. Hang on." Schubert patted his left lapel and found Eugénie's letter in the pocket beneath. Schubert tossed it onto the table with a flourish. "Here, Misha. Take it with my blessings."

Vogl picked up the paper and ran his eyes over it. When he reached the end, his head snapped up. "*Fünf?*" he cried, his voice a mixture of amazement and outrage.

"Five what?" asked Schober.

"I never sang 'fünf,'" said Vogl.

"Of course you didn't!" said Schubert. "Fünf is unsingable."

"You altered the text, Franz!"

"What of it? A single word, a syllable. You should thank me."

"Thank you?"

"I did it for your sake! At first I thought of 'sechs', but I know your voice, Misha and picked 'acht'. Please don't take this the wrong way, but you sing the "ah" vowel better than "eh" in that register."

"I sang eight when there were five," Vogl muttered, no longer heeding Schubert.

"Most expertly," said Schubert. "But I can't claim too much credit. Any competent composer would have done the same."

"That's what Eugénie meant," Vogl continued *sotto voce*. Then he recovered. "Please excuse me, I have some important business."

"But, Misha, you just got here, and you haven't taken any refreshment," said Schubert.

"And you don't mean to be rude to Fraülein Rosa," Schober added.

Vogl intended to go to von Neulinger's without delay, but Kunegunde's presence changed his mind. He wouldn't involve her with the count, and he couldn't entrust her to Schober. He agreed to one drink. When it emerged that Schubert, as usual, hadn't eaten all day, he enacted the usual charade, and ordered food for them all. Other than placing the orders for food and drink, he allowed the subsequent conversation to proceed without him.

Two Franzes talked mostly about their evening plans—a true "Schubertiad" at the home of Ludwig Mohr. Kunegunde became interested.

"What occurs at a Schubertiad?"

"We prepare nothing in advance," Schober told her. "Some artists gather with their friends and events follow naturally. Sometimes we discuss the events of the day. Sometimes we share things we've read or written. Sometimes there are *impromptu* performances. Other times we just chatter. More often than not, Volker the Minstrel shows up, before the evening ends."

Schubert squirmed uncomfortably.

"Volker the Minstrel?" Kunegunde said. "Who's that?"

"You're sitting next to him," Schober said.

"Herr Schubert, you?"

Schubert nodded and stammered, "Mohr owns a nice piano."

"No one uses his real name at a Schubertiad," said Schober casually. "Lately I've become 'Hagar', not to be confused with the guardian of civil order," he added hastily, when he observed Kunegunde's shocked expression. "'Hagar' with an 'a'. It's all in good fun."

"Do outsiders attend a Schubertiad?"

"There's no formal guest list," Schober assured her. "Mohr, or someone, sends out invitations to a few of us, and we bring whomever we like. Would dear 'Juliet Schikaneder' like to become one of our guests?"

Vogl emerged from his introspection, suddenly alarmed about the direction the conversation was going. "At Schubertiads I've attended, the guests are generally all males," he said.

"Not tonight," Schober said, "Mohr has a charming sister. In all seriousness, will you join us, Fräulein?"

"I'd love to, but my parents expect me at home."

"We'll send word that you're with us," Schober assured her.

"Herr Rosa won't like that," said Vogl.

"Then we can escort you home and present ourselves in person."

"Don't let me delay you," Kunegunde said.

"No trouble at all, Fräulein. We'll hire a coach."

"I must object," Vogl said. The other three looked at him. "It's not safe."

"What do you mean, Misha?" Schubert asked indignantly. "You know what goes on at Mohr's. You go there yourself. We are all honorable men," he concluded with a naïveté Vogl could have predicted.

"Surely you don't fear for Fraulein Rosa's honor," said Schober with a smirk that Vogl did not find reassuring, although he personally had seen no worse behavior than immoderate drinking and a few aesthetic or linguistic improprieties at any Schubertiad.

The remark emboldened Kunegunde. "Herr Vogl, I can look after myself."

"It is not you, Fraülein, of whom I am thinking. It's 'Volker' there."

"Me?" said Schubert.

"Have you forgotten that someone tried to kill you?"

"Impossible. There must be another explanation."

"Can you think of one?"

"Not just now, but I'm not very clever," said Schubert. "Anyway, the attempt failed."

"The assassin might try again."

Vogl's comment hit home. Eventually Schubert said, "What can I do about it? An unknown enemy pursues me for a cause known only to himself."

"The situation is not all that bleak," Vogl reassured him. "Your assailant—"

"If there was one …" Schober inserted.

"If there was one," Vogl went on unflustered, "didn't attack you openly. He's probably afraid to. Stay among friends, and you should be all right."

"I can't do that forever," said Schubert.

"No one is asking you to. The danger will probably pass in a day or two."

"What makes you say that?" asked Schubert.

"Apparently, Franz, Michael knows more than he's revealing," Schober said.

"That's not true. I'm simply looking at the attacker's plan—a mixture of haste and stealth. I may know the reason for the attack. If I'm right, disposing of Franz won't help."

Kunegunde spoke up. "You know the reason without knowing the person? Herr Vogl, how can this be?"

"Franz altered the text of '*Die Sonne und das Veilchen*'."

"Oh, come now, Misha. One simple vowel change?"

"Your song evoked a strong response from the countess."

"Yes, she fainted," said Kunegunde.

"That's right Fraülein, she fainted. At the time, I didn't understand why, but it must have been because of the change."

"She said nothing to me about it," said Schubert.

"Why should she? She told me I'd 'ruined everything'."

"But why blame you? You didn't know what I did. No one knew."

"Except the countess," Vogl continued, "and at least one other person who was also misdirected by the misinformation we provided—Eugénie's killer. The killer wants the secret of 'Das Veilchen' to remain a secret—to die with Franz Schubert. As soon as Franz's secret is out …"

"I'm safe again," said Schubert. "I'm safe now, come to think of it. Now you all know what I know, or—" Schubert's face darkened, "we're all in equal danger. I'm sorry, Misha."

"The danger isn't great for the rest of us, or for you, either, once word about the song gets out. I'll take both Eugénie's version of the song, and yours, to the authorities at once."

"By all means, Misha," But as he rolled up the manuscript, Schubert paused. "Shouldn't I deliver this?"

"No. A killer is pursuing you. Stay with Schober and go to your Schubertiad. Stay there all night, if you can. Under the circumstances," and here Vogl turned to Kunegunde, "Fraülein Rosa can't join you."

Vogl's position proved unassailable. A few minutes later Vogl and Kunegunde traded noisy good-byes with die Zwei Franzen in the Café Lindenbaum's well-lighted doorway. Vogl stowed *"Die Sonne und das Veilchen"* under his cloak.

When the quartet separated into two duos, a biting wind blew in the faces of Schubert and Schober, but at the backs of Vogl and Kunegunde. The young woman latched onto the arm of the older man as the wind drove them towards the Belvedere Gallery.

Kunegunde asked, "Herr Vogl, is Herr Schubert's music really connected to that horrible business with the countess?"

"Why do you ask?"

"While you were explaining things, I started thinking back over that evening. "

"Yes?"

"I remember how joyful everyone was until the countess fainted, then how everything changed. I was in the back along with the count's son."

"Heinrich."

"Heinrich, that's right. Did you know that he is a play-wright, like Herr Schober?"

"He told you that?"

"Yes. When we were upstairs dancing. Rather," Kunegunde

said with a blush, "I was dancing, he was observing. Anyway, he told me he was a playwright."

"So?"

"He said that his stepmother encouraged him, while his father disapproved. That's all. What strikes me is how excited he was before the song and how crestfallen he became afterwards."

"Well, his stepmother fainted."

"Yes, I suppose that was it. Could the song have anything to do with his family?"

"Fraülein, it is unwise to speculate. But I believe that the song more likely conveyed some information on a business matter, not one of the hearth or heart. Something to do with a metal called platinum."

"Oh. I heard about that, too. Actually, I overheard—" Kunegunde stopped for a moment.

"Overheard what?"

"As the guests were leaving, one of the German guests…"

"Barenberg or Himmelfarb?"

"Yes. One of them, I can't remember which. The man with the longer beard, I think. He told the English gentleman that some Lord, Walls, or Wallace—I didn't catch the name— could have it."

"Platinum?"

"I suppose. I didn't recognize the word. I don't know English, and since the word was unfamiliar to me, I thought that the professor had attempted an English pleasantry. The Englishman did not look pleased when he heard it. It's odd how that song affected people. Until you mentioned it, I never realized."

"Someone considers that song a matter of life or death," said Vogl. They neared the Belvedere Gallery.

"Herr Vogl, one more thing."

Vogl waited patiently.

"You were serious when you said that you didn't know who is behind all this."

"Quite serious."

"Then you must be very careful yourself," Kunegunde said.

"I appreciate your concern."

"We do have a performance tomorrow, you know," said Kunegunde lightly. "Only you can handle Frau Donmeyer. Good night."

With Fraülein Rosa inside her father's house, Vogl turned towards von Neulinger's. After a few steps he stopped—stopped and sighed. Fraülein Rosa had consciously complimented him. He thought he'd never see the day. The realization disoriented him. He turned around in the street and took a step back towards the Belvedere, but a cold blast of wind returned him to sanity.

But sanity, in this case, offered no reassurance. Now alone, Vogl felt his confident veneer disappear. He had no better plan to protect the youths whom he had instructed than to stay out of sight. He could not assess the ruthlessness of Schubert's pursuer. What if he remained nearby? Schubert, and all those with whom he associated that evening could be dead by morning. For that matter, Vogl, now that he was taking an active hand in the game, might not survive himself. The sooner all he knew was in the hands of the authorities, the better. It was not too late to stop by the Ministry of the Interior.

Then Vogl changed his mind. Probably it was nothing,

but one of Kunegunde's remarks made him pause. She noticed Heinrich's change of mood after hearing "*Die Sonne und das Veilchen*". If the cause of the subsequent trouble was domestic rather than political, the person to tell was the count. He stood a full minute in the increasing wind, now scattering bits of fresh snow about. Vogl felt his wits scattering with it.

He decided on a third course. Instead of going to the count's home, he went straight to his own. He half feared that he'd find an official summons waiting for him—one he couldn't disobey. With relief, he learned that there had been no callers for him. Forgoing offers of refreshment, he went directly into his study and locked the door. Until he was safely ensconced, he did not even remove his cloak. Carefully, he placed Schubert's song and Eugenie's original letter down on the room's central table.

He stared at them for quite a while, yet they told him nothing. There was that one discrepancy. Eight not five. How could this small change produce disaster? Whom did it affect? No answers came. It wasn't long before Vogl had paper before him and pen in hand. He started jotting down various names, von Nuelinger (Georg, Eugénie, Heinrich), Diederich and such servant names as he knew. He reviewed the guests who had seemed most affected, Barenberg, Himmelfarb, Tagili, Bellingham, and a few others. As he did so, he experienced a spasm of horror.

If one of the Auslanders killed Jennie, he still wasn't safe. For the sake of Vienna's stability, Jennie's murder would have a public solution, and a criminal would go to justice. If the real criminal was, for some reason beyond the reach of the count and his associates—either out of the city or too high ranking in aristocratic circles or foreign diplomatic services, there could be a substitute. As he realized before, no one suited that role better than he, Vogl.

With a shudder he wrote down the names Millstein and Nordwalder, representatives of the Ministry of the Interior, who had some interest in the party beyond the entertainment offered. Nothing became clear other than that any one or group of these people had the capacity to kill without compunction, and the high likelihood that within a day or two, someone's blood would avenge Eugénie's death.

Vogl thus adopted a new line of reasoning, that of a potential victim. Were there available means to protect himself? Unless he could tell what the others could not—who killed Jennie and for what reason—he could not. What did he know that others didn't? Only that Schubert altered Eugénie's text. Who else knew of the alteration? Only Eugénie.

At that moment, Vogl decided that what began in Eugenie's world would play out there. Intrigue, deception, bluff, and bravado were her means, all of them anathema to Vogl. What was Eugénie really after that night? Who caught sight of her plan? Who chose to thwart it so brutally?

Vogl dismissed many terrifying answers to those questions with another one—What would Jennie do? Throughout her career she had instigated many dangerous situations, and, until that night, always managed to escape their negative repercussions. She juggled many contingencies, and she knew how to use her considerable gifts to move people out of her way. Someone that night remained immovable, for once one step—only one—ahead of Jennie. With one other turn, Jennie could have attained the upper hand again. Then Vogl knew his course. Right or wrong, he decided the terms upon which he would risk his life.

He sent for more paper and fresh ink. For perhaps the first time in many years, since the horrible days when he first grappled with life without Jennie, he passed a sleepless night, writing between frequent bouts of pacing the floor. By dawn the writing was done. Jennie might not approve of what he said, but she'd certainly understand what he did. Vogl hoped her killer would do likewise.

Chapter Forty-two

I gnatz Nordwalder had had enough—enough of his underlings' incompetence, enough of reassigning personnel taken from their daily duties to investigate inconsequential matters, enough of the obscurities and absurdities of the English language, and more than enough of the angst generated by his encroachment on extremely dangerous territories outside his own ministry.

He summoned Captain Millstein and Count von Neulinger to report his conclusions, for conclusions they were. The official inquiries into the deaths of Eugénie von Neulinger and Gert Timmerich were, willy-nilly, about to end.

"*Guten tag mein Herren,*" Nordwalder began when the men were closeted in his inner office. "I won't take much of your time. We have a delicate situation before us. You two men are the most affected by it. Vienna has suffered two unsolved murders recently: that of your wife, Herr Count, and that of your subordinate, Captain. I am now convinced that the same person committed both atrocities. It's time to exact retribution."

"Congratulations for resolving matters so quickly," von Neulinger said, with a trace of irony.

"That's how we do things these days," said Nordwalder, with equal irony. "Let us look at the case. Here's what we know: approximately two weeks ago, some irregular economic negotiations set events in motion. Your wife, who had the reputation of being highly skilled in such matters, took part. Is this correct, Count?"

"Completely correct."

"You knew what your wife was doing," Nordwalder continued. "Come now, Georg. I commend your attempt to maintain the your household's reputation, but you must admit the truth. Nothing said here will go beyond these walls. Am I correct in assuming that you encouraged your wife to facilitate a secret exchange of platinum rights and technologies?"

"You are correct."

"Thank you, Georg. We'll return to the point in a moment. But tell me this. Was your wife's plan to consummate the exchange at her musical *soirée*?"

"It was. At any rate, she promised me she'd do so."

"Good. In the event, her offer was conveyed through a song performed that evening."

"That's right, Doktor, but …"

"Georg, did you know in advance what method your wife selected?"

"No, I didn't."

"Just as I thought. So, the negotiations fell through. I only bring up the matter to point out that the music was important to someone. I then conclude that the same person killed your wife and Timmerich. Timmerich worked for you, did he not, Captain Millstein?"

Millstein merely nodded, so Nordwalder continued, "Tell us what he did, Captain."

"I assigned Timmerich to observe the movements of Franz Schubert, the composer."

"Why?" asked von Neulinger. He asked this question simply to disconcert his subordinate. Nordwalder himself compelled Millstein to unleash Timmerich.

"His unexpected appearance at your house, Herr Count, so soon after your wife's demise made us suspicious."

"We now believe that Herr Schubert himself is completely innocent, but his song is important," Nordwalder continued. "Has a written version of the song turned up, Millstein?"

"Our … my efforts to recover it have come to nothing. The song has almost certainly been destroyed."

"Precisely. Now we must speculate. The last time anyone saw the song was the morning of the countess's death, when, with Millstein's permission"—Nordwalder paused to let the blow land with full force—"Schubert carried it out of the house. Within hours, Schubert was under steady surveillance. His rooms have been searched. One of two things must have happened. He could have destroyed the manuscript himself in the short time between leaving your house until the proper deployment of our watchdogs. This seems unlikely since he had no knowledge of the manuscript's significance.

"The second possibility is that someone else took it. Perhaps Timmerich himself did. More probably it was someone Timmerich observed. In either event, Timmerich became a threat. His killer needed to eliminate him and the song."

"You still haven't explained why."

"Bear with me just a little longer, Georg. Captain Millstein, see to it that Timmerich's death appears in the papers as an accidental drowning. The count and I will see that his death receives more appropriate, private vindication. Timmerich was devoted to his work. He had few unusual vices and no enemies interested in his sudden elimination. He died in our service. It is up to you, Captain, to quash any outside inquiries. You're dismissed."

Millstein, delighted to be set at liberty, rose hastily, bowed and left.

"Exit our *capitano*," Nordwalder said. "With the buffoon out of the way, we'll talk more seriously, Georg."

"I am all ears, Herr Doktor."

"Let's first clear up this enigma of the song. Timmerich died for it, yet it seems to have no intrinsic worth."

"What do you mean, Herr Doktor?"

"We assume that the song conveyed a disquieting message the night your wife was killed. We know the substance of that message."

"Tell me, Herr Doktor …" von Neulinger said, half rising from his seat.

"Patience, Georg. The countess wanted the song to convey some sort of fiduciary offer. Whatever it was, the terms were unacceptable."

"You have no details?" von Neulinger asked.

"I don't need them," said Nordwalder. "It is unwise to ask, as well as unnecessary. Unwise because the offer concerns platinum, which, I'm sure you know, remains of great interest to Metternich. Unnecessary because once the offer was conveyed, your wife had no further interest in it."

"I don't follow you."

"Think a minute, Georg. Suppose you offer me a hundred krone to do a service for you, and I want two hundred. You convey a compromise offer through a third party, which I again reject. Can you think of any reason for either of us to dispose of the third party?"

"Well, if the offer demands secrecy, the third party now knows the secret."

"That won't do, Georg. We are rival negotiators. If one of us kills the countess, the other will know. In the actual case before us, the negotiations were between a Russian and two Germans with the British hoping to step in. If one of the Germans or the Russian killed your wife, the innocent parties would eagerly point us toward the guilty one. The secret—her offer—was made public through the song. Only the countess's murder allowed us to learn of the song's hidden meaning."

"Eugénie's killer may have miscalculated."

"Possibly, but since no negotiator accused any other, it seems clear that no negotiator turned into an assassin— or hired one. And consider the method: Decapitation with a saber hardly seems a calculated economic decision. The circumstances surrounding the crime suggest, what I've thought all along, that passion, not business is at the root of it."

"The song has no bearing on the case?"

"The contents of the song did not motivate the murderer. Do you see what I'm driving at Georg?"

"In all honesty, I do not, Ignatz."

"I'll tell you. However, I'll mention no names. To do so would obligate me to arrest the killer. A trial would follow. Baron Hager does not like to encumber our judges with cases involving sensitive politics. Timmerich would have been my usual recourse in this sort of situation. Unfortunately, he is no longer with us.

"However, if you, properly informed, acted in advance of the justice system, I guarantee that you will face nothing but a few minor formalities afterwards. No man will blame you for avenging your wife. You won't be prosecuted. I assume you can find a suitable method to exact satisfaction."

"You have my complete attention, Ignatz."

"Here is the situation: *'Die Sonne und das Veilchen'* is a song contrived to deceive—to relay information to an 'enlightened' few over the heads of an unenlightened many. Discovered deceit is humiliating. There are two people, aside from those who understood the song's inner meanings, who might feel that humiliation: those who performed the song. There are now two possibilities. The pianist and the singer."

"There is a third," von Nuelinger inserted, "the person assigned to turn pages."

"I haven't forgotten him, Georg. His name is Franz Schober. "Fortuitously, he fell into the clutches of one of our agents last week …"

"Or she fell into his," von Neulinger added, showing that he understood.

"Precisely. They met in a house on the Annagasse. Suffice it to say that they spent a lot of time together on that occasion. Schober is unusually talkative between events, and he brought up the murder to impress her."

"I see."

"Schober didn't confess, nor did he try to plant a false scent. His chatter concerned his heroic attempts to warn and then to rescue the countess—pure nonsense."

"You're certain of this?"

"I can show you Annika's report if you like … after the actual murderer is punished. I must again emphasize the need for haste in this matter."

"Please continue, Ignatz. I won't interrupt again."

"Danke. Now, as I was saying, either the performer did not know that he was doing something underhanded, or he did. In either case, once he realized the song's true purpose, his shame impelled him to destroy the countess. When the countess fainted, he understood that he was only a pawn in one of her games, perhaps not for the first time. The knowledge infuriated him.

"More likely, our killer knew the song's purpose and saw the ploy fail. Perhaps the countess offered some special payment—dare I say 'favor'—for success, and he, having discharged his part of the bargain faithfully, still expected his reward. Now do you see my meaning, Georg?"

"I do. I'm impressed by your logic, Ignatz. A scorned suitor, suffering the deepest shame, proceeds to obliterate all traces of his humiliation."

"Exactly," said Nordwalder. "By trailing Schubert, the unfortunate Timmerich stood in his way, hence Timmerich had to be eliminated."

Von Neulinger rose. "Thank you, Herr Doktor. I see my course. I thank you also for letting me resolve this affair personally."

Bows were exchanged, followed by an unwonted handshake.

"Herr Count. There's not much time. Hager expects a full report by the end of the week. His patience is not unlimited."

"I think a day, two at the most, will be sufficient. I won't rest until this matter is concluded."

"Good, Georg. That is what I wanted to hear."

𝄢

Von Neulinger's homeward journey displayed his agitation. He spurred his horse with unusual vigor, almost upsetting a baker's push cart on the street and definitely upsetting the baker, who controlled his curses until the count was well out of earshot. Von Neulinger's mind whirled, but he soon resolved on a course of action. As Diederich took his cloak, and the count removed his gloves, he ordered, "Send at once for Michael Vogl."

"That won't be necessary, your Excellency."

Von Neulinger's face purpled. "How dare you!" he said, lifting his gloves in preparation to strike.

Unperturbed, Diederich responded, "Herr Vogl is here, Excellency. He waits in the grand salon."

Von Neulinger handed his gloves to Diederich, turned on his heel, and entered the salon.

Chapter Forty-three

Vogl sat at the piano but stopped playing on the count's entrance. He rose at once.

"I did not expect you, Herr Vogl," Von Neulinger said, closing the paneled doors of the salon behind him and locking them. "To what do I owe this unheralded visitation?"

Vogl caught the peculiar strain in the count's word selection but ignored it. "I come to fulfill my duty," he said, "my two promises."

"Two?"

"Heinrich and I have talked about his play."

"Very good," said the count. "What happened?"

"Do not fear your son's embarking on a theatrical career."

"Do you mean that Heinrich has no talent?" said the count, his color rising.

"It is not that, your Excellency. Heinrich has a decent way with words, and he is not devoid of sensibility."

The count began to pace. Vogl calmly held his position

at the piano, as the center of the count's semicircular path. "What, then, prevents him from continuing as a playwright?"

"Some practical considerations. In its present form, his play is unproducible. Heinrich lacks experience in stagecraft, but I won't tire you with a technical discussion. If he wanted to, Heinrich could master the mechanics. No, the reason is deeper, and I daresay, more permanent."

"What is it?"

"Heinrich no longer needs to be a playwright. He had things to say, and he set them to paper. Now they're out of his system."

"How do you know this?"

"Intuition mostly," Vogl confessed, "infused with experience. Did he ever show you the manuscript?"

"I know nothing about it. I believe that Heinrich conceived of the play to spite me. He knows I disapprove."

"It's called—was called—*Phaedrus*. It chronicles a young man's complaints about the condition of the world, a world redeemed, temporarily, through love, the subject of almost every play these days."

"I will take your word for that, Herr Vogl. Why is Heinrich's play unworthy to join the others?"

"He wants to change it. Again, I won't bore you with details. Heinrich no longer sees the world in the sentimental terms that characterize *Phaedrus*. When he asked me to review his play, he was a soul in torment. Since then, the cloud has lifted. *Phaedrus* sprung from Heinrich's emotions. He now exercises his reason."

The count stopped pacing and turned to look at Vogl. "Enough about Heinrich. If, as you say, playwriting is 'out of his system', I am indebted to you. You said two promises."

"The other is only implied. You see, I have learned something about Herr Schubert's song, '*"Die Sonne und das Veilchen"*', the song commissioned for the *soirée*." Vogl paused.

"Continue."

"Schubert altered the text."

"That's interesting," said the count.

"He changed the word '*fünf*' in the last line to '*acht*'. I can only guess why five violets matter more than eight violets, yet the change caused Eugénie to accuse me of 'ruining everything'."

"Undoubtedly," said the count, who became very still.

Vogl pushed onward. "I give you this information first, as you will best know how to use it."

"*Danke.* Have you anything else you wish to tell me?"

"No, your Excellency. I have fulfilled the purpose of my journey."

"Good. Now I have a question for you: How do you wish to die?"

This thunderbolt did not catch Vogl completely unprepared, but when he actually heard the words, he was taken aback. "I beg your pardon?"

"Scoundrel, choose your weapon! I have a complete selection here. What will it be? Pistols? The saber?"

"Neither, your Excellency. I have no chance against you."

"You prefer, then, to be found floating in the canal, like some miserable cur?"

"I prefer not to die," said Vogl gently, raising a hand to forestall a response from the count. "I suspected that coming here might be dangerous for me, so I came armed." Vogl's hand reached under the lapel of his coat. "For a weapon, I chose the pen."

In the graceful, practiced manner with which he customarily traversed a stage, Vogl swept by von Neulinger and dropped three sheets of paper, folded into thirds on the table behind him. Vogl inwardly thanked his acting experience for masking the agitation he felt. The count spun around to observe the maneuver.

"I present you with a copy of a letter I've composed. Will you read it, or should I tell you what it says?"

Except for a slight narrowing of his eyes, von Neulinger remained immobile.

"The other copies are sealed and bear the instruction 'to be opened in the event of my death'," said Vogl, "'or after my unexplained absence of more than forty-eight hours'. The contents explain my theory of why you murdered your wife."

The count reacted to these words by unconsciously clenching and releasing his right fist.

"There is, of course, no doubt that you did it, or about how you did it. No one hindered you." Vogl supported this partial bluff with all the confidence he could command.

"Doktor Nordwalder believes that death occurred late at night," said the count, retrieving his voice, "while there was still enough snow falling to obliterate any tracks."

"Doktor Nordwalder is a brilliant investigator, no doubt, but he does not realize that you killed Jennie. He found no evidence of escape because no one tried to escape."

"Preposterous! An intruder, lingering after the *soirée* murdered Jennie while the rest of us slept."

"There was no intruder, and if the contents of my letter

register the truth, you were not asleep. You waited to see your suspicions confirmed, and then you acted. You slashed Jennie's throat and tossed the saber out her window."

The count made no further attempt at denial. Vogl expected none. Aristocrats did not bare their souls to commoners. "The baffling question is why you did it. The answer must be pride. You couldn't let Jennie make a fool of you."

"She never did that."

"She never intended to do that," Vogl corrected, "but we both knew Jennie. She demanded her own way regardless of the cost, and she believed she could get whatever she wanted."

"What could she want that I didn't supply?" asked the count. The attempt to match Vogl's studied self-assurance did not succeed.

"What Jennie always wanted—what she lived and died for—power. Not exclusively the vicarious power of influencing men such as yourself behind their thrones. She wanted to be an empress. Instead she worked with what we supplied her. Allowing her to take a hand in the negotiations over platinum was a stroke of genius on your part. However," Vogl again raised his hand to forestall the count's interruption, "it wasn't enough. Jennie wanted to gain ascendancy over you as well. And to that end, she made a fatal miscalculation. She enlisted your son."

"Leave Heinrich out of this!" The count clenched both fists.

"He figures prominently in my letter," Vogl continued quietly. "Somehow Jennie ensnared Heinrich—to a degree that was intolerable—for both of you."

"For both?" For a moment, the count's animosity abated.

"Here I have the advantage of you. Heinrich's play. Did not Jennie encourage him to write it?"

"Suppose she did," said the count. "The theater is not a suitable career for Heinrich. Yes, Jennie and I had words about it. But a nettlesome domestic dispute over my son's literary aspirations hardly justifies her murder."

"Nor was it the precise cause," said Vogl. "One has but to note the title of the play to see why you decided to stop Jennie."

"The title?"

"Phaedrus. It is not a common name. I haven't run across it in the works of the ancients."

"You're the scholar," said the count.

"But the name is suggestive. Phaedrus is the masculinization of Phaedra. Phaedra was an unfortunate woman who, against all her inclinations, found herself in love with her son-in-law!" Vogl let the remark hang.

"Disgusting," said the count after a moment.

"Yes, and how insensitive of Heinrich to invoke the legend. As I say, I don't know anything specific about Jennie's encroachment into Heinrich's soul, but the encroachment was continuing. Here '*Die Sonne und Das Veilchen*' makes its unfortunate appearance."

"Stop this madness, Vogl. Doktor Nordwalder informs me that the song contained arcane information about platinum."

"I'm sure it did. The ploy certainly bears Jennie's mark, but your Excellency, we both know never to underestimate Jennie's inventiveness. This time, Jennie underestimated you."

"Here's what my letter says," Vogl continued under the count's glare. "You may correct any misstatements."

In spite of himself, the count nodded.

Vogl continued, "You witnessed Heinrich's developing fascination for Jennie. Heinrich, given his youth, couldn't adequately conceal his feelings. Jennie noticed them. So did you. Thus Jennie encountered her final temptation. She seized the opportunity to dominate your household. With Heinrich in her thrall, through him she could manipulate you. In the letter, I take a charitable view suggesting she only desired to further his artistic aspirations under your nose and against your wishes. She knew the risks. Knowing that you were on the alert, she proceeded with utmost caution. When she undertook the platinum negotiations, I presume with your blessing, she came to a number—five.

"I accept Doktor Nordwalder's conclusion that international platinum concerns hinged on that number, but Jennie outfoxed herself: the number held significance for Heinrich also. It identified an hour when Jennie expected him. In terms of time and secrecy, 'five' is most suggestive. At five in the morning everything is still. By eight in the morning, everyone is up. Heinrich could not expect a private audience then. So Jennie had me leave a note for him on the table downstairs telling him to go away. He would arrive at eight and find the note. She didn't expect you to read it and deduce its implications."

"A most imaginative account, Herr Vogl," said the count, "but not very credible."

"I hardly believe it myself," Vogl said almost affably, "and I only committed it to paper after you attempted to poison Franz Schubert."

"Schubert the flunkey?"

"Schubert the composer, Schubert the pianist, Schubert my friend."

"Herr Vogl, you astonish me. Schubert's life is insignificant. One doesn't get on in the world with friends of so little consequence."

"Your Excellency, Franz Schubert possesses something which neither you, nor I with all our worldliness and—ruthlessness—can ever aspire to: a unique talent. In posterity, his life may amount to more than yours and mine put together. If he dies betimes, who knows how much great music the world loses?"

Von Neulinger's voice displayed contempt. "If you say so. To me, Schubert has nothing to do with anything."

"But he does. Franz Schubert altered Jennie's text. Her 'five' became Schubert's 'eight'. Only he knew the song's original lyrics. Removing him prevents the change from coming to light."

"I'm sorry to burst your bubble, Vogl, but Schubert has been under continual surveillance since the day my wife died. We carelessly returned his music to him, and Nordwalder wanted it back. Do you suggest that Doktor Nordwalder and the Ministry of the Interior condoned the destruction of their only hope of retrieving the song?" The count's eyes remained fixed on Vogl's letter.

Vogl followed the count's gaze to the pages on the table, hoping that his performance was convincing. "You escaped Nordwalder's notice somehow, not a difficult maneuver for one in your privileged position. Nordwalder wanted the music, but you wanted to destroy its composer. Safety was not your chief concern. To you '*Die Sonne und Das Veilchen*' remains a source of shame, a chronicle of your weakness, the legacy of your perfidious wife. It must disappear from the earth"

"Accepting your absurd premise for a moment, why are you so certain that I tried to harm Schubert? My son could have an equally strong desire to dispose of him."

"Not Heinrich. He didn't come back to the house from the time he left the *soirée* until eight the following morning— long after Jennie died. I met him on the stairs."

Silence reigned for several minutes. Then von Neulinger said, "Very well thought out, Vogl. Ingenious. Of course you can't prove any of this nonsense."

"No, your Excellency, I cannot. Nor do I want to." Vogl returned the count's steely gaze. "Only my death or disappearance gives credibility to my writing."

Again silence hung in the air. This time, Vogl broke it. He spoke softly. "Your Excellency, I am an actor, trained to observe and to empathize. Before composing my letter, I imagined myself in your painful position. Having felt my own humiliation at Jennie's hands, I can envisage your rage at her cruelty. I respect the importance of the von Neulinger name. What greater shame, even as unsubstantiated gossip, than to be constantly reminded that your wife was carrying on with your son? If it is any consolation to you, from my observation of Heinrich, I don't think that the possible horror we both imagine actually occurred. Today, unlike two weeks ago, Heinrich walks about like a man with a clear conscience."

The count acknowledged the remark with a slight bowing of his head.

"But, Herr Count, we face a terrible impasse. For the sake of public order and your family's honor, Jennie's death must be avenged. As her long-time friend and victim, I fit the role of the murderer neatly. However, I decline the role. Hence, my letters, and hence I make this pledge to you. Once I am freed of suspicion, all copies of the letter, except the one I leave with you, will be destroyed. I have kept the ones destined for the newspapers—forgive me if I don't tell you which ones— and Doktor Nordwalder at my lodgings, to be mailed out this evening unless I reclaim them personally. The others have gone to trusted, sensible friends who will not open them prematurely. I will do everything in my power to preserve your family's reputation. That's the best I can do."

There was more silence. Eventually the count said, "You have done enough, Herr Vogl. Now I must act. I remember saying on the morning that my wife was found that whoever killed her would feel the full extent of my anger. I will keep that vow. Now go!"

With his firm military stride, the count went and unlocked the salon's door.

"*Auf wiederseh'n*, Herr Vogl."

"*Auf wiederseh'n*, your Excellency."

Chapter Forty-four

On the evening of Tuesday, February 26, 1822, at the moment Count Georg Von Neulinger ended his life with a bullet to the temple, Doktor Ignatz Nordwalder was at the home of his friend Kurt von Merlinbeck, seeing him off on a trip to the mountains of Graz.

"It will be chilly at first," he counseled Merlinbeck, "but soon it will warm up, and everything will be different. Don't worry, Kurt. I will look after affairs here," he finished with a cynical smile.

Merlinbeck suffered a dutiful farewell kiss from his wife, and when the coach pulled away he reached into his greatcoat for the bottle concealed there. He paid no attention to his wife and superior entering his house together.

The week following Merlinbeck's departure was more hectic than Nordwalder anticipated. While becoming better acquainted with Zdenka, he labored to justify Count von Neulinger's suicide as the action of a man "deranged by grief."

Eventually Nordwalder explained to Captain Millstein that the count, after skillfully tracking down Timmerich, who had forced himself into the countess's *boudoir* and murdered her when his advances were rebuffed, was cheated of proper revenge by Timmerich's untimely accidental drowning. "How much this disappointment contributed to the count's momentary madness, we will never know," he concluded.

Millstein managed to commit the explanation to paper and see it published in appropriate places.

The narrative was not completely convincing. For one thing, how did Timmerich ever come to know the countess in the first place? Nordwalder casually instructed Captain Millstein to add Timmerich's name to Eugénie's final guest list, posthumously. If suspicions of some other explanation lingered elsewhere, no one came forth to voice them.

Fixing this and other details took diplomatic skill, cajolery and coercion, but the stability of Metternich's Vienna remained what it always was, and Vienna looked like Metternich and Baron Hager expected it to look.

𝄢

Heinrich von Neulinger, at the decisive moment, was finishing up a latish dinner at his lodging. He barely knew what he was eating, because he was enthralled in revising *Prince Flamminius's Triumph* (previously *Prince Phaedrus' Ordeal*). Never before and never again would he come as close to resembling Franz Schubert. Within weeks, he abandoned his play, indeed all his artistic longings. Over time he became a worthy inheritor of the von Neulinger establishment, although his service to Austria never achieved the notoriety of his father's works. It is said that providing for his family, which grew to include a wife and five children, consumed most of his time.

𝄢

But that was the future. On this late February evening, Michael Vogl was on the stage of the Hofoper, singing his short first act solo in *The Empress of the Common*. Kunegunde Rosa managed to leave the maypole intact. She stood within a few feet of Herr Vogl echoing his sentiments as Bildman's score required—"She's approaching fast! The gate is passed! She's here at last!" Anne-Marie Donmeyer's entrance, predictably, created a great sensation, and the little dog, "Schmutz", was rewarded for his squirming in her clutches with the customary gales of laughter and applause.

Many of Vogl's friends and acquaintances were in the audience, among them Thomas, Lord Bellingham, who "at the drop of a hat" decided to "take in the play as his swan song" to the city he "planned to leave on the morrow forever." No Austrian serving or spying at the embassy fully deciphered Lord Bellingham's utterance. To everyone's relief, he didn't sing. He "left all that to professionals." And he did enjoy the flawlessly executed maypole dance near the end of the first act.

The audience also included many members of Vienna's artistic community, both old and young. Oddly, three in one party were named Franz. The young playwright Franz Schober, who rarely attended the theater as a spectator, was there in the company of his friend, Franz Seraph von Bruchmann and his sister Justina. Schober joined the party at the last minute "in the spirit of adventure," and found himself enjoying the on-stage performance just as much—exactly as much—as Justina did.

On Justina's other side, sat the third Franz, the up and coming composer, Franz Schubert. He, too, rarely attended the theater—he could rarely afford tickets. This time, however, he was the guest of Michael Vogl, upon whom Kunegunde Rosa had prevailed to sponsor the outing.

Perhaps the most eminent member of the audience that night was the composer Carl Maria von Weber, whose own opera *Der Freischütz*, was to open in a week and take Vienna by storm.

As the curtain descended, smiles were to be seen throughout the audience and on the boards. Franz Schober and Justina Bruchmann exchanged whispers of delight; Michael Vogl and Kunegunde Rosa signaled silent mutual congratulations for their so far flawless contributions to the performance. Franz Schubert caught Carl Maria von Weber's eye and the men traded the cordial smiles that can only be fully understood by two people who recognize and respect each other's genius.

Thus concluded the dramatic events of February 1822 in Vienna. Spring, with its attendant promise of change, was in the air. As Count von Neulinger repeatedly promised himself, all would be well.

the end :|

Postlude:
Moderato

Author's Note

Vienna in Violet is entirely a work of fiction. As it features more than the usual number of people who actually walked the earth and events that actually occurred, I want to distinguish the historical portions of the story from the totally invented ones.

Of the main characters, all of the von Neulinger and Merlinbeck families, their attendants and retainers are pure inventions, as are Ignatz Nordwalder and Captain Millstein. The platinum hunters, Barenberg, Himmelfarb, Tagili and Lord Bellingham are also inventions, but Lord Wollaston, with his interest in acquiring vast quantities of the platinum ,was real.

About the real Franz Schubert a great deal is known, and most of the personages and the non-criminal events surrounding him did happen at approximately the time they occur in the story. Schubert met Carl Maria von Weber and attended a concert with him on Sunday, February 24, 1822.

He submitted to Weber the score of his opera, *Alfonso und Estrella*, whose librettist was Franz Schober. Weber expressed initial interest in it, although the opera was not produced in Schubert's lifetime by Weber or anyone else. Schubert was the friend and accompanist of the actor/singer Johann Michael Vogl then, indeed for most of his adult life.

Nonetheless, Schubert, Schober, and Vogl are also fictional creations. I consulted several biographies of Schubert before embarking on my tale. My bible for ready reference was *Schubert—a Biography* by George Marek, published by Viking in 1986. Though unanimous about Schubert's talent, biographers do not agree regarding Schubert's personality, degree of shyness, degree of impoverishment, sexual orientation, degree of innocence or degree of earthiness. Thus I felt free to mold a hypothetical Schubert to fit my story.

I followed this same principle in developing Schober and Vogl; I tried to remain true to the contours of their characters when historians were in agreement about them. Schober was known to be dissolute, Vogl was known to have a fondness for Epictetus, for example, but I felt free to invent their manners, words and actions during the week of their lives I appropriated.

I consulted only one full biography of Weber in English (written by John Warrack). Aside from anything Weber says directly and his method of approaching drinks, my portrait of him is derived heavily from that biography. Still Weber, too, is more my creation than the actual composer.

I took my greatest liberties with Kunegunde Rosa, who in fact was the daughter of the first curator of the Oberes Gallerie in Vienna. She was a pupil of Michael Vogl, and they married in 1826. I found no record of her ever having trod the boards anywhere, and I did not learn anything of her actual personality from the materials I consulted.

Aside from "*Die Sonne und Das Veilchen*" all other references to Schubert's music mention pieces that he had written or was working on by 1822. "*Der Erlkönig*" ("Erlking").was published in 1815, and arguably was Schubert's best-known work. The other *soirée* songs mentioned or alluded to are "*An Den Mond*" ("To the Moon")1815, "*Die Forelle*" ("The Trout") 1817, "*Der Tod und Das Mädchen*" ("Death and the Maiden")1817, "*Gretchen am Spinnrade*" ("Gretchen at the Spinning Wheel") 1814, "*Heidenröslein*" ("A Hedgerose") 1815, "*Lob der Tränin*" ("Praise of Tears") 1817, "*Frühlingsglaube*" ("Faith in Spring") 1820, "*Geheimes*" ("The Secret") 1821, and "*Ganymed*" ("Ganymede")1817.

The quotation from "*Gehiemes*" (pp.68-69) reads in German,

> *Blicket sie wohl In die Runde;*
> *Doch sie sucht nur zu verkünden*
> *Ihm die nächste süsse Stunde.*

The English version I cite is by Sergius Kagan.

The two mentioned instrumental pieces by Schubert are his "Wandererfantasie", finished and published in 1822, (first mentioned on p.173) and not the famous "Unfinished" Symphony (number 8) in B minor, but his fragmentary 7th Symphony in E minor (referred to on p. 244). Schubert began work on his 8th Symphony in October of 1822, more than six months after the meeting with Weber.

All mentioned works by Mozart, Beethoven, and von Weber, are of course, real. A work by Friedrich Schneider was performed at St. Stephens before Weber, Schubert and Salieri on Sunday, February 24, 1822, but I did not find the actual composition. Hauptnegler, the pianist and Bildman with his *Empress of the Common* are complete fabrications.

Another musical selection may merit some further attention. In 1822, modern Germany did not exist, even as a concept. A sense of national unity among German states was just sprouting, though the sense of unity was strong among German speakers. There was no German national anthem. The song, "Heil dir in Siegerkranz" (p.127) was sung to the tune of "My Country, 'Tis of thee." The words of the first verse are: *Heil dir in Siegerkranz,/Hersher des Vaterlands,/Heil Kaiser dir!* (Hail to you in the victor's crown,/leader of the Fatherland/ Hail, Kaisr, to you) were written by Heinrich Harrier in 1790 as a patriotic anthem for the King of Prussia. Later in the nineteenth century, starting around the time of the Franco-Prussian War, the song was commonly used to welcome the German Kaiser when he traveled and was associated with a greater unified Germany.

I close with a few small scraps of information to tie up some loose ends for my historical characters. Franz Schober continued in the theater for several years, attempting to work more as an actor than as a playwright. He was never a successful thespian. He suffered through a legendarily unhappy marriage and lived until 1882. He often was consulted about his memories of Schubert and helped promote Schubert's greatness after the composer's death.

For Vogl, Weber and Schubert, 1822 marked turning points. All three men reached pinnacles in their lives. Vogl, after his long, successful acting career, retired from the theater later that year. He continued to sing recitals and give readings until his permanent retirement in 1834. He died in 1840. He always was a great promoter of Schubert's memory and music, both before and after the composer's death.

Weber went on to write two more operas after the triumph of *Der Freischütz*: *Euryanthe, and Oberon*. Neither matched the former's success. The strain and effort literally killed him (along with tuberculosis), as he died in London, in 1826 just days after getting *Oberon* up and running. He allowed Schubert to attend some early rehearsals of *Euryanthe* in October of 1823. He also had a different Franz Schubert working as a production assistant on the opera. Schubert the composer made it known that he wasn't thrilled with the new work. At about that time Weber lost interest in *Alfonso und Estrella*, which had to wait until 1854 to reach the stage. It has never made it into the standard repertoire.

In February, 1822, Schubert approached his worldly, although not his creative, zenith. Through the rest of the year his star remained in the ascendant. He received increased public notice and inspiring critical accolades. However, some time near the end of the year, or the beginning of 1823, Schubert became seriously ill and stopped working for several months. When he recovered sufficiently, by the fall of 1823, his outlook on life seems to have changed. At any rate, his music changed. A reigning theory is that he became aware of his mortality and turned from writing as a means of immediate advancement towards writing for the ages. In his last years he produced works of great musical depth. He died, almost certainly of syphilis, on November 19, 1828.

About the Author

After wrapping up a forty-year teaching career teaching English mostly at the high school level and producing plays for thirty-four years at The Roxbury Latin School in Boston, David W. Frank has continued his literary and dramatic pursuits in non-academic settings. His adaptations of Ibsen's *The Pillars of Society* and Henry Fielding's *The Mock Doctor* were published online, and his adaptations of Gozzi's *The Love of Three Oranges* and Aristophanes' *The Clouds* were performed, as well as the revue, *Musical!* for which he wrote the book. His original play, 4'33" *In Rehearsal* was also performed onstage. David's life-long hobby, classical piano, introduced him to Schubert at an early age, and his education includes a year at the Eastman School in Rochester, New York. *Vienna in Violet* is his third published novel, the first with a historical setting and the second to feature a musical maguffin.

CPSIA information can be obtained at www.ICGtesting.com
Printed in the USA
LVOW11s1021220915

455177LV00003B/3/P